About the author

Tony lives in Auckland with his children, pets, and an incredibly understanding (& clairvoyant) wife.

Visit his website at **www.tonyprice.net**

Also by Tony Price

Kicking Out
Moving On

Acknowledgements

Writing a book takes patience, perseverance and, most of all, a great deal of support. Thanks to the readers who were forced to endure early drafts: Jill & Trevor Price, Malcolm and Christine Attree, Bill Somerville, Marie Cooper and Julie Pethers. Thanks also to Mary-Ann Attree for her wonderful design efforts. And special thanks to freelance editor Louise Russell who improved the narrative flow enormously.

But my deepest gratitude goes to my wonderful wife, Kiri, for selflessly allowing me the opportunity to give this a go.

First published 2011
by Starting Gun Books,
Auckland, New Zealand.

National Library of New Zealand Cataloguing-in-Publication Data

Price, Tony, 1965-
Kicking out / Tony Price
ISBN 978-0-473-18283-0
I.Title.
NZ823.3—dc 22

Cover design by Mary-Ann Attree
Cover image: Zane Price
Printed by Lightning Source

KICKING OUT

TONY PRICE

'We fear violence less than our own feelings.
Personal, private, solitary pain is more terrifying
than what anyone else can inflict.'

Jim Morrison

'Life is like a ten speed bicycle.
Most of us have gears we never use.'

Charles M. Schulz

28 November 2000, Friday mid-morning

ONE

It happens so suddenly.

The explosion rips through the office behind me, lifting me off my feet and into the meeting room I was walking towards. The abrupt feeling of helplessness is as crushing as the shockwave of air that blasts into my back. I feel small and insignificant as I fly through the air in terror.

I land in a sprawling heap. Pieces of debris shower over and around me. Shredded paper mingled with shattered glass, ash and fabric fills the air. As I try to reconcile my position, I find myself staring at a large black leather shoe. The world around me has become strangely silent and I lie unmoving, watching as fragments settle on the carpet nearby. With my heart hammering in my chest I try to rise, but can't. My entire body just trembles.

I don't understand what has just happened.

Only moments before I'd been wading through seemingly endless paperwork at my desk – and now I'm face down on the carpet, deafened, and I think I'm bleeding.

Without warning, the shoe before me moves abruptly and slams into my face. I cringe with the pain. With blurry vision I shift away instinctively, and something sharp pokes into my upper arm. Then a hand settles on my shoulder, roughly shaking me, rolling me over. I suddenly realise I can hear something, but it's only a loud rushing sound, a sort of a high-pitched hum.

The hand rolls me carefully onto my back and a face eventually comes into focus above. Steve Cassidy. His lips are moving. He's speaking but I can't make out the words.

He coughs and I notice he's bleeding. A steady stream of blood runs down his face from a cut just below his eye. It reaches his mouth and I watch as he silently tastes it, then wipes at his face with his sleeve. He frowns in annoyance and coughs again.

My vision is still a little blurry and I have to blink to regain focus. Pulling myself up onto an elbow, I try to avoid leaning into the glass and debris beneath me. My face hurts where Steve accidentally kicked me, but I don't think he even realises what he did. I begin to cough too, my throat tasting like burnt toast. I turn to stare back out the doorway I've just flown through to see a thick bank of smoke billowing slowly towards us.

I panic, sitting up quickly and trying to scramble back – away from the smoke – and bowl Steve over in my haste. He topples over me, landing on his side between my scrambling legs. He cries out, probably swearing, but I can't hear properly and I just see his lips move in a snarl of obscenity. Instinctively I draw my legs together and press down on my skirt, hazily wishing I'd worn something longer, or trousers, today. Steve is unceremoniously pushed away and rolls towards the doorway, towards the rapidly encroaching smoke.

The hum in my ears finally recedes, only to be replaced by a low buzzing. Through it I hear Steve's curse this time, his voice distant and muffled, and I become aware of a siren howling somewhere nearby. It pulses insistently, demanding attention. My throat constricts as the smoke reaches us and we both resume coughing.

Then, thankfully, it starts to rain.

Cold water sprays down onto us from above, like an urgent storm-shower blowing in an open window. In moments everything is wet, dripping, and the smoke begins to dissipate. Almost immediately, drifting through the clamor of the siren, I hear the unnaturally faint but unmistakable sound of screaming. Voices are shouting, calling out names, some screaming for help, others just wailing.

I shudder. The high-pitched hum had been infinitely better.

Shaking my head, I try to clear the sounds away and to focus. Steve manages to right himself and turn to me. His coughing has eased and he speaks again. His voice is muffled and seems to swirl down a long tunnel. This time I understand his intent if not his actual words. He reaches out a hand, offering to help me up. He wants me to get up and go with him.

I just stare at his hand. I'm desperately confused and too overwhelmed to move, yet he seems oddly calm and composed. He leans closer and I finally reach out and take his hand. Pulling me to my feet, he adjusts his grip and turns, beginning to lead me directly towards the dissipating smoke. I follow reluctantly. My low-heeled shoes crunch on the broken glass with each step and I'm instantly thankful that they didn't come off as I'd flown through the air.

Looking up I finally understand that sprinklers set into the ceiling are providing the unusual effect of indoor rain. Everything is now becoming completely drenched, but at least the smoke is quickly clearing.

What I see next, as Steve steps aside at the door, will haunt me forever. The scene of devastation that had so recently been my workplace is almost unrecognisable. I freeze on the spot, my hand slipping from his grasp.

My workplace was on the far side of the room from where I now stand. But it is no longer there. The area around and beyond my desk is now nothing more than a smouldering black space. There has been a massive explosion and clearly it happened somewhere very close to where I normally sit. A sickening feeling overcomes me as I realise that if I'd been at my desk, as I had been only moments before the blast flung me across the room, I would probably not be alive to see this. My knees almost give out. If Steve hadn't called a few minutes before and demanded an urgent meeting I would have been sitting right there, right next to my friend Janet.

Dread consumes me and I have to grab the doorframe for support. Where is Janet? Disoriented, I look back into the meeting room, and then to my right and left. Yes, my workplace should be directly ahead – right where the blackened space now smoulders. Janet's desk is the next one along from mine, closer to where I stand, further from the centre of the blast, and it's empty. It's also burned, blackened and smouldering too. There is no sign of Janet.

I scream, shout Janet's name and start towards the desk as I feel a hand grab me forcibly around the wrist. Steve again. He's saying something, and shaking his head at me. He tries to pull me back, away from the charred central area. He hangs on tightly as I fight to free myself. His eyes are blank, emotionless, as he pulls me towards him and motions towards a blackened lump on the floor over to the right of Janet's desk. The lump has wisps of blonde hair and appears to be wrapped in the remains of a tattered pink blouse.

Janet is face down and she isn't moving.

Steve pulls on my wrist again, trying firmly – yet relatively gently – to draw me away from the grim sight. He still seems so calm. I shudder and feel the floor waver beneath me. Struggling for breath I feel myself slide towards a deep, gnawing horror. I manage only one more, very brief, look around the devastated office area, which only minutes ago had been quietly humming with activity before my senses become completely overwhelmed and I succumb to darkness.

* * *

6

The jarring revives me. That and Steve's warm breath on my neck. Each step he takes down the stairs bounces and jolts me gently as my head lolls against his chest. He carries me in the classic bride-through-the-doorway hold, so that my arms wrap naturally around his neck and my face lies on his shoulder. His cheek is soaked with blood, but his arms around me are like an iron cradle and the unusual image of being abducted by a bear forms dimly in my mind. Steve is a big guy, your classic tall-dark-and-handsome, and he is carrying me easily.

Becoming suddenly and irrationally embarrassed I struggle in his arms and he falters on the step, having to lean against the wall of the stairwell to stop us from falling. Still I push at him and he releases my legs, setting me on my feet lightly.

'I can walk,' I insist, but quickly realise he can't hear me. He has to be suffering the same buzzing in his ears that I am. I can't actually hear myself speak. Still embarrassed, I try to smile my thanks and speak louder, 'I'm okay, I can walk.' He nods assent and carefully releases his hold.

When I immediately stumble he catches my arm, keeping me from falling. Someone is trying to push past. It takes me a moment to realise that the stairwell is actually crowded. Hordes of panicked people are trying to escape the building. Steve pulls me closer and lets a few of the frenzied crowd flow past, and then we start moving downwards again, together.

My mind is spinning. I feel unbalanced, lost. Everything around me seems so unreal. That damn siren is definitely still howling away somewhere nearby and, although I'm dripping wet, my throat is unbearably dry. I start to cough again, desperate for a cold drink of any kind.

The stairwell is only semi-lit, but I'm relieved at the absence of smoke and rain.

We keep moving downwards. People jostle and cry. Meredith, from legal, keeps staring back over her shoulder at us. It takes me some time to realise that we are both filthy, and Steve is still bleeding. Everyone else around us appears a bit damp, but otherwise fine.

Steve continues to hold my arm, which definitely helps, now that I've overcome my embarrassment. I'm forced to accept that I'd most likely just stumble again if he wasn't guiding me.

We had only been on the third floor, but the stairwell seems endless as we trudge along with the other escaping office workers. I watch my feet most of the way, fearful of tripping; only occasionally looking up at the other frightened faces around us. Then, abruptly, the stairwell ends and we are in a long, dark concrete passageway. There is light up ahead.

Salvation.

We step out into the mid-morning daylight. It's warm and sunny, a lovely day outside, but I shiver from the dampness of my clothes. People are milling about everywhere. They seem muddled and directionless. Steve leads me to a bench in the open courtyard and we both sit down. I no longer resist him.

The scene around us is chaotic.

While my ears buzz annoyingly I spot a man I recognise as Jason from IT. He's normally a bit smooth, but right now he looks absurd in a bright fluorescent-orange vest. He's standing motionless, clasping a clipboard to his chest and staring vacantly around the courtyard. Clearly he never expected this when he volunteered to be a fire warden.

To his right I spot my friend Nikki looking wide-eyed amongst a cluster of ladies from Customer Services. They're talking feverishly across each other and anxiously gesturing this way and that, while another small group from IT huddle protectively together nearer to where I sit with Steve. Their manager, Don, is trying to keep them calm, and together.

I'm struck by the incongruity of the familiarity of the faces and the abnormality of the situation.

Hector, a guy who works in Sales with Steve, is staring blankly up at the windows above us, an odd look on his face. He appears more deeply affected than the fluorescent-vested Jason and I notice that he's bleeding too, from a gash on his arm where his shirt is sliced open.

Brendan, our Marketing Manager, is babbling away into his cell-phone, his back to both the building and a group of his staff. His behaviour seems out-of-place, but it's the most natural thing I've seen since sitting down.

The new girl from Finance stumbles past – I can't remember her name. She's soaking wet, covered in dripping ash and crying. A man I've seen in Legal – Dennis, I think – takes her arm and guides her away, comforting her.

A girl named Tiffany, from Marketing, points at me and Steve and I become aware that he is still holding my arm. I gently try to slip it out of his grasp. He's been surveying the crowd too and when he turns his face towards me I'm shocked at how much blood is on it now. No wonder Tiffany is pointing – we're a mess. I silently gesture at his face. He raises a hand and touches his own cheek. It comes away slick with blood and he frowns again. He just seems irritated, not frightened.

I think he says, 'Stay here,' but it's hard to tell. He gets up and wanders off into the bustling crowd. Quite a few eyes follow his movement in awe.

I look down at myself. I'm bleeding too, but only a little. My bare legs and arms are scratched and dirty. My clothes ruined. I remember the charred black lump that I'd seen lying on the floor of the office upstairs. The patches of blonde hair and the pink blouse.

Janet is dead, surely. But I am alive.

Anguish overwhelms me and I start to cry. Sobbing uncontrollably, I curl up into a ball on the bench and try to convince myself that this is just a bad dream.

TWO

Sometimes he likes to think of himself as a phantom.

Mysterious and enigmatic, able to move with a ghost-like grace. But today, once again, he is more than that, and it feels good. Actually, it feels great. He can feel the excitement coursing through him. He loves the rushing and tingling within his bones. The feeling of power, of righteousness.

But unlike Charles Bronson in the *Death Wish* movies he so enjoys, or even Eastwood's *Dirty Harry*, he doesn't like guns. No, he won't use them. They're too simplistic and too direct, with none of the right energy. He'd have to be standing out there, in the open, right in front of his target. He doesn't like that at all. He prefers to be anonymous. But he does like to watch, so his bombs are perfect.

He crafts them with his own hands, each one created with love and pride. He knows he is a talented man and he truly enjoys electronics, finding the building of his explosive devices to be deceptively simple, especially as he plans well and works methodically. These are his strengths. And he considers his devices to be a form of art, things of beauty. Simply meant to be shared, and admired.

Being here, amongst the turmoil in the courtyard, it's hard to contain himself. He knows he must keep a straight face, even try to look a little upset, but it's not easy. He's bursting with pride and with satisfaction even though he is bleeding a little. But the wound is worth it. He'd been a bit too close, underestimated the power of his work. But he'd done good. He'd done great!

As people continue to leak out of the building and into the courtyard, he keeps his face as expressionless as he can, watching with joy in his heart at the chaos he has created. The excitement continues to tingle feverishly within.

Today he is Thor, God-of-Thunder.

THREE

Events at the hospital are a blur as grief and denial overcome me. Later I am unable to remember how I got there, or much of my interaction with any of the doctors or nurses. Faces come and go. People scurry around, rushing from one emergency to the next.

The police try to talk with me, but I'm too confused and deafened to understand what it is they want to know.

Eventually I'm cleared for discharge and someone helps me outside and into a taxi. I don't recall giving the driver my address, but soon I find myself being dropped off at home and I shuffle mindlessly towards the front door.

It is late Friday afternoon now, school is out and Rosie – my ten-year-old cousin who lives next door – calls out to say hello. I think I manage to wave back, but I'm in no mood or condition to be sociable. As expected, no one else is home so I take myself off to bed without a thought for food and cry myself to sleep.

I awaken mildly disoriented – and very hungry – the next morning. I still can hear little more than a constant buzz, my throat is dry and my body aches all over. I sit up in bed and look myself up and down. I'm still wearing my ruined clothing from yesterday and I have dressings and bandages all over my legs and arms. A number of dark bruises leer at me from the exposed skin between them, and then I discover a wider bandage wrapped around my left upper arm, which I can't bring myself to look beneath. Feeling anxious, I gingerly ease my way across my bedroom to survey my face in the mirror.

There is no real damage, thank God. Just a couple of light scratches and a darkening bruise beside my left eye. I quickly realise that I've been very lucky as the blackened and smouldering image of Janet suddenly springs up in my mind. I'm immediately overwhelmed with both grief and anger and sink to the floor before my bedroom mirror, sobbing.

Eventually I compose myself enough to lurch stiffly through to the bathroom. I strip off my clothes, ignoring the multitude of dressings and step under the hot shower. The water is scalding and stings my battered body but I stay under the steady flow for what seems like hours. Maybe if I stay here long enough the downpour will wash away not only the grime from my horrific experience but also the ache in my heart.

After what seems like an eternity, I drag myself away from the cleansing waters as I succumb to my stomach's growls of hunger.

With my hair wrapped in a towel and my bathrobe on, I walk carefully through to the kitchen to make breakfast. Toast and strong, hot coffee. Fast and simple. I light a few of my own home-made aromatherapy candles. A couple of lavender ones to help relieve tension, and a sandalwood one to reduce stress. God, but I need them today.

Slowly, through the persistent buzzing in my ears, I become aware that the phone is ringing, more so from the flashing display than by any audible sound. I pick it up and say hello, but can only hear faint sounds of a voice somewhere distant.

'I'm sorry,' I shout, 'I can't hear you. Can you speak up?'

I am pretty sure the voice begins shouting back, but I still can't make out the words.

'I'm sorry, but I can't hear you. I have to hang up. I'm sorry,' I apologise and push the 'end' button. I realise I'm a little relieved. I'm not ready to talk, at least not yet. I put the phone down and go back to bed.

I'm drifting fitfully in and out of sleep when I realise there's someone knocking at the front door. At least I think that's what I can hear. My bedside clock tells me it's still morning. I sit up sharply and listen. My left ear remains plagued by a persistent buzzing, but it seems to have faded from my right ear considerably.

I reach the door with my hair still damp and bedraggled, hugging my robe tightly around me. Through the frosted glass panels in the front door I can see the shape of a big man, wearing blue, and another slightly smaller shape just behind him. My immediate impression is of police officers, and I feel a rush of panic.

Opening the door – only a crack – I confirm my visitors are in fact a uniformed police officer and a middle-aged woman. Before I can speak the uniformed man introduces himself as Officer Something-or-other and the woman as Detective Someone-else and asks if they may come in. I open the door instinctively, but the woman reaches out to stop the man from entering. She is watching me intently and her eyes show some concern. I must look a mess.

'Are you Lillian Grace MacDonald?'

Her voice is a bit distant through the variance of humming in my ears, but I hear the question clearly enough.

'Yes. Lily,' I reply, possibly a little louder than necessary.

She smiles kindly, 'Lily, we need to talk with you about the explosion at your workplace yesterday. Would it be con-venient to come in and ask you a few questions right now?'

I don't really want to talk about it, but know that I will eventually have to, so I nod reluctantly. The detective smiles again. She is tall and lean, and carries herself with a calm air of authority. She speaks again, 'Thank you. Perhaps you'd be more comfortable if we let you dress first?'

Suddenly I feel foolish, standing there in nothing but a robe. Pulling it tighter I usher them in, close the door and quickly slip away to get dressed.

I answer their questions as best I can. Many seem odd, but I feel sure they have their reasons. First they ask me to run through everything that I remember directly after the explosion and then they probe for a while about anything I can remember happening just beforehand. Did I see anyone unusual on the floor? No. Had there been anyone I didn't recognise? No. Had there been any unusual activity, such as a person moving more quickly than usual? I didn't think so. Do I remember seeing anyone using a cell-phone, or anything similar? No. Were any of my co-workers acting strangely? No, not really, other than Steve. I'm asked to explain Steve's odd behaviour.

'Well, it was nothing really,' I hesitate, unsure what to say. 'Steve called me just minutes before the explosion and asked to meet with me straight away. He didn't say why, just that he needed to ask me a couple of questions quickly as he had to hurry to another appointment.'

'And this was directly before the explosion?'

'Yes, just moments before. If Steve hadn't called I would have still been sitting at my desk when it went off . . .'

I tail off as the realisation sinks home again, and involuntarily shiver. The lady detective reaches out and steadies me, telling me to take a minute to breathe, to relax. My thoughts spin feverishly and I close my eyes, hugging myself tight as I fight to hold back a wave of tears.

After a few minutes I open my eyes and try to blink myself back into the here and now. When she thinks I've recovered sufficiently the detective speaks again.

'Can you tell me a little more about Steve please, Lily?'

I try to focus. Eventually I tell her that Steve Cassidy is one of Hawthorne Building Supply's salesmen, responsible for promoting the company's services to the building trade. He's good too, a top performer. He's been with HBS for a couple of years and is doing very well. He's big, good-looking, early twenties, with a reputation as a ladies man. Otherwise, I don't know much more about him. She asks if I think his call might have been about business, or was it possibly a social call? I say I don't know. I tell her that he had asked to meet with me, in private, and straight away. I noticed there was no one in the meeting room on my floor so suggested it as a meeting place. He'd agreed and hung up. I'd left my desk as soon as I saw him step out of the lift and headed towards the room.

The male officer produces a floor plan of the entire third floor. It's reasonably detailed with offices, meeting rooms, cubicles and storage areas clearly marked. There is an ominous, large circle sketched at one end of the floor.

He asks me to point out my desk, and where Steve and I met. My stomach lurches as I wave my finger vaguely at the circle on the plan.

'That's where the explosion happened,' I say, horrified.

He hesitates, deferring to the detective who is watching me carefully. She confirms what is obvious, 'Yes'.

I feel my head shaking robotically in disbelief as I point specifically. My workplace is almost at the centre of the sketched circle. The bomb must have been positioned very near my desk.

Choking back a strong urge to vomit I then wave my finger back down to the far end of the floor plan to the small meeting room, just near the lift doors.

'This is where we were going to meet.'

'And you were in this room when the explosion occurred?' the detective asks.

'No, not quite. Steve was at the door. I was just arriving.'

'What happened then?'

I take a deep breath and describe what I remember of the impact of the explosion, and then how we had picked ourselves up and made our way down the stairs, with Steve helping me. She asks if Steve had a cell-phone with him. I don't recall seeing one. Do I remember seeing anyone in the building or outside, that looked out-of-place? No. Or someone who didn't appear to be upset or in shock? Not that I can remember.

I ask her if anyone has been killed. I know in my heart that Janet is dead, but had been too confused yesterday to confirm anything more. She sits back, this time deferring to the male officer. In a careful tone he tells me that there have been casualties with a number of other people injured.

Without pause the detective then asks me if I have any enemies? Initially I think it's a stupid question. No, of course not. But as she starts asking more questions about my private life – do I gamble or take drugs, am I politically active, have I travelled overseas recently – I realise that she's wondering if I may have been the intended target.

My God, the bomb was right beside my desk. Was I the target? Was someone trying to kill me? But that's just not possible. I'm not important. I've never hurt anyone. Why would anyone want to kill me? I start to lose it and turn from them, curling up into a ball, choking back tears.

She waits fairly patiently until I restore some semblance of control. But then she starts in again with questions about my workmates and the company and I start to feel exhausted. The interrogation is relentless and repetitive and eventually my answers ebb away to become little more than monosyllabic uttering. I'm emotionally drained by the time they decide I have little else to offer and finally leave.

What a relief. Talking about it over and over, and so clinically, hurts too deeply. I really need to be alone for a while. After dragging myself back to bed I stare numbly at the ceiling until I somehow drift away.

Mid-afternoon I force myself outside to sit in the back yard and soak up some sun. I curl my legs up beneath me on the porch swing-chair and force myself to eat a sandwich while hugging a large, hot coffee to my chest.

I feel leaden and miserable. My ears still buzz, but I can now hear traffic noise from around the front of the house and other neighbourhood activity: a lawnmower a few houses down, loud music from somewhere else.

The phone has been ringing intermittently all day and I've turned the ringer volume down so that it won't bother me. I did answer one call from a reporter wanting to talk to me about the explosion. I hate to think how he got my number and hung up on him quickly. I understand that people will be interested. It'll be big news. But I really can't face the thought of talking to anyone else today, not about the bomb, not about anything.

Weatherwise, it's a beautiful day again. I want desperately to be relaxed and enjoy it, but I can't. My nerves are all edgy and I just can't get the horrific images out of my mind. Nor can I shake the detective's earlier line of questioning.

Was I the target? Surely not. And why had Steve called me to that meeting? He'd saved my life without a doubt. But had it been an incredible stroke of luck, or was it intentional? Had he known about the bomb? Did he save me deliberately?

I almost scream when a cat suddenly appears on the swing-chair beside me. It recoils too, mirroring my fright, but overcomes its surprise more quickly. It steps forward onto my legs and rubs up against me. It's just a kitten, probably only a few months old. I relax and reach out to pat it and it butts up towards my hand. In only a few seconds of stroking it is purring like a jack-hammer and I feel my tension easing.

It's amazing how comforting a small amount of affection from a cat can be. I actually smile. The kitten is just curling up on my lap when my cousin Rosie appears.

'There you are, Twinkle, you naughty puss,' she announces, striding purposefully up onto the deck where I am seated. 'I'm sorry, Lily. Twinkle shouldn't be over here.'

She reaches out, taking the errant kitten into her arms.

'It's only her second time outside and I'm trying to teach her to stay in our yard. She wasn't bothering you, was she?'

'Not at all,' I reply, surprised at how disappointed I am at having the kitten taken away. 'In fact she was being very friendly.' I look at them together: a picture of innocence at it's brightest. 'She's a lovely wee cat, Rosie. How long have you had her?'

Rosie beams with pride. 'About two weeks, but she's only been allowed outside this weekend and I'm making sure she doesn't get into trouble.'

Rosie's a cute kid with big green eyes and beautiful long strawberry-blonde hair. Her mother is my Dad's sister, and, as she's an only child, she's often looking for someone to play with or chat to. I can't help thinking that getting her a kitten is a great idea. It will give her somewhere to focus all that youthful exuberance.

'And who named her Twinkle?' I ask.

She smiles. 'Me. Do you like it?'

'It's beautiful and it suits her. Well done.'

Rosie is staring at me now, curious. 'What happened to your face, and your legs? You're all bruised and cut. Did you fall over?'

I find myself frozen by her question. How do you explain to a child that you almost died in an explosion at work? How do you express the horror of being lifted like a rag doll by the force of the blast and thrown across a room?

'Something like that,' I eventually say. 'But I'm okay, no real damage.'

Fortunately she accepts the vague response and doesn't push the subject. Instead she launches into an enthusiastic discourse on the responsibility of raising a kitten. She starts to tell me about Twinkle's litter tray and how she is feeding her special kitten food when I unexpectedly find myself overwhelmed by a deep feeling of despair. My chest tightens and I feel like I'm going to burst into tears yet again. I close my eyes, fighting it, and take a deep breath to try and calm myself. I become aware that Rosie has stopped talking and open my eyes.

'Are you all right? Should I go get my mum?' Rosie asks.

'No, no. Don't do that.' My aunt is a good person, but we don't always see eye to eye and I have no desire to deal with her right now. 'I'm okay, just a little tired. Maybe you should take Twinkle back home now?'

Rosie nods quietly. 'I hope you feel better soon,' she says as she turns and slips away with the kitten wrapped tightly in her arms.

I hope so too, but I doubt that I will.

FOUR

I return to my coffee and it perks me up slightly. Slipping inside the house, still moving quite gingerly, I retrieve the cordless phone from the kitchen and go back out to the swing-chair. Despite a growing sense of dread I have decided that I need to know more about yesterday and I know just who to call.

Nikki answers on the second ring. 'Speak to me,' she demands pleasantly.

'It's Lily,' I say quietly.

'Lily, oh my God. Are you okay? What happened to you yesterday? Where are you? Are you at the hospital? Are you all right? The bloody police wouldn't tell me. Neither would the people at the hospital. You're not hurt, are you?'

I wait for her to take a breath and confirm that I'm not really injured, I am all right, I'm at home, and definitely still in one piece. I manage to explain how I was well away from the explosion and how Steve Cassidy had pretty much carried me out of the building.

'Oh, babe! Steve Cassidy – you're kidding me. He is sooo hot, and now a real-life hero to boot. I might just say yes the next time he asks me out.'

Nikki isn't being flippant, Steve asks her out at least once a week and she always turns him down. Mind you, Nikki is a living, breathing Barbie doll and almost every single guy at work has asked her out at least once. But, in her mid-thirties, she's at least ten years older than Steve, probably fifteen years older than me, and she doesn't date younger men.

But Nikki, who is the CEO's secretary, is also the heart and soul of the office gossip tree, so I'm certain she will know everything there is to know about the explosion at work yesterday. And, of course, she does.

'Tell me,' I ask tentatively, 'is Janet . . .' I can't say the word. There is a moment's silence on the phone and then she speaks softly.

'I'm sorry. I know you two were good mates, but Janet, umm . . . no, she didn't survive.'

I hesitate, feeling sick, then ask, 'Who else was hurt?'

She sighs. 'The police are being cagey, but the best I can tell is that three people died, including Janet, and four others were injured, not including you and Steve.' She pauses momentarily and I wait, knowing I don't have to ask. 'Adam Mitchell and Henry Warrington were also killed in the blast, and Mike Smith is in hospital. He was pretty badly hurt. John was there too, but he's relatively okay.' Then she names the other injured people, but tells me that none are serious, just a few bad cuts and bruises.

I can scarcely believe it. The dead are a significant part of HBS's senior management team. Adam Mitchell, who, I sadly recall, only recently turned thirty, was our Chief Financial Officer and Henry Warrington was my boss, the Administration Manager. Mike Smith, whom I get on with really well, is our Sales Manager. I'm so glad he's alive. And the 'John' that Nikki has mentioned is our CEO, her boss, Jonathon Green. She tells me that he was very lucky. He'd just ducked under a desk to pick up a dropped pen when the bomb went off, and that act saved his life. All of the other injured are women who work in either Finance or the Administration Department with me on the third floor. And then there's Janet.

My good friend, and supervisor, Janet Tripp. Small, blonde and bubbly, with an infectious laugh and a deviously sharp sense of humour. My friend Janet, who wore little round-framed 'John-Lennon-style' glasses, and who mentored me with care and affection over the last two years. She taught me so much. Not just about time management and other work-related things, but also about dealing with people, managing their expectations and getting along. She was simply amazing at diffusing conflict and could honestly name every employee in the company. Janet was a natural leader, calm and assured and I know that I am going to miss her incredibly.

The memory of a blackened body with wisps of blonde hair and the remains of a pink blouse flashes before me and I let out a sob. I feel numb again and go quiet.

Nikki is unnaturally silent too for almost a whole minute, and then she kindly offers to come around and sit with me. I should really say yes, but I still just want to be alone. I can't face company today.

Eventually I convince her I'm okay, promise to call her tomorrow, and hang up. The phones display starts to flash again almost immediately and I'm thankful I still have the ringer volume off. I put the phone face down on the chair beside me and try to ignore it.

I think of the floor plan the detective showed me earlier. Across the aisle from my desk was a large meeting room, one that was practically the centre of operations for the senior management team at present. I vaguely recall seeing Adam wandering past my desk just as the phone rang with Steve's call. He was going into the meeting room for yet another discussion about the merger HBS is in the middle of.

I sit and stare vacantly into the garden as my mind reels.

Adam Mitchell and Henry Warrington are both dead, and so is Janet. Mike is badly injured. And some of my other workmates are bruised, bloody and battered, as I am, too.

I sit in a daze for hours before realising it's getting dark. I take myself back inside and crawl into bed again.

I awake the next morning to more knocking at my front door. As I stagger out to open it I'm able to make out a diminutive figure through the frosted glass. Of course, I finally realise, it's Sunday morning. Megan is here for our weekly long run. I let her in.

'So you are still alive,' she snaps at me, 'I was getting bloody worried.'

I smile crookedly at her. Megan isn't one to mince words. We've known each other since primary school and I'm now impervious to her forthright manner. In fact I quite envy her ability to say whatever she thinks and damn the consequences. I'm always too polite.

'Christ,' she exclaims, 'you're a mess! Look at you. You *were* in that bloody bombing! Why the hell didn't you call me, or at least answer your god-damn phone? I've left a dozen messages.' She glares at me angrily, and then finally softens, 'Are you all right?'

For the first time I answer honestly, 'No, not really.'

Megan steps into the house, swiftly closing the door behind her and wraps her arms around me. It feels good to be held. I start to sob, yet again, and lean into her embrace. She leads me through to the couch in the lounge and we curl up together as I cry in her arms. For a few minutes she whispers softly as I shake and sob, and then I take a deep breath, determined to control myself, and am still.

'You want to tell me all about it?' she asks gently. I don't, but I think I need to.

She listens patiently as I talk through the horror show that my life has become since going to work on Friday morning. I tell her about the call from Steve, being flung through the air, the glass and debris, the smoke and the rain. I tell her about the charred shape that lay on the floor where Janet should have been, the feeling of disorientation, the aching in my bones, and the pit of despair that now languishes in my heart.

When I finish talking she just holds me tight and I soak up the strength of her. Maybe I should have called her yesterday, but I was too numb to talk. Too lost within myself.

'Jesus,' she finally mutters, 'that was one crappy Friday.'

Her blunt summation works wonders for me. I smile a little and almost laugh.

'So, are we going for a run now or are you going to offer me a cuppa?' she asks.

I know she's just trying to lighten the mood and I'm glad. Megan is like a sister to me, and we even look a bit alike too. We're a similar average height, both with long dark brown hair. She's a fraction heavier on the hips and I'm a tiny bit fuller in the chest, but we are still able to share our wardrobes easily when the mood takes us. Only our eyes set us apart, with mine a deep brown and hers a bright blue.

Those clear blue eyes look me up and down slowly as she sits back and asks, 'So, what's under there?' pointing at the bandage on my left arm.

'I don't know,' I admit. 'I've been too afraid to look.'

She immediately begins to unwrap the bandage, revealing a wound a few centimetres long that has been stitched up tidily. 'Oooh, nice, that's going to leave a cool scar,' she says. 'Is that it?' I stretch my legs out to display the mosaic of plasters. She reaches out and strips one off before I can object. Beneath it is a small cut. 'You're kidding, what a waste of a good plaster. Is that it?' she asks again, teasing.

'I think I was pretty lucky.'

'You can say that again. You look like you went a few rounds with a rose bush, but that's about all.' She points at my head, 'No concussion, or anything?'

She is making light of my injuries, trying to downplay them. Again I am grateful.

'No, I'm fine. But I'm not going out running today. I think I've earned a day off. Do you still want that coffee?'

While I pull together some coffee and breakfast in the kitchen, Megan chatters away, clearly trying to talk about anything other than my traumatic experience. But after a while she slips back to the subject and asks if the police have come to see me yet. She's curious, I knew she would be. She works at the local police headquarters in an administrative role, a civilian position. But she loves police work and is always talking about one or another of those millions of crime shows they have on TV these days. Getting the job at the station was a dream come true for her and she is one of the few people I know who trots off to work with real excitement each day.

I tell her about the visit yesterday morning, a little embarrassed that I don't remember either of the officers' names. However, I don't need to describe them as, apparently, they only have one female detective on staff at present, Natalie Dowd. Megan seems to like her and tells me she is smart, but there is a bit of envy in her voice. When I describe the way Natalie focused in on Steve's call, just minutes before the explosion, Megan is intrigued.

'Wow, that does seem pretty suspicious, doesn't it?'

'Suspicious or not, I'm pretty pleased he called.'

'Oh yeah, for sure.' Megan pauses, contemplating something. 'You know, the media think there may be a connection with the bombing at the City Council carpark a couple of weeks ago. If I heard right yesterday, the guys at work think it might be the same bomber.'

I don't know what to say. Of course I'd heard about *that* bombing. Who hadn't? Only it hadn't yet occurred to me that they might be linked. But suddenly it's obvious though. Two bombings in a matter of weeks in a place the size of Hawthorne. They really have to be connected, don't they?

'But why? Why would someone bomb both HBS and the Council?'

Megan shrugs, 'I don't know. I guess that's why I'm a lowly admin clerk who's not making any waves in the detective pool. But someone must have benefited, surely. There has to be a reason. Some kind of link. I guess that's who Natalie will be looking for. Someone who has gained something from both bombings. Don't you think?'

She's probably right, but talking about it is making me uncomfortable and I don't answer. Naïvely, I wish I could just put it out of my mind and pretend it never happened. As if not thinking about it might change something. But it won't.

Sensing my discomfort Megan lapses into silence too, holding her coffee mug in front of her and staring into it, deep in thought. As I watch her I suddenly have a strong feeling that she is thinking about her father, worrying about him. Without thinking I hear myself speak.

'Don't worry, it's not as bad as they first thought.'

Megan blinks and looks up at me sharply. 'What?'

'It's not as bad as they first thought,' I repeat. I can't help myself. The words come from nowhere and just tumble out of me. 'Your dad's thing, it can be fixed.'

She stares at me for a long moment, a touch of wariness in her eyes. 'How do you know about my dad's thing? He made us swear to secrecy. I haven't told anyone.'

I feel myself flush with embarrassment. I don't under-stand what I've just said, or why. 'I'm sorry Meg, I just . . .' I have to pause, suddenly totally unsure of myself. 'I just . . .' I start again and tail off. Her dad had just popped into my head and I'd felt utterly compelled to share the thought with her. But the truth is, I'm just as confused as she is.

Megan frowns, her cheeks starting to flush, but then something seems to draw her back from the brink of an outburst and she calms herself. She watches me carefully for a minute before asking, 'You don't know what Dad's thing is, do you Lily?'

I can't trust myself to speak so just shake my head a little. I have absolutely no idea.

'So, where did that come from?'

'I . . . I don't know. It just came out,' I reply hesitantly.

There is an uncomfortable silence for another few seconds and then Megan brushes it off, thankfully changing the subject.

'You going back to work tomorrow?'

'I guess so,' I answer quickly, keen to move past the weirdness. I lift my legs off the floor and wave them at her, 'See if I can find another rose bush to do battle with, eh? There's still a little fight left in me.' I grin hopefully and she offers a fractured smile in return. She seems to have forgiven, if not forgotten, my strange comment.

I try to push it out of my mind. I have more than enough clutter in there for now.

Megan stays until early afternoon. We just chat and hang out, but it is positively therapeutic. I open up and talk a little about Janet and the others from my work and she listens attentively, allowing me to process some of my pain. It helps more than I expect and the weight of my grief eases slightly.

After she's gone I think about going for a run on my own, to clear my head further, but decide not to push myself so soon. Instead I light a couple more candles (Jasmine, to try and lift my spirits), run a deep bath and, after peeling off all my annoying little plasters and turning up the stereo, I soak myself in soothing lavender bath salts until the water goes cold. For a while there I almost manage to forget my sorrow. Almost.

Once I finally drag myself out of the bath and get dressed the house suddenly feels very empty. It's been lovely here for the last week – my own peaceful haven with Greg and Cheryl away – but now it seems forlorn and bleak, the house too quiet.

I've only just turned twenty, so am not ashamed about still living at home, but I know I should be thinking about going flatting and challenging myself a bit more. I have a relatively comfortable arrangement here at home with my Dad and neither he nor my step-mother Cheryl are putting any pressure on me to move out.

That said, I have to admit that up until today I had really been enjoying having the house to myself with them away on their big annual holiday. This year they're somewhere in South America, possibly cruising the Amazon, or perhaps trekking their way up to Machu Picchu. It's planned as a three-week trip and I haven't so much as glanced at the itinerary they left behind since they went last week. I could easily work out where they are if I want to try and make contact with them, but I don't feel the need. Physically I'm okay and I have no desire to upset their holiday over a few scratches and bruises. I'll just catch them up on my horrific Friday when they get home.

I spend the afternoon and evening mooching around the house. I think about making a few new candles. I have a new mould I've been meaning to try, but I just can't seem to summon the enthusiasm. So I watch a little TV instead, then read for a bit and generally try to occupy my mind with superficial stuff. I remember that I'd promised to call Nikki back today, but can't bring myself to do it. I'm sure she'll understand.

Eventually I head to bed and sleep fitfully.

FIVE

I'm normally quite cheerful on Mondays. I actually like my job and genuinely enjoy the companionship of the people I work with. But today is different.

I arrive at the office at my normal time and just stand in the courtyard outside, looking up at the windows, watching my co-workers milling around inside. I have no real sense of foreboding, but I'm desperately uncomfortable. Three people died here only a couple of days ago. Many others were injured. Working here will never be the same again.

A little disconcertingly I'm surprised that very little of what I see looks different to life before the bomb. I'm not sure what I expected. There are no longer police, fire or ambulance vehicles littered around the courtyard. The only item out of the ordinary is a large rubbish skip tucked around the corner from the main entrance. I assume it's now full of charred furniture or waterlogged and smoke-damaged carpets.

Everything else looks normal. The smokers are gathered for a last good puff before lock-down and others are just going about their business.

I've worked here for just over two years now and, until Friday, had been enjoying it. I decided not to go to university, opting instead to get a job straight from high school. My first job, as a sales assistant in a fashion boutique, wasn't really me. After that I tried my hand in a bakery for a few months, but I hated the odd hours. This job, where I work as an Administration Assistant, seems to much better suit my natural organisational skills, and with a larger staff it's a lot more sociable after hours.

As I will myself to get a grip and enter the building, a hand comes to rest gently on my shoulder. I jump in surprise, letting out a squeal of shock.

Nikki pulls her hand away quickly and puts both hands up in the air in a pose of surrender.

'Sorry, babe, I didn't mean to frighten you.'

'That's okay,' I reply. 'I was just gathering my thoughts.'

She smiles at me with her warm eyes and wraps her arm around my shoulder, pulling me in for a hug. 'Today will be a better day, little one,' she announces positively and then leads me gently into the building.

Nikki guides me to the lifts and we make our way up to the fourth floor, one level above my normal workplace, and straight into a small kitchenette.

'Let me conjure you up a coffee and then we'll get you sorted for the day. It's all still pretty messed up round here.'

I'm grateful to her and just nod compliantly. Soon, with a hot coffee in hand, Nikki fills me in on the latest.

'No big surprise here, but level three is out-of-bounds. The police have it sealed off at the moment, but we've been told it will be released to our cleaning crew by midday tomorrow. Fortunately all the mess was only on that floor, so everyone else is still able to truck along "business as usual". Until they get your area sorted out, I've made arrangements for Admin to run from the boardroom here on level four. Claire and Lauren are already in there.'

'And Edna?'

'She wasn't hurt, but she's taking a week's leave – to recuperate.'

Edna is another of my co-workers in Admin. She's older, near retirement, and probably could have used a break even without the bombing.

'What about our files, and computers?'

'All sorted, babe. Well, in part anyway. I dragged in some of the IT geeks over the weekend and they've already set up temp systems for you guys up here, and for the bean-counters down on level one. You'll each have one of the pool lap-tops for now, until they can get level three restored and you move back in.'

The thought of going back to my floor sends a chill through me and I flinch. Nikki notices this and frowns, concern in her eyes. But she doesn't say anything and resumes her briefing, watching me carefully.

'Apparently all your electronic files will still be accessible, so you haven't lost everything. But all your paper files are pretty much history. You'll need to reprint a lot of it.' She pauses, then reaches out and takes me by the hand. 'Come and see the boardroom. Laurel and Hardy will be glad to see you.'

Nikki shows me through to the boardroom where my equally bruised and battered co-workers, Lauren and Claire, are already seated, trying to patch together their systems and working structures.

I'm surprised by how pleased I am to see them.

Claire is a middle-aged, slightly overweight mother of four with a fairly caustic tongue. She still looks the same, with no apparent injuries. Lauren, on the other hand, has two lines of stitches across the right-hand side of her face. She's around the same age as Claire and has always had a perpetually mournful outlook. The stitches will obviously leave some pretty dramatic scars.

We all stare at each other uncertainly. Without Janet, there is a huge void between us. Then Nikki ushers me into a chair at the big board-meeting table and sits down herself. I hold the coffee mug tightly as she sets about updating us.

'Okay guys, I've been asked to let you know that the supermen at Head Office have already arranged for one of their guys to fly over and stand in as Admin Manager – until a full appointment can be made to replace Henry.'

This makes me oddly uncomfortable. Henry was in his early sixties and had been with the company for years and years. The poor man has only been dead for a matter of days and a replacement is already on the way. It feels wrong.

'But that won't happen,' Nikki continues, '. . . until the merger is finalised and everything gets sorted out. The nice man from HQ is expected here tomorrow, so babe here will be holding the fort for today – for anything that can't wait till tomorrow.'

I nearly choke into my coffee cup.

'Oh God, you can't be serious,' I splutter. 'Why me?' I'm genuinely surprised and look to Lauren and Claire for support. Both of them have been with HBS much longer than me and should be considered senior. But Lauren just gives a small shrug and shakes her head.

'Don't look at us like that,' Claire snipes, rolling her eyes. 'They're not going to put me in charge of anything, are they? For crying out loud, Lily, you and Janet were running the show anyway, we all knew that. Makes sense to me and it's only one day.'

Lauren offers a small smile and nods softly, confirming that she is okay with the decision too.

'Just for today,' Nikki repeats.

Without Henry and Janet, the Admin team is in tatters and I realise that I am now the only person alive, other than Jonathon Green, with a reasonable overview of the planned merger process. I am to be the interim Admin Manager, just for a day.

I sigh theatrically in resignation. But if I'm honest, I'm more than a little flattered.

Then, just as Nikki is about to press on with other news, Dave, one of HBS's mail runners, strolls in.

'So this is where you lot are hiding now,' he announces. 'I found the Finance girls down near us on level one, jammed in like sardines. This is much better.'

Dave is part of a two-man team that works out of a small space on level one. He and his colleague Reuben are responsible for distributing mail, stationary supplies, and other odd jobs around the company. They're also part of the Administration Team. Dave is a small man, aged somewhere in his forties, who tends to strut around the building with his chest out and shoulders back, displaying a general air of arrogance rather at odds with his lowly position. He's an odd man.

'So is anyone else being moved about?' he asks.

No one immediately answers him. Nikki stays silent and looks over at me. Normally Janet oversees Dave and Reuben, and it takes a moment for me to realise that they are all waiting for me to respond. What a short memory. Today I am in charge of the Admin team. I finally find my voice.

'Sorry, Dave, not that I know of. Actually, Nikki was just about to update us a little more. Do you want to sit in?'

Initially he seems surprised at the invitation, but nods self-importantly and quickly makes himself at home. Neither of the mailroom guys are the sharpest tools in the shed, but both are fairly industrious. Letting Dave sit in means that he can brief Reuben on everything too, saving me from that little job. We all then look expectantly at Nikki, who loves being the centre of attention.

'Right then,' she says, puffing up a little. She quickly repeats the news about an interim Admin Manager coming from Head Office tomorrow and reconfirms that I am team leader for the day. Then she moves on to other pressing issues.

'Sean Peterson will be picking up the CFO role and Hector Lawson will be filling in as Sales Manager for Mike Smith while he's in hospital. And, as Dave's just said, they-who-control-the-purse-strings have been re-housed on level one for the time being.'

Neither of the management appointments are a surprise. Both men are very capable, but I do notice Claire wrinkle her nose as Nikki mentions Hector from Sales. A brief image from the courtyard last Friday hits me. Hector standing alone, staring up at the building, his arm bleeding. He must have been on level three when the bomb went off, though I don't remember seeing him there. Claire flashes a look at Lauren who just shrugs again, passively. Hector is one of those guys who is brilliant at schmoozing the customers, but is often rude and insensitive when dealing with our own staff. Claire hates Hector and makes no secret of it. To be honest I'm not really that fond of him either.

Nikki continues, choosing her words carefully.

'And, as I understand it, Head Office has advised that they still need the human resource realignment proposal for the merger completed by this Friday.'

'You can't be serious,' I say in surprise.

'Apparently they're adamant.'

I'm appalled. 'But surely, given all that's happened . . .'

She makes a face. 'I know. I'm sorry, babe, but they've made it very clear. No delays. The word is that deferring the merger would cost too much, and the Board won't accept that – because losing money tends to upset the shareholders. So that's why they're sending their pinch-hitter down so urgently. Sorry, but it seems that delaying the CCS merge is not an option.'

I struggle with this news.

Our merger with the smaller Commonwealth Construction Supplies has been the number-one priority around here lately, and the realignment proposal is a highly sensitive part of it.

To put it simply, the HBS Admin team's job – the realignment proposal – is to work out how many people the new organisation (to be called Westwood Building & Construction Limited once merged) will need, and in what roles, and then set a process in place to make it all happen. The result will see a fairly significant reduction in total head count from both companies.

We had been on schedule to deliver the realignment plans by this week's deadline, but I just presumed last Friday's tragedy – where we lost two of the draft proposal's key architects, Henry and Janet – would have changed that. Head Office couldn't be serious, surely.

Unexpectedly, Lauren puts her two-cents-worth in, the stitches on her face making her words sound even more strained.

'We can do it, Lily. We can get it finished by Friday.'

'Yeah, sure we can,' Claire says peevishly. 'And maybe the guy they're sending from Head Office will actually be helpful and not just get in the way.' Sarcasm is Claire's default-setting. I say nothing.

'Hey, come on,' Nikki weighs in. 'They're not going to send down a complete drop-kick.'

'No, they'll probably drag some geriatric out of retirement and he'll make us work out the numbers on an abacus,' Claire retorts. 'Or he'll just want to draw names from a hat.'

'That's not going to happen,' I interject, trying to shut Claire down before she really gets on a roll. Once she builds up steam she's hard to stop. I turn to face my co-workers. 'Whoever they send, we'll make the best of it and make it happen. Okay?'

There is a moment's silence and then, to my surprise, Claire just shrugs and lets it go. Lauren nods and tries to force a smile. I'm pretty sure Dave hasn't got the faintest idea of what we are talking about, but he nods too. I feel a little relieved, just for a second before the reality of the task before us begins to sink in. Previously, with Henry and Janet responsible for the outcome, I'd approached the restructure with some level of detachment. All care, but no responsibility. But now, abruptly, I find myself in the unenviable position of having to make some very serious recommendations that will affect many people's lives. It's more than a little overwhelming.

I turn back to Nikki. 'Okay then. Is there anything else we need to know?'

She starts to say something and then changes her mind. 'No. I think that's plenty to be getting along with for now.'

I nod to her and then turn to Dave. 'Would you mind updating Reuben for me please, Dave?'

He stands and salutes me, with an odd smirk on his face. 'Sure thing, boss,' he says, turning quickly and leaving. I frown. Was he mocking me? I'm not sure.

Nikki rises too and moves over to stand right in front of me. She looks me straight in the eye. 'You can do it, babe. I believe in you.'

I take a deep breath, steeling myself, as Nikki turns to leave. Then she stops and faces me again quickly. 'I'm sorry . . . did I mention Janet's funeral?'

I look back at her blankly. She didn't.

'It's this afternoon, at 4 pm, Five Rivers Cemetery.' She adds softly, 'Would you like me to take you?'

I nod gently, a tear already forming in my eye.

SIX

Nikki appears by my side later that afternoon without fanfare, but this time I don't recoil in surprise.

The day has been intense and literally flown by, but we are making progress and I'm beginning to think that we may actually get things running reasonably smoothly fairly soon. I've already found that whenever I need help from one of the other departments they now assist meekly, probably in some form of reverence to our losses. Much of the posturing of previous weeks has been knocked out of the other managers, while the guys standing in are going out of their way to be helpful. Even the Marketing people, who are usually so full of themselves, have been cooperating. I can't help wondering, a little cynically, if this will last.

I decide not to try and take any work home with me. I feel pretty sure I won't feel up to it once I get home from the funeral, which I have been trying to push out of my mind all day. But it keeps looming into my thoughts.

I hate funerals.

I haven't been to many, but attending my own mother's – when I was only nine years old – has pretty much put me off for life. Most of my memories of my early childhood are hazy, but the grief and anguish of the days around Mum's funeral remain with me as clear as day. I don't want to go to Janet's funeral, but know that I have to.

God, I hate funerals.

We arrive at the cemetery to discover that it is to be a closed-casket affair, held outside at the open grave. Just like my mother's. Fortunately, as if I'd known in advance, I've dressed sombrely today, so don't feel out of place. There are quite a few people from work, including Lauren and Claire, but also a good number of others I don't know. I recognise Janet's husband but can't bring myself to walk over and say hello. My chest feels so tight that I don't think I can speak without bursting into a river of tears.

A clergyman of some type draws the crowd together by the casket and begins his eulogy. Nikki and I move towards a small group of our workmates and stand silently, listening to the man talking about Janet.

He speaks about what a wonderful inspiration she was, what warmth and caring she bought to her relationships, what joy and laughter she shared with us all. He speaks as if he truly knew her.

It's then that I start to feel anger all around me. The feeling of frustration that suddenly engulfs me is palpable, but it feels odd. It's not the way I normally experience this emotion, and I abruptly realise that this anger and frustration isn't my own. Rather, I'm somehow sensing it from someone nearby. Inexplicably, disjointed phrases form in my mind.

I sense the words;

–not just me–

and, don't ask me how, but somehow I just know that it's Janet.

–not just my life–

I can hear these words, or rather feel them, as clear as day. I look around wildly in surprise. Janet? All the other mourners are silently watching the clergyman or the coffin as more words come to me.

–it isn't right, my baby . . . it's just not right–

And immediately I understand.

Janet had been pregnant.

I don't understand how I know this, or why this knowledge should consume me in this way, but the feeling is strong and intense. Janet was pregnant, only a few weeks, but definitely pregnant. The lucidity of the revelation startles me and I realise that I have spoken something out loud because Nikki has suddenly grabbed me by the arms, staring into my face with a look of deep concern.

'Lily, are you all right?' she asks anxiously.

Everyone is staring at me. I'm overcome with embarrassment and blush deeply. 'I'm sorry,' I mumble. 'I didn't mean to interrupt. Please. I'm so sorry.'

The clergyman saves me by starting to talk about grief and how it is good to let your feelings out as I take a couple of steps back from the gathering and try to clear my head. Nikki follows me, concerned.

'What did you mean?' she asks in a whisper.

I can't answer. I don't know what I said.

'When you said "You didn't tell me", what did you mean?'

I'm dumbstruck. I don't remember thinking that, let alone speaking it aloud. But I immediately know what the words mean. You didn't tell me. Janet hadn't told me that she was pregnant. It was an accusation. Had I berated her aloud for not telling me this?

I feel dizzy. I'm suddenly confused at my own thoughts and feelings, but also absolutely certain that the revelation is true. Janet had been pregnant. But how can I be so sure?

I just shake my head at Nikki, not trusting myself to speak. But I feel cheated, betrayed. Janet didn't tell me she was pregnant. She was my friend, she should have told me.

But then I feel Janet again, this time a sudden flash of warmth in my heart, and I know. She was waiting until she was certain. She wanted to be sure the baby would take.

I relax a little and look past Nikki at the gathering around the graveside, once again becoming intensely aware of Janet's frustration and anger.

I somehow understand that she has accepted her own passing, but knowing of the life within her that will never come to be is tormenting her relentlessly.

I want to do something, but feel helpless.

After the ceremony the small crowd filters away towards their waiting cars. I stand aside and wait, having asked Nikki to meet me back at the car shortly. I need to speak to Derek, Janet's husband, alone.

When the opportunity arises I'm shaken by his immense sadness. His eyes are red and puffy, his face ashen and he seems to have shrunk considerably since we last met. He is a stocky and prematurely balding man, but he usually wears a mischievous smile, like he is just about to play a practical joke on you. Today I barely recognise him, he seems lesser somehow and there is no hint of that smile at all. I approach him as he stands by the open grave, tears gently tickling his cheeks. He looks as if he is considering throwing himself in after his wife.

'Derek, I'm so sorry,' I say gently as I come up beside him. He turns slightly and gives me a small smile of acknowledgement. I don't think he's able to talk. I stand beside him for a full minute, trying to work out what to say. Finally I just blurt it out. 'You knew she was pregnant, didn't you?'

He barely moves. After a few moments he gives a slow nod. He's still staring down into the open grave.

'I'm so sorry, Derek. I don't know what to say,' I hesitate, desperately searching for words of comfort, but finding little of any value. 'She was a wonderful person,' I manage.

He draws in a deep, sobbing breath. 'Yes,' he finally speaks, his voice cracking. After a moment he turns to me, with a faint smile. 'She wasn't supposed to tell anyone. Not yet, anyway. She was terrible with secrets. I suppose everyone knows?'

I look into his eyes. He isn't upset. He loved her way too much to be mad at her now. But I still feel that I need to defend her, to pay respect to her character.

'No, she didn't tell anyone. Honestly, not even me.' I realise it sounds confusing even as I am saying it. 'I just knew,' I add lamely.

He just looks at me, clearly bemused. I feel a sudden rush of emotion and find myself blurting out, 'You were her rock, Derek. You must know that. When you held her she felt invincible. She drew her strength from you.' I want to stop but the words just tumble out of me. 'But she needs to be forgiven for the kiss. She can't move on until you truly forgive her. She is so very, very sorry.' My mind is reeling and Derek's eyes have flown wide. 'I'm sorry, I don't know where that came from,' I apologise breathlessly.

-make him swear, make him swear-

The words form suddenly in my mind, pleading and desperate;

-must truly forgive me-

Words tumble from me again. 'When she kissed your friend Terry last year she was drunk. She wasn't thinking. She needs your forgiveness.'

I can't help myself, I simply have to let the words out. I somehow just know that Derek needs to hear them.

—make him swear—

And that Janet needs him to know.

—hurt him so bad, all my fault—

'Please, Derek. She needs you to forgive her,' I implore.

Derek just stares at me in shock.

'When did she tell you this?' he asks, looking around to see if anyone remains within earshot, but the others are all gone. We're alone. 'Why would she tell you this?' He looks hurt, astonished and confused, all at the same time.

I don't know what to think. I want to just stop and run away, but something is compelling me to stay and push forward. Like expressing this is my duty somehow.

'She didn't . . .' I start to say, and abruptly cut myself off. 'I don't know. All I know is that right now, right here, I need you to tell me that you forgive her.' I'm getting a little angry now, I don't know why.

–please forgive me, please–

I can feel Janet's pain. I can feel her need and it fires me up. 'She knows that she hurt you and she is so desperately sorry. She just needs your forgiveness. For God's sake, Derek, if you loved her just forgive her!'

'Lily, hey . . . calm down,' he replies soothingly, putting his arm around my shoulders. 'It's okay. We're both just badly shaken up here, all right? This has all been so sudden.'

I start to shiver. He pulls me in and hugs me tight.

–please, I'm so sorry, make him swear–

I gently push myself out of the embrace, staying close enough to look up into his tortured eyes. 'I know this is really weird and I don't really understand it myself, but please Derek . . .' I pause and wipe away a tear. 'Please, can you tell me that you forgive her for the kiss? Can you swear to me that you forgive her for that?'

I watch his eyes as he struggles to understand my demands. With a jolt, I abruptly understand that I have it wrong.

Derek has already forgiven her, and a long time ago.

It is Janet that has never really forgiven herself.

But Derek finally complies with my pleas. 'Of course I forgive her. And I've already told her so, many times.' He looks deeply concerned, 'Where is this coming from, Lily? Did Janet say something to you? Why are you asking this?'

Again I'm stumped for a response. We never discussed any kiss, ever. We've told each other a number of private things about out lives, but she'd never mentioned this kiss.

Nor did she mention anything about being pregnant. Everyone has their secrets, I guess.

I suddenly feel incredibly claustrophobic and step back. I look at Derek, seeing the confusion and worry in his face. Am I going mad? How do I know these things?

I finally find my voice. 'I'm sorry, Derek, I don't know. I just miss her, that's all.'

I can see he finds this response hopelessly inadequate, but I'm becoming frightened now. Something is wrong with me. There are voices in my head. No, not voices, but feelings, strong feelings that form into words. How is that possible?

I need to be alone, desperately. I apologise to Derek again and dart away quickly, leaving him bewildered beside the open grave of his wife and unborn child.

I avoid the carpark and drift away to the furthest corner of the cemetery I can find to be alone. I don't trust myself to be near anyone right now. My mind is spinning with panicked thoughts of impending lunacy.

What is happening to me?

SEVEN

I sit beneath a large old tree and hug my knees to my chest, curling up into a ball of confusion, and rock myself slowly.

I'm cracking up.

The explosion has scrambled my mind somehow and now I'm hearing things. Words, phrases, in my head. Not actual voices – that would be really crazy – just words, sharp and clear, and feelings. How do you hear feelings? My stomach lurches.

What the hell is going on? Is this some kind of reaction to the shock of the explosion, and my dead workmates, or to the gnawing belief that it should have been me? I'm reeling. Why was I saved? How is this fair?

Suddenly Nikki is there, yet again surprising me, trying to calm me. I'm crying and muttering to myself and she holds me until I stop. God, I'm seriously losing it here.

She gets me to my feet and leads me back to the car. I'm embarrassed, but also deeply frightened, isolated, adrift, alone. Am I losing my mind?

I can't talk to Nikki during the ride home. She can't possibly understand. How can I tell her about my crazy conversation with Derek? What could she say? I sit there miserably and try to clear my thoughts, realign myself. I'm okay. I'm fine. It's just the shock, I think, over and over again like a mantra.

'Do you want me to come in?' says Nikki as we pull up outside my place. I could throw some dinner together.'

I shake my head. 'No. I'm all right,' I lie. 'I'm just sad. I hate funerals.' I pause, taking a deep breath. I like Nikki, but she would never be my first choice as a confidante. She's too good with the gossip, but that's a double-edged sword. To be in the loop you have to give to receive and I don't want her sharing details of my insanity with anyone else at work. I try to smile for her. 'Thanks anyway, it's a nice offer. But I think I'll just run a hot bath and soak myself for a bit. That'll fix me.'

She isn't buying my act, but I can sense that she realises I'm not suicidal.

'Okay, babe,' she says softly, 'but you take it easy, all right?'

I nod, thank her again for the ride and for taking care of me, and climb out of the car. She watches me for a moment and then drives away as I give her a wave.

As I make my way inside I think about calling Megan and asking her to come over but I'm not sure I really want to share my craziness with her either. For now I decide I'm better off on my own.

When I arrive at work the next morning there is a post-it note on my lap-top in the boardroom. *'Meeting, John's office, 9.30 am,'* is all it says, but I recognise Nikki's handwriting. I wonder vaguely why she didn't send an email or a meeting request through the automated system. Perhaps she thinks my systems aren't working properly yet.

I spend a bit of time chatting with both Lauren and Claire, attempting to reassure them (and myself) that things are under control, while also trying to ensure they both have their portions of our massive workload planned out and prioritised, despite our unfamiliar surroundings. I try to joke with them and praise their efforts, just as I used to watch Janet do before. She was so good at managing people, and I desperately want to live up to her example.

So far the three of us haven't spoken about Janet to each other, not yet. Eventually we will, but for some reason we're all keeping our feelings bottled inside at the moment, probably because we're afraid we will publicly crumple and break down in tears.

At 9.30 am I arrive at John's office. Nikki is already there, arranging seating for what looks like a crowded gathering. Donald Swain, our IT Manager, is blushing faintly – as he always does around Nikki – while he helps her set up. Don is a pretty average guy all around, in height and size, but he wears his hair a little too long and never quite succeeds in dressing trendily. Although he is married, he's hopelessly smitten by our Nikki and would leap through a burning ring just to earn a smile from her. But Nikki has that effect on most men. And I note that she is clearly dressed to smite today – wearing her favourite and tightest little black dress. I idly wonder what the special occasion is.

Brendan Armstrong and Sean Peterson, our Marketing Manager and acting CFO respectively, are already seated. Brendan is a complete bastard, if I can be so frank. He shaves his head so no one can tell how bald he is getting and wears bright shirts that are supposed to look modern, but make him look like a clown. Sean is entirely different and I'm hoping he gets appointed fully to the CFO role once all is said and done. He's tall and lean, a genuinely nice guy with all his own hair and teeth. I like him.

Hector Lawson, the arrogant little acting Sales Manager, arrives as I take a seat near the door. He sits down next to me and raises his eyebrows quizzically, silently asking if I know what's going on. I just shrug and he frowns.

Others arrive and it starts to look like a full management team meeting, but cramming everyone into John's office is a bit odd. I guess with level three unavailable we must be low on meeting rooms.

Don finally stops trying to impress Nikki and sits down, noticing me for the first time. 'Hey Lily, how are you? Are all you Admin folk settling in to the boardroom?' he asks earnestly. Despite his all-too-obvious infatuation with Nikki I generally think of Don as a nice guy. I suddenly realise that getting all the computer systems re-set up over the weekend would have taken him and his staff quite some time.

'We're good thanks, Don. Everything seems to be working okay. We're just missing a lot of paperwork.' I almost add 'and some good people', but choke back the thought.

He smiles. 'You just call me if you ladies need anything else.'

I nod, starting to feel a little uncomfortable. It makes me sad to think that, despite the special effort they've put in over the weekend, Don's IT team is likely to take a fairly big hit in the coming restructure, especially as they're currently well overstaffed. Like most companies, HBS hired extra IT people to prepare for the dreaded Y2K bug that never eventuated. And I'm pretty sure that CCS have an excess of IT people as well, so something is definitely going to have to give there.

I realise that Nikki has wandered off and it strikes me that I am now not only the youngest person in the room by a large margin, but I'm also now the only woman. All the men around me are in their forties or fifties, with only Don in his late twenties. As the men in the now quite crowded room make quiet banter with each other, I sit silently, wondering why I have been invited here.

Then a man I don't know arrives and hovers in the doorway. He's dressed in a sharp grey suit and seems relaxed, but a little uncertain about what he's walking into. Suddenly Don jumps up, smiling, with a look of surprise on his face.

'Bobby, hey,' he cries, thrusting his hand out. 'How the hell are you?'

The room goes quiet as the stranger takes Don's hand and shakes it effusively. They're about the same age but the new man, Bobby, is taller and broader, quite good-looking really.

'Donald Swain, my God, this is a surprise,' he replies with a smile. 'Don't tell me you work here?'

'Damn right, Manager of Information Technology,' Don grins back. 'So what are you doing here?'

Just then Jonathon Green, HBS's CEO, enters the room and Bobby hesitates. 'Sit down, Don,' he says quietly. 'All will be revealed,' and he takes a seat himself.

Rather than moving around to sit behind his desk, John stops and perches on top of it, facing the occupants of his now quite crowded office. I notice Nikki move in to join us also, quietly pulling the door shut behind her, her face impassive. What's going on?

John waits for a moment, seeming to gather his thoughts. He is entirely bald but, unlike Brendan Armstrong, carries this off with both grace and strength. As always he seems to radiate confidence, which I find both a little attractive and also intimidating. I'm surprised to see him back at work so soon after the explosion, but he only has one small plaster on his mildly bruised face while his left hand is swathed in a white bandage. Other than that he looks as sharp and focused as usual. You would never guess he'd been hospitalised over the weekend and only released yesterday.

Finally, once he is certain that all eyes in the room are on him, he addresses us.

'Good morning, team. I must apologise for the short notice about this meeting, but it's been a trying few days for us all and I wanted to get you all together quickly to ensure everyone is up to date.'

He pauses. No one speaks. You could hear a pin drop.

'Obviously, many of us have been through an incredibly frightening experience last week. Some of us involved a little more closely than others.' He pauses and looks directly at me. He'd been a lot closer to the blast than I was, but he seems to want to deflect attention away from his own miraculous survival. All eyes turn my way and I feel my cheeks start to burn. Don catches my eye and I suddenly remember him leaving level three just before the bomb went off. He stepped into the lift that Steve had stepped out of. How incredibly lucky. John continues.

'And in that terrible incident we have suffered the enormous loss of some wonderful people. Some exceptionally talented and caring people that we have all worked alongside. Some of us for many years. These people will be a huge loss to the company and I feel sure that those of you here today will want to ensure that we honour their memories appropriately – and we will.'

The address goes on for another fifteen minutes or so, in which time John offers kind words about Adam, Henry and Janet and also updates us on Mike – who is improving in hospital, but unlikely to be out for some time. Then he tells us that the police are doing all they can to solve the crime, but there is nothing he can tell us about their investigation or any possible suspects.

Next he goes to great pains to speak directly to each of the managers in the room and particularly to Sean and Hector about their temporary roles, assuring them that he will be spending time with each of them over the next few days. Then he talks about how important the merger is, and finally gestures to the new man that Don greeted as Bobby, and introduces him to everyone.

'Gentlemen, and ladies, I'd like you all to meet Mr Robert Davis. I am very grateful that he has agreed to join our team as acting Administration Manager, for an undefined period. Robert is with us from Head Office in Auckland and brings with him a wealth of knowledge in business continuity planning and a fair bit of experience in mergers and restructuring. And so, with the able assistance of Lily and the rest of the Admin team, he will be assuming responsibility for completing our merger realignment proposal.'

So this is the guy from Head Office? Surely not. He's much younger than most of the management here, and easily the most handsome. There are mutterings of welcome and introduction as everyone shakes hands all around. But it goes quiet again very quickly and I note the looks of surprise on almost every face, including Don's. His expression makes me wonder how the two men know each other.

I glance across at Nikki. The corner of her mouth curls up ever so slightly and she flicks me the faintest of winks. I try to keep my face straight. Clearly she thinks he's cute too, hence the special dress today.

It's now Bobby's turn to address the meeting. He sits forward in his chair, trying to make eye contact with everyone in the room as he speaks. He starts off by insisting that everyone call him Bobby (not even my mother calls me Robert, he says charmingly) and then gives a little speech thanking us for the warm welcome, sharing his condolences about our workmates. He then goes on to tell us that if we all work together he is confident we can get through the next few weeks comfortably, without missing any of the realignment proposal deadlines.

He has a lovely smile and his blue eyes flash with life and passion. He speaks positively and enthusiastically and I find myself more than a little entranced. It's hard not to immediately take a shine to him.

Perhaps Head Office did send us a Superman.

After Bobby's short address John announces that a brief memorial service will be held on level three later today.

Apparently the police have released the floor this morning and a clean-up is now underway. A memo will be circulated soon. He wants to ensure that all of the management team attends, and he instructs that they are to allow any of their staff who wants to be there unfettered time away from their work. John is adamant that, even if it means shutting off the phones and closing some work areas down completely, no one is to be denied the opportunity.

He looks to Bobby and me and tells us that it will take some time before level three will be ready for staff to recommence work there. They are hoping to move the Finance team back in by the end of this week, as their area was the least affected, but we probably won't be able to return until sometime the following week. He makes it sound like the repairs are all happening too slowly, but it seems like an awfully fast timeframe to me.

Then, abruptly, the meeting is over.

As it breaks up and the other managers head away, Bobby catches me just outside the office door and more personally introduces himself. As I shake his hand – it's warm and firm – Don springs up alongside, interrupting us.

'So how long have you been with Westwood, Bobby, and up at Auckland?'

'Hey, Don. Umm, not that long. Just under a year, I think. Are you still living in Wilton?'

'No, I'm down in Fernleah now, but I've still got the old family yacht moored at the marina up there. My God, how long has it been since you skipped town, you rogue?'

Bobby offers a guarded smile, clearly a little embarrassed. 'Um, let's see . . . I left in '92, so I guess it must be about eight years ago now.' Then he quickly raises his hands in surrender, trying to cut off Don's line of questioning. 'But we're going to have to catch up another time, all right? I'd love to charge up and down memory lane, but I really need to chat with Lily here about the Admin team right now, so . . .' he pauses, 'how about dinner tonight, are you doing anything? My treat.'

Don grins. 'Done deal. I'll call and let the good woman know I'll be working late tonight.'

'You're married? Or do you mean your mum?'

'Ha, ha. Funny guy. You haven't changed a bit. Do you remember Sue Chatwin?'

'Sultry Sue from the chess club?'

Don grins, flashing his eyebrows. 'My lovely wife.'

'No way.'

'Yes, way. She works at the City Council now, just been promoted–'

Nikki gives a loud cough behind the two men, intentionally interrupting, and asks Don if he will help her rearrange the chairs. Don instantly forgets Bobby and me and scurries away after Nikki, eager as a puppy-dog to do her bidding. If only Sultry Sue could see him now.

Bobby turns quickly back to me.

'Sorry, Lily, I didn't expect to bump into Don. Quite a surprise actually,' he apologises, gesturing that we should move away from John's office. 'I think we need to have a chat about the realignment proposal, if you can spare a few minutes,' he says as we move towards the boardroom. 'I know you've been thrown in the deep end on this, but I'm reliably assured that you are without doubt the best person possible to run this whole merger thing for the company – and I plan to ride on your coat-tails all the way.'

He is obviously laying the charm on thick, but I still feel myself blush involuntarily.

EIGHT

His mood is dark again today. He is annoyed.

The rage feels hot and leaden in his belly, dimming his thoughts further. Not only has he somehow failed to crush them, but things aren't working out as he'd planned. It incenses him. Yet he quickly realises that if he wants to secure the right outcome he will need to take action again, and soon.

He tries to calm himself, to temper the anger and funnel it. He needs to re-plan. He needs to find another opportunity. There has to be another way.

Swiftly he decides that it will be unwise to place another device at HBS, there's too much risk. He will have to open his mind wider, call upon his limitless intelligence, and take a different approach to achieve his goals.

Then, in a flash of inspiration, it comes to him and he almost laughs out loud.

Of course, it's so ridiculously simple. He already knows the territory, he saw directly into the room in question while he was setting up the first one. He would just go back there, it would be easy. And they wouldn't suspect a thing. How could they?

This lightens his mood considerably. He's still annoyed, but at least he now has a new way forward. A new goal. He closes his eyes and takes a long, deep breath to control the anger that boils within him, using it to centre himself, to refocus his mind.

Thor will strike again. And soon.

NINE

After introducing Bobby to Lauren and Claire, who are both instantly captivated when he insists they too call him 'Bobby', we settle in at one end of the big boardroom table to run through our progress on the realignment proposal. He asks smart questions and picks up on the more detailed issues quite quickly. I'm impressed. He immediately notes that Janet and Henry had been trying to achieve a ratio of around 70/30 in favour of retaining our HBS staff over those coming onboard from Commonwealth. He is also careful not to criticise their plans, and asks my opinion on favouring staff with a longer history with either company versus those who are more productive. He carefully probes around the sensitive issues to establish my personal thoughts and discover whether I am going to help or hinder him in his new role.

We chat away amicably until I realise its past my usual lunchtime and the morning has flown past.

'This is all looking really good, Lily,' he smiles at me warmly. 'I think you guys actually have this completely under control and don't need me here at all.'

I recognise that he's managing me, but still I feel some satisfaction as I thank him.

'Why don't you go and grab yourself a bite to eat? After that, if you wouldn't mind, I'd be keen for you to have a go at tackling another draft of the realigned Finance team while I meet with the managers for Sales and then Customer Services. Okay?'

Just then Brendan Armstrong arrives at the boardroom door. I don't enjoy dealing with Brendan and feel sure he's about to, yet again, launch into a lengthy moan (which he would call a healthy debate) about the levels of personnel his marketing team will need. Janet and I had already endured a vast number of these visits in the last few weeks and I can't bear the thought of suffering another.

I decide to leave poor Bobby to get his first taste of our Marketing Manager's egotistical worldview. Just outside the door I almost bump into Reuben, the other mailroom guy, and have to stop. Like Dave, Reuben is short with a slight build. But he's a little older, somewhere in his fifties with greying hair and a limited and unkempt wardrobe. He hesitates at the door, first frowning at me, then at Brendan who is semi-blocking the boardroom entrance and finally peering through his too-thick glasses at Bobby, whom he won't have met yet.

'Hey there, Reuben,' I say, offering a small smile. He takes a half-step back to put me in focus, raising his eyebrows. He's an odd-looking man who has been, as I understand it, with HBS all his adult life.

'Busy today?' he murmurs and I nod.

Behind me I can hear Brendan telling Bobby how important his marketing team is and decide it's time to flee. I step aside and allow Reuben to shuffle in and drop a number of files to Lauren. He doesn't hang around, moving on hastily to continue his appointed rounds. I pause to listen a little more to Brendan's tirade and then beat a hasty retreat myself.

I feel a little guilty though. Janet was always so incredibly patient with Brendan and I briefly consider going back and offering Bobby some moral support, as I know Janet would have done. 'Everyone has a valid opinion and it's our job to listen,' she would say. God, I miss her.

I pause again, halfway to the lifts, but finally decide that I'm too hungry. Bobby can fend for himself. A good chat with Brendan will build character. I smile furtively at the thought and finally slip away for some lunch.

After picking up a fresh sandwich for lunch I'm deep in thought as I enter the ground floor lobby to return to work. Drifting along absently I almost walk headlong into Steve Cassidy as he comes out of the lift. He's reading a letter and not looking where he is going either as he steps out between the sliding doors, almost bowling me over. In unison we both release mumbles of surprise and stop.

He seems angry, but not at me. At the letter.

Again in harmony, we both offer apologies for not looking where we were going and then stop again, self-consciously. We haven't seen each other since the explosion last Friday and I immediately feel awkward. But he seems distracted.

'Sorry,' I apologise again. 'I've been meaning to drop by and say thank you. You know, for helping me out of here last week . . .' I tail off, unsure what else to say.

There is another uncomfortable moment. He's obviously troubled by whatever is in the letter and, as he begins to stuff it into his jacket pocket, I notice the crest of the Hawthorne City Council on it. With no way of really knowing this I suddenly feel – with absolute certainty – that he is being kicked out of his home. *Evicted. Final Notice.* The phrase *'out in the damn street'* springs into my mind from nowhere. The idea is so strong and so clear I feel a small jolt of shock course through me, but I manage to force myself to say nothing.

Steve doesn't seem to notice. It's clear he's making some effort to try and focus his attention on me, but struggling. He's angry, distracted, and can't hold my gaze.

'You don't need to thank me,' he finally replies in a muted tone, 'I was there. I didn't really do anything.' He even looks a little embarrassed, but I can tell his thoughts are still elsewhere. With the Council almost certainly. Since they're evicting him.

'Are you okay, you seem a bit off?' I ask.

'Really? No, I'm fine, just got a few things on at the moment.' He pauses, but not for long. 'Sorry Lily, but I actually need to be somewhere else. Can we catch up later?'

He's brushing me off. I want to ask him why he called me last Friday but don't get the chance. Before I can open my mouth again he is gone.

Once again I simply don't know what to think. How can I possibly know that the Council is evicting him, and why would I feel it with such absolute certainty? My mind has sure been playing some crazy tricks on me since the explosion. Am I still feeling after-effects of the trauma? Or has my brain been rattled somehow? Should I go and see a doctor?

The lift door slides open in front of me and Don Swain and Hector Lawson spill out, embroiled in a heated debate. I step aside quickly as they bustle past with Hector fuming away at Don over something he seems reluctant to help Hector with. Some technical thing, I presume, not wanting to get involved.

I step into the lift quickly, still puzzled and a little frightened over my brief interaction with Steve. What is happening to me? Then the bell pings and I step out of the lift.

Immediately I feel a swelling surge of anger and despair. The feeling is immensely strong and I physically recoil, backing myself up against the wall beside the lift door.

As a wave of resentment washes over me I realise that I've walked out into level three by mistake. I must have pushed the wrong button instinctively, drifting on auto-pilot after being distracted as I entered the lift.

Fury pounds at me. It's close to suffocating, but there is no immediately obvious cause. Before me the long room is almost bare. It's stripped back to a concrete floor and nearly all of the ceiling panels at the far end are missing. There are building tools and equipment scattered around and two men are busily reconstructing the framing for the meeting room near where my desk had been. They don't seem to have noticed me though.

I lean against the wall and shudder in horror as a picture of the room as it had been last Friday flashes into my mind's eye. I see the smoke and the rain and the blackness of everything and my chest tightens, my stomach lurching. Then that terrible roaring hum explodes in my ears again and I see Janet, charred and still, lying on the floor up ahead. Sliding down the wall, I end up seated with my knees drawn up to my chest. I sit there shivering, rocking slightly and clutching myself tight.

Like waves pounding on a rocky beach the sense of anger I'm feeling is overwhelming and despair surges forth and washes over me again. Words leap into my mind, sharp and clear.

—damn them, not fair on team . . . how will they cope—

I feel an extreme bitterness in the phrases.

—just babies, can't be without me, won't go—

The force of the words is much stronger, more violent than anything I've endured before.

—I won't go, can't go—

I gasp involuntarily at the intensity.

—this isn't right . . . a mistake—

And then the words are abruptly gone, leaving me breathless and frightened and I slump in relief.

In that instant I know it's Adam. I don't know how, or why. But just as I'd known the feelings that had burst into my head at the cemetery were Janet's, I know these words are Adam Mitchell's – HBS's former CFO – who died right here last Friday.

Only this time I don't understand the message. He seems to be worried about his team. But why? None of the Finance team is in danger, are they? And they're not babies.

Suddenly the anger returns, yet again swirling within me. It's terrifying. I can't stop it, I can't control it, and I don't know what to do. It surges through me like an electric current and I hear;

–I won't go, I can't leave them, my team needs me–

I must have screamed at that point because when I open my eyes, I find a man standing there. I think it's one of the builders. He looks startled.

'Oh God, he's so angry,' I tell him.

The builder just stares at me in surprise. He looks like he's just found a rattlesnake in his kitchen and doesn't know what to do. Will I attack him if he moves?

I quickly scramble to my feet, both embarrassed and relieved. My heart is racing but the bitterness has left me.

'Are you all right, Miss?' the man asks cautiously.

I nod vigorously. I need to get away. I start pounding on the lift button with my hand.

'I'm okay,' I manage. 'Don't worry, I'm okay.'

He stares at me. His hands are out in a gesture of assistance, but I can sense that he really doesn't want to touch me. He's either terrified that I will scream sexual harassment or, worse, that I might bite him.

The lift door finally springs open and I all but leap in, thankful that once again there is no one else inside. I try to offer the builder a friendly smile, but I probably just grimace and frighten him a little more. Terror is coursing through me as I quickly hit the button that will take me back down to the entrance lobby.

I want out of the building, and fast.

TEN

Nikki unintentionally sneaks up on me yet again, making me jump. I'm a bag of nerves and it doesn't take much. She tilts her head and smiles at me. 'Hey there, babe. You okay?'

I nod, embarrassed. I've been back at my desk for a while now, pouring myself into my work as a distraction from the strange things that have been going on inside my head.

'The memorial service will be starting soon,' Nikki tells me gently. 'Are you coming?'

The dread pours through me like warm treacle. I've known this is coming and still don't know what to do. The service is to be held on level three and I don't want to go, but know in my heart that I have to. I owe it to Janet and the others to be there. And as a survivor – God, that's a scary way to describe myself – I know all the other staff will expect me to be there. Lauren and Claire have already gone, and I feel sure that the Finance team will all be there. I simply have to go.

I draw a deep breath, steadying myself, and stand up. Nikki smiles and walks with me to the lift doors. It's only one floor down but everyone always uses the lifts. The stairs are bare concrete, poorly lit and only ever used for fire drills. Last Friday was the first time I'm aware of that they have actually been used for their designed purpose.

As we ride silently downwards my stomach clenches in anticipation. Was it just shock that overwhelmed me before? The surprise of finding myself confronted so abruptly by the scene of my horrific memories? Or did I really feel Adam down there? His anger and hurt. I'm so frightened. What if something happens and I collapse? What if I scream and have to run from the room? Everyone will see me flipping out. I'll be the laughing stock.

The lift door slides open quietly.

My heart seems to stop beating.

But the scene before me is surprisingly different to my expectations. I relax a little. The room has been transformed significantly since my last brief visit. While there is still no carpet, all the ceiling panels have been replaced and there are large bouquets of flowers dotted around the walls. Soft music is playing in the background and, most startling of all, the room is almost completely full of people.

I step forward hesitantly. I feel as if all the eyes in the room turn towards me, but they don't. People from every department of the company are gathered together in little clusters, much like they had been last Friday outside, talking softly and glancing around curiously.

My heartbeat slows to its normal rhythm and I relax a little more as we step out of the lift.

I spot Bobby over to the right, chatting quietly with Don Swain and Sean Peterson. Lauren and Claire are together quite near them. Steve is standing a little further away, looking distracted. I notice one of the Customer Service girls, Kylie, subtly flirting with him. She is pretty, but he hardly notices her. Dave and Reuben are huddled together in a corner to our left, neither of them really mixes well and they both look almost as uncomfortable as I feel about being here.

Nikki leads me to a space, to the left, about a quarter of the way into the room. We pass some of the Marketing girls, who look bored, and then a small contingent of the remaining Finance team. As we pass Jason, the pushy guy from IT, he offers me a phony smile but I turn away, not comfortable meeting his eye. We stop just as Jonathon Green steps up to a low podium to address the crowd.

He welcomes everyone and pays special thanks to our visitors for attending. Standing near him I recognise Derek, Janet's husband, and an older woman, Henry's dour-faced wife – I can't recall her name. Had he ever even told us her name, I wondered. There are others I don't know, including an attractive blonde woman standing with a little dark-haired girl by her side and holding a baby in her arms. It's as I watch them that the feelings of anger and resentment suddenly begin flowing over and through me once again. And I instantly know.

They're Adam's wife and children.

They were his team. I don't get why. But it is somehow so absolutely clear to me. I just know.

John is outlining the horrific events of last Friday, praising those who evacuated the building without panic, when I sense the words;

–you bastards, I won't leave them–

The words tear through my consciousness with a force that terrifies me.

–they need me . . . I won't go, it isn't right–

This time it is even stronger than before and I feel myself sway.

–can't leave my team, won't go–

My knees buckle, and I think I'm going to faint.

Nikki supports me and I see concern on her face as I lean into her, trying to stay on my feet. Resentment and fury drive through me like a mid-winter gale and I know it is Adam. He's here. He isn't ready to leave this world, not yet. He is desperately angry and bitter and I feel his hostility lashing me like a storm, punching right through me.

–this isn't right, shouldn't be me–

Now I'm staggering and Nikki holds me, guiding me through the crowd.

–it's a mistake, no one understands–

We lurch along, Adam's fury surrounding me, tearing at me like a tornado, driving me almost to my knees and as we near the lift doors I feel a terrible pain inside my head.

–IT'S NOT RIGHT–

A large display of flowers in front of us suddenly shakes, then tumbles and falls from a small table, the vase shattering onto the bare concrete.

We both stop and stare in surprise. No one was near them.

Nikki quickly guides me the other way, away from the fallen flowers, towards a meeting room near the lifts. The frenzy of resentment swirling in my head has abated slightly, but I can still feel Adam's pain. It's horrible, unbearable, and I feel like I'm going to throw up. I struggle to hold it back as Nikki leads me inside the meeting room, closing the door behind us and steering me into a chair. I collapse into it thankfully.

As my thoughts start to clear I realise we're in the same meeting room that Steve and I were blown into when the bomb went off. The glass has been replaced and the door re-hung, but it is definitely the same room.

Nikki pulls a chair over and sits directly in front of me, holding my hands. 'You look like you've seen a ghost. Are you okay?'

How am I supposed to answer that? I feel like I've more than seen a ghost. I feel like a ghost has somehow been pummeling me like a desert sandstorm.

Adam is here. On level three. And he is really, really pissed off. Does no one else feel this? I can see the crowd outside the meeting room, a few of them glancing over at Nikki and I, but most have now refocused on John's address.

No. They don't feel it, I realise. Maybe not in the same way at least. It's just me. I'm the only one that's apparently going mad. I'm the only one hearing voices, or rather –

feeling words and phrases from a dead man inside my head, his emotions assaulting me.

I try to re-focus, to concentrate on Nikki.

'I guess I'm not safe to take anywhere at the moment,' I murmur, trying to force a smile.

'I think you're just in shock. You've been through a lot in the last few days. Maybe you need to take some time off?'

I nod. But it's more than just shock, isn't it? I'm clearly going crazy, losing my mind. Although the feelings of anger have drifted away somewhat and I no longer feel so nauseous.

'Do you want some water?' Nikki offers. 'Can I get you something?'

She's being a real trooper about my apparent episode and I feel desperately grateful. I peek over her shoulder again at the crowd outside. I don't want to be alone in here, but I don't want to go out and face that crowd either.

'No, thanks. I'm okay. What are you going to tell everyone?'

She looks at me carefully, tilting her head to one side. 'I think we should tell them you've been drinking, that you're plastered,' she smiles as she says it. 'How does that sound? Or we could say you're on some really heavy drugs?'

I smile back. 'Perfect,' I reply. 'Or maybe we could just tell them I was reliving an alien abduction, or something?'

'Mmm, that could work,' she grins again before quickly becoming serious. 'I'm pretty sure it's just shock, Lily. You're going to be okay, you just need to work through it. You've lost a good friend and you've been through a frightening experience. Shock is natural, it's your body's way of coping with the tragedy. You just need more rest, and more time to heal. To come to terms with it all.'

I do feel quite a bit better now, but I'm still not comfortable sharing the full extent of my experiences with

Nikki. I can't bear the thought of anyone else knowing that I am going crazy, so I just nod again, slowly.

The memorial service only goes on for another ten minutes. Nikki opens the door and we both stand in the doorway to listen as it wraps up. I immediately feel Adam's resentment, but it's more subdued now, the anger diminished. It's bearable this time, but I still hold onto the door frame for support.

Feeling more composed, I listen to John talking about the merger now, reassuring everyone that they will have a fair and equal opportunity to remain with the merged entity. But he also makes it clear that the same fairness will be shown to the existing staff of the other company. He speaks positively and somehow manages to make it sound exciting, but the crowd shuffles nervously as they anticipate the possibility of having to go out and seek new jobs, regardless of how hard they have worked in the past. Then he returns to the main theme, remembering our fallen friends and co-workers, and finishes up with a minute's silence to honour them.

As it ends, Nikki has to slip away. She is supposed to be with John looking after the invited guests – Adam, Henry and Janet's families. The crowd starts to drift away, but it will take some time as they all need to exit via the lifts. I move back into the meeting room, still embarrassed by the earlier drama, and wait for a chance to slip away alone.

As I stand there I watch John escorting Henry Warrington's widow towards the lifts. He's talking to her in a soothing tone. I can't hear his voice, but suddenly there are words creeping into my mind once again.

—never dreamed so many would come, can't be for me—

But these feelings are much softer than the earlier ones, conveying more a sense of surprise, or disbelief.

—not here for me . . . for the others—

And I know it's Henry. He's overwhelmed by the turnout and John's touching tribute.

He had thought nobody liked him. I'm struck by his feeling of regret, that he hadn't made more of an effort to befriend his workmates. He knew he'd treated the other employees as resources, and deliberately tried not to think of them as people. He'd seen so many come and go. It had been easier for him that way.

I look at his widow, a grey-haired and frail-looking woman. I know that he'd treated her well. She was the only person he truly cared about. She was his world.

I feel a compulsion to go to her and share this information with her, but fight the urge and hold myself back. She already knows. She doesn't need me to tell her. Let it go. Leave the poor woman alone, I tell myself, you don't want to cause another scene.

Stepping back into the meeting room, I sit down to once again try and compose myself. The crowds are still dispersing, everyone waiting their turn to squeeze into a lift and escape level three. I take a deep, calming breath.

But then I feel Adam again, a small resurgence of anger, although more tempered this time. There is a stronger feeling of self-pity now and it wrenches my heart. I look out and realise I can once again see his family through the thinning crowd. Nikki is with them, the two strikingly attractive blonde women standing out from the crowd. Nikki has taken the baby while Adam's widow is holding the little girl tight, comforting her. The girl looks about eight years old and I feel my heart breaking for them all. The baby isn't even a year old.

—no 'a' in team anymore, no 'a'—

The words come from nowhere, and I suddenly understand.

It's simple, a family thing.

I have never met them and don't recall ever chatting with Adam about his family, but I know somehow, and with absolute certainty yet again, that their names are Tracey, Elizabeth and Mark. Including Adam, their first-name initials spelled 'team' but without Adam it doesn't work any more.

–isn't fair, not right . . . why me–

I shudder, burying my face in my hands. I wish that it would all just stop. That I could turn back the clock and undo the terrible things that have happened to these people. But more than anything I wish I could turn off the feelings that are suddenly coming at me from all sides.

'This must be hard for you,' a warm voice says, startling me.

I look up to see that Bobby has quietly entered the room and is crouching down in front of me with surprising tenderness in his eyes. I try to force myself to relax. Oh, God, you don't know the half of it, I think self-pityingly. But I just nod, not trusting myself to speak, and start wishing for a tissue. I must look a mess.

'You knew them all well, didn't you?' he asks softly.

I nod again and sniff, wiping my cheeks with the back of my hand. His words are gentle.

'It's good to grieve when you lose someone close to you. It's important to let it all out, all the pain you're feeling. It can help you to heal.'

I'm quietly touched, but I can't think of an adequate response. There's a warm understanding in his wonderfully blue eyes.

'I'm sorry, Lily. I'm not very good at this sort of thing so, if it's okay with you, I'm going to just change the subject.'

He looks apologetic, but I actually think he's doing pretty well. His hand has slid down from my shoulder and rests comfortably on my forearm. I make no effort to remove it.

'I need to meet with some of the management from Commonwealth tomorrow morning and I was hoping you'd be available to join me? I know you've been working pretty closely with our own managers on this damn merger and I think you'd be really useful to have alongside tomorrow.'

I'm incredibly surprised, and very flattered too. He probably only wants me there to take notes, or as some kind of a power accessory, but it will get me out of this awful place. The thought of escaping from the office tomorrow, if only for a few hours, is immediately very attractive. A wonderful distraction from the misery that is literally haunting me here.

And while my joining him might not be normal protocol, I think that it will also help me to put faces to the lists of names we have been bandying around the last few weeks. I quickly think of Henry and the depth of remorse he seemed to be carrying. How he regrets the way he thought of the people he worked with. How he had dealt with them all as resources, to be managed as you would stationery. The idea of meeting these people feels right, a positive thing.

'Sure, of course. If you want me there,' I blurt a little too enthusiastically. 'What do you need me to bring?'

He smiles and squeezes my arm gently.

'Not much. Just your latest realignment notes for Sales, Customer Services and Marketing – and your best smile. We'll wing it from there.'

ELEVEN

I manage to escape level three without further incident and eventually arrive home a little before 6 pm. But while I think my day has surely been weird enough, it hasn't finished with me yet.

My little cousin Rosie appears to have been waiting for me and staggers through a gap in the hedge as I arrive at my front door. She often comes over for a chat, but today something is clearly wrong and she's acting very strangely.

She also has a huge white plaster cast on her left arm – from her wrist to her shoulder. She's holding it to her chest with her other arm folded over the top. It makes her look defensive, which is very unlike Rosie.

She moves slowly, watching me as she edges closer, as if I might suddenly leap forward and attack her. Again, very unlike Rosie.

I consider pretending that I haven't seen her and just go inside, but that would be rude. I've had an awful day, but I still can't bring myself to just dodge her.

'Hey there, Rosie,' I finally say, my voice sounding strained and tired. I'm hoping she'll take the hint and go home. She is staring at me curiously, but her head seems to loll to one side, as if she's having trouble holding it up. Without reply she shuffles forward another two steps, almost tripping over her own feet. She manages to keep her balance and stops, looking up at me rather blankly. I'm really not in the mood for this, but something is clearly wrong here. I sigh in resignation.

'Are you okay, Rosie? What have you done to yourself?'

She barely seems to register my question. Her eyes are hooded and seem a little glazed, and I notice a large bruise on the left of her forehead, peeking out from under her fringe. She stares at me, leaning forward to peer at my face as if short-sighted. Then her left eye flutters awkwardly and she sways. Her mouth sags open limply but no words emerge.

She could almost be sleepwalking. It's kind of creepy.

'What are you doing here, Rosie? Are you all right?'

Then, just for just a moment her eyes clear briefly and seem to focus. Standing a fraction straighter she finally speaks, but in an incredibly quiet voice, her single word thick with uncertainty.

'Lily?'

She doesn't sound like Rosie at all. What's going on?

I take a step forward, frowning, and bend down slightly to try and see her face more clearly. But she sways back away from me in slow-motion recoil, not quite toppling.

I can see that her eyes have glazed over again, yet they seem to stare right through me.

'Yes,' I answer, pausing. 'Rosie?'

And she suddenly straightens, her shoulders pushing back as her head snaps up. Her eyes fly wide. 'Lily,' she says my name again. This time louder and clearer. Recognition, not a question. But the sudden alertness doesn't last. She slumps again quickly and staggers. Eyes closing, her head drops and she shuffles uncertainly two steps backwards.

Now I'm really concerned. 'Rosie, are you all right?' I reach out to her. Has she taken too many painkillers for her broken arm?

But she doesn't seem to hear me. Her eyes slowly open again and she tries to speak, attempting to form a new word but not succeeding. It's like watching a fish out of water, in slow motion. My stomach tightens as I begin to wonder if she's having some kind of seizure. Her eyes have gone glassy again, clouded like ammonia-filled water. I'm not sure if she can see me or not.

Then she falls.

I'm not fast enough. For a moment she rocks towards me and I'm horrified to see her eyes roll back in her head. Then she lurches and suddenly topples backwards, beyond my grasp. She hits the ground with a surprisingly soft thud and lies still.

Dropping quickly to my knees beside her I desperately try to remember my first aid training. Is she breathing? I lower my head to her face, turning to watch her chest. I freeze for a moment in dismay, not seeing any movement – and then it rises and falls ever so slightly and I feel a very soft, very gentle breath on my ear.

Yes, thank God, she's breathing.

What to do now though? I need to get help, but I don't want to leave her here. I could easily lift and carry her but I don't want to move her. I don't know what's wrong with her. What if I move her and it makes things worse?

I snatch my cell-phone out of my handbag and search through the list of contacts I have pre-programmed. I hastily find my Aunt Louise's number and hit 'Call'.

Just twenty minutes later, feeling truly numb, I finally slide my key into the door at home and drift inside.

Rosie is okay, for now. Louise had rushed over, dropping to her knees, crying softly and stroking her daughter's face as I called an ambulance. They arrived very quickly and made us step aside. While they checked Rosie over I asked Louise about my little cousin's plastered arm.

It turns out that she fell out of the big totara tree in their backyard on Sunday, trying to rescue her kitten, and broke it. I'm more than a little ashamed to realise that I didn't hear a thing. Rosie took Monday off school and had been fine, so they cautiously sent her off to school this morning. Again, all had gone well, but she'd come home extra tired – they assumed because of lugging around all the added weight of the big plaster cast. She had been lying down napping when Louise last saw her. Then I called.

Within a few minutes the paramedics decided Rosie should go down to the hospital for a more thorough examination and loaded her onto a gurney. Louise rushed off to grab her handbag and then leapt into the ambulance to ride with them.

I was left standing in my driveway, suddenly alone and emotionally exhausted. What a day.

The next morning I'm ready early, waiting nervously for Bobby to pick me up as we'd arranged.

A few minutes earlier I called Louise to check up on Rosie and was pleased to hear that she seems to be okay. The doctors actually sent her home last night after a few hours of observation, diagnosing the episode as nothing more than a fainting fit. Louise sounded hopeful that that was all it was.

Bobby is right on time. I wait until he starts to get out of the car before I step out of the house, trying to look casual.

Today I have dressed to impress. Nothing too obvious, but I know this outfit makes me look both professional and a little sexy at the same time. As I slip into the car I can tell that Bobby notices, just a little something in the way he smiles, but he simply says 'Good Morning'. He looks pretty tidy too.

I know it's wrong to get any romantic ideas, especially as he's my boss and quite a bit older than most guys I've been out with. But the age gap isn't *that* big, and he's only in town for a short time. Besides, something about him just makes me tingle a little. What the hell, Lily, I tell myself. You only live once.

We have a good twenty-minute drive ahead of us. Bobby opens the small-talk. 'Nice house,' he says, 'do you own it or rent?'

I'm immediately embarrassed. 'It's my parents' place,' I reply, feeling myself flush slightly, 'but they're away on holiday right now. They won't be back for weeks.'

My God, did I really just say that?

'Oh, okay. So have you always lived around here?'

'Yes, actually. In that same house. All my life.' Why am I so nervous? 'Where are you staying at the moment?'

'The Mt Wallace Hotel. It's not flash, but it's comfy enough.'

'Oh,' I'm surprised. From Mt Wallace he'd have had to drive quite a bit out of his way to pick me up. It would have made more sense for him to pick me up from the office than from my home in Wilton. 'I didn't realise,' I pause, deciding to leave it alone. 'So you must know the streets around here quite well, or are you just a good map-reader?'

He gives me a little half smile. 'Actually, I grew up around here too. I know it pretty well.'

'Really? So that's how you know Don Swain?'

'Yep. We were mates at school, at Wilton Comp. He used to live just down the road. We got up to a fair bit of trouble together back then,' he actually looks a little wistful. It's cute.

'So you did the whole reminiscing thing with him over dinner last night then?' I ask.

'Yes,' he laughs, a little embarrassed. 'It's amazing how much some people's lives can change in a few years. I could tell you a few things about Don,' he pauses, '. . . but I won't.'

He glances over, flashing a cheeky smile. I like the way his smile touches his eyes.

'So you grew up in Wilton, around here?' I ask, keen to get him talking.

'Yes, up on Wilton Road, opposite Fraser Park.'

I know the road, it's not far away. Close to Lake Breckenock. I run along there often. 'Do you still have family there?' I ask.

I'm surprised as his mood changes abruptly. He frowns, his face darkens slightly as if a cloud has passed over, and he doesn't immediately respond.

'Ah,' he starts, but then pauses, clearly struggling to find the right words. 'Probably . . .' he tails off, going quiet, and I suddenly feel uncomfortable. And then I somehow know. And just as I've done a couple of times in the last few days I find myself speaking without thinking.

'They'd love to hear from you,' I blurt. 'They both would.'

Oh crap, what am I saying? Where did that come from?

He glances across, confused. 'Sorry? What was that?'

'Nothing, I'm sorry, it was nothing,' I babble, embarrassed. 'Just thinking out loud.'

He looks a bit annoyed, but more puzzled than angry. His eyes fix onto the road ahead and he lapses into silence.

I become angry at myself, and scared. Why can't I control what I'm saying any more? Where is this stuff coming from? How on earth do I know that he hasn't spoken to his parents in many years? I shouldn't, but I do. I just know. A sense of deep bitterness floods over me. But the feeling is Bobby's, not mine. It's his shield against a father who he feels doesn't love him. His birth was an accident and he rigidly believes that his existence is just a nuisance to his father.

I try hard to refocus, to shed the bitter feelings, and to think of something that will change the subject.

'So, umm . . .' I struggle for a second, and then opt for work, 'have you been able to talk with all the HBS managers to gather their thoughts yet?'

I hold my breath. This is safe territory, our easy connection and I'm relieved when he relaxes visibly.

'Most of them, briefly. They all want to keep their own people – as you'd expect. But that's just not going to be possible. We have to bring at least thirty per cent of the others on board.'

'It's going to be tough, isn't it? What do the Commonwealth guys expect?'

'They probably believe it will be a 50/50 merger, but that won't work. We're going to need to help them understand that this morning. I hope you're not too nervous?'

'No. I'm fine.'

There is silence again for a moment, I want to keep him talking, hoping he will forget my remark from earlier. I search my mind frantically for another subject.

'So what about Admin? Are we going to need as many people?' I try to sound casual, but know that I don't.

'Don't worry Lily, you and your mates in Admin won't be going anywhere. We may have to change some things a bit. I mean, most companies are calling their Admin departments something like Human Resources or Recruitment now. "Admin" is a pretty old-fashioned term and, with payroll almost fully automated and ordering decentralised, the focus is moving towards Health and Safety, Counselling and other "People" issues.' He pauses. 'Things might change a little, but you'll all be fine. Trust me.'

I'm not completely sure what he means, but I nod and smile back. It sounds like Lauren, Claire and I won't lose our jobs, but I doubt that Edna will want to return. Then I remember Dave and Reuben – the rest of the Admin team.

'What about the mail guys? Will they be realigned in the restructure?'

'I'm not too sure,' he says, sounding a bit hesitant. 'I'm actually not convinced we really need mail runners at all any more. They're a bit old-fashioned, you know, what with email and other changes in communication technology. We may need one of them, but even then . . . well, I don't know.'

He's being evasive. It's obvious he doesn't think we need any and it makes me a little uncomfortable. But to keep him talking I ask about other departments and before long he's grumbling about the issues he's having with the Marketing team – no surprises there – and I feel relieved that my odd comment about his family now seems to be safely forgotten.

We arrive at our destination a few minutes early. Commonwealth Construction Services has smaller offices than ours, and less staff. But it operates out of a newer building centrally located in downtown Hawthorne. We park in a multi-storey parking building next door and I feel a jolt of shock when I recognise where we are.

'Oh my God, Bobby. This is the parking building where that man was killed in the car bombing,' I exclaim. It had been all over the news a few weeks back.

'There was another bombing?' he asks, surprised.

'Seriously, you didn't know?'

He shakes his head. We've just gotten out of the car and we both look around, possibly a little nervously. This is definitely the building. I point to our right.

'See over there, that's the City Council offices. The guy worked in there and he parked his car in here.' I find myself a little breathless as I try to explain it for Bobby. 'He was returning to his car after work and it exploded when he reached the door. Not like on gangster movies when they turn the key in the ignition, but just as he got to the door. He didn't even open it. Apparently he was on the top floor.' We both look up at the roof above us. We're on the ground floor. 'He was blown right off the roof, and he landed in the street.' I turn to get my bearings, and then I point behind us. 'Right out there.' A cold shiver runs down my back and I pull my hand in quickly, as if I've just touched something nasty.

'When was this?' he asks.

'Only a few weeks ago,' I say. 'About two weeks before our bomb.' He nods slowly. A soft 'wow' is all he can manage.

'They reckon it was the same guy,' I add softly. 'He'd have to be crazy.'

'Crazy or desperate,' Bobby offers. 'I'm not sure there's much difference sometimes.'

I really can't think of any response to that. I shiver also, wondering what it could take to drive someone to do such a terrible thing.

'We should get going,' Bobby says gently to get me moving.

I nod and move a little closer to him as we walk, drawing some strength from being near him. I have no real need to be nervous, but my stomach is now tingling in dread.

TWELVE

His observation post is almost too perfect.

From where he sits on the second level of the parking building he has a direct and unobstructed view of the target area. And if he leans out over the edge just a little he can see clearly into the room that he'd so recently passed through. There was no security whatsoever. He just walked straight in earlier in the day, before most of the workers had arrived. No one had seen him, or if they had no one had noticed him. He can move like a phantom, can't he? He can be invisible when he needs to be.

And today the God-of-Thunder is well prepared.

He is also very, very excited. This will be yet another spectacular display of his incredible skills. Of his artful and delicate handiwork. He feels the rushing and the tingling once again as he waits for just the right moment. The excitement within him threatens to explode, just like his beautiful, perfect device that waits silently below.

He watches quietly, barely moving, savouring each moment. Anticipation surges through him as he caresses the small plastic shape in his hand. It is warm from his touch. He is ready. The device is ready. His stomach knots with a thrill of expectation. Any minute now, any second.

Then his target appears and he starts to smile, but his target is not alone. He pauses, frowning slightly. Then he realises that this is a good thing. It will help to confuse the issue for his pursuers, and he will be further protected. His smile widens as he readies himself.

He rises slightly, stretches his arm out directly towards the target area and squeezes down on the large blue button on the small plastic box.

THIRTEEN

We are waiting in Commonwealth's main reception area, making small-talk with the receptionist, when a strong feeling of anxiety overcomes me, and with it:

—no, no, don't do it—

sharp words from a presence I do not feel I know;

—don't be a bad boy, not again—

frightened words, mournful and helpless;

—you'll get in so much trouble—

and I feel terror overwhelm me in an instant.

Something bad is about to happen, and very soon. I just know it. I suddenly realise that both Bobby and the receptionist are staring at me with puzzled expressions. I must have turned white with alarm. Did I say something out loud?

Then it goes off.

The boom of the explosion is incredibly loud, close to thunderous. I recoil immediately, dropping to the floor and curling up small, shielded from the blast by the receptionist's large wooden console. Bobby keels over beside me, tripping over a low coffee table and sprawling to the floor just in front of me. I close my eyes and cover my head.

After what feels like an eternity I peek out.

Once again I see smoke and dust and hundreds of tiny pieces of paper billowing through the air before me. It's all coming from a corridor just beyond the reception area. My hearing seems to be gone again.

It's like déjà vu.

Bobby is on his back directly in front of me, seemingly unscathed, but wide-eyed and clearly terrified. He kicks out, trying to stand, but he just scrabbles along a bit and then stops. Either he can't get up or he thinks better of it and sinks back to the floor. Suddenly he becomes aware that I'm watching him. He blinks a few times rapidly and shakes his head. He's disoriented and probably can't hear either but he tries to speak, saying something that I can't hear. I'm not a good lip-reader but I think it's 'are you all right?' or something like that. I nod.

My heart is racing furiously and I take my hands away from my head. I'm surprised to find I can actually hear better than last time. Perhaps I was further away from this explosion, or that there was a wall protecting me. I can't work it out. I can hear an alarm, or siren, sounding outside, but nobody seems to be screaming – thank God. Then suddenly I feel faint.

My vision starts to funnel and I feel my body start to shake, shivering violently. It's all too much, just far too much. I curl up, close my eyes and start to sob uncontrollably. Then someone is holding me, pulling me close, and I snuggle in for safety. My mind is reeling. This simply isn't possible. I can't be in two explosions in less than a week. That just doesn't happen.

There are no sprinklers this time. At least my favorite outfit might be able to be salvaged. Shame suddenly overwhelms me. How could I be thinking about my outfit? How totally inappropriate. I suddenly remember the receptionist we had been chatting with and begin struggling. Bobby releases me and I stand up too quickly. My head spins but I force myself to blink away the dizziness. I peer over the console. The girl is about my age, maybe a bit younger, and she's sitting up in her chair, swaying, with blood running down her face. But she's alive. Thank God.

Bobby appears on his feet beside me and sees the girl too. Without a word we round the reception desk together and help her to her feet, and start guiding her outside. Behind us smoke and ash drift on the breeze from the corridor, but no one emerges. I cradle her in my arms as Bobby produces a handkerchief and presses it firmly to the wound on her head, trying to stem the flow of blood.

The alarm is louder outside, but I can still hear the whine of the ambulance and police sirens above it.

Help is on the way.

It's mid-afternoon by the time I arrive home, dragging with me that familiar feeling of despair. Only this time I remember a lot more about getting to, being at, and finally leaving the hospital. Perhaps the shock has been lesser this time? I don't know. But I do feel like an old hand at it, almost like I'm following a steady routine. What I don't understand is just why the hell buildings keep blowing up around me?

At the hospital I even made an effort to visit Mike Smith, our injured Sales Manager. But he was sleeping and they wouldn't let me in. All they would tell me was that he was improving, but nothing else. I'm not family.

So I arrive home, once more, to a silent and empty house. And while my ears still ring somewhat, yet again I have suffered no new injuries. I've been very, very lucky – once more.

But others weren't so fortunate. Word around the hospital was that two people died and another was seriously injured. The 'seriously injured' guy had just entered the corridor. The blast had thrown him back through the door from whence he came.

I didn't ask too many questions, mainly because it's hard to make conversation with your hearing all messed up. But I do understand that they want me to return in a few days to check that my hearing hasn't been permanently damaged.

I take a slow, deep breath as I look around the house. So familiar and usually so welcoming, it once again seems devoid of any joy. Then, sharply, I realise it isn't the house, but me. I am the one devoid of joy. I'm also still in shock. How can this possibly have happened to me twice?

A shiver of anxiety runs through my body. Am I the target? Have other people died because I didn't? Dread drops like a stone into the pit of my stomach. Tears start to well up in my eyes and I drag myself through to my bedroom. I was going to shower but suddenly can't find the energy, or the will, and just drop onto my bed once again.

I weep myself to sleep.

Knocking at the front door wakes me. It's late in the day, but still light. Probably the police again, I think, sighing deeply. They must think I'm a suspect now after surviving two bombings. If I didn't know better I would put myself at the top of their suspect list too.

I drag myself out of bed and stagger to the front door. The knocking is persistent. Someone really wants to talk to me.

But it isn't the police, it's Rosie.

'Did you know that I stayed at the hospital last night?' she asks earnestly. Her eyes are bright and alive. She actually seems pretty excited. 'And I went in an ambulance.'

I hesitate. My mind is fuzzy from sleep and my ears still hum softly. Instinctively I just want to send her packing and crawl back into bed, but something about seeing Rosie standing there – all animated and full of enthusiasm – makes me relent. This is the Rosie I know. Vibrant and energetic. I manage a wry smile.

'Yes, I know,' I manage to reply as pleasantly as I can. 'Your mum told me.'

She looks briefly disappointed, but then grins.

'They let me have ice cream for breakfast today. You didn't know that, did you?'

I smile back. It's hard not to feel a little uplifted by her relentlessly positive spirit.

'No Rosie, I didn't know that. What flavour was it?'

Her eyes light up. 'Vanilla. It was really yummy.'

'Hmm,' I nod conspiratorially.

'You haven't seen my cast, have you? Isn't it gross? It's sooo heavy.'

I just shake my head and try to keep smiling.

'They say that next week I'll get a new one – and I'll get to choose the colour.'

'Wow that's awesome. What colour will you get?'

'Pink,' she says firmly. 'They do a really cool bright pink. They showed me. And I don't have to go to school tomorrow, isn't that great?'

'So what was the best thing about going in the ambulance yesterday?' I ask.

'I don't know. I don't really remember,' she shakes her head, 'but Mum said they came to our house, and they put me on a bed with wheels, and they carried me along on it, and they flashed all of their lights.'

'Actually, they came here,' I correct her. 'They picked you up from right over there.' I point to the place where she'd collapsed just yesterday evening. 'You don't remember that?'

She looks confused and frowns. 'No. Really?'

I'm not sure what to say. I begin to wonder if Louise has deliberately misled her for some reason, and that I should say no more, or if the story has just got mixed up in the telling. Clearly she has no memory of coming here and collapsing, or being taken away.

I'm still trying to decide how to respond when I hear Louise calling Rosie's name from next door. The cries quickly become urgent and Louise suddenly appears at the hedge looking frantic.

'Oh, my lord, Rosie. There you are,' she exclaims as she spots us.

'Hi Mum, what's the matter?' Rosie asks.

'You're supposed to be lying down young lady, not wandering about the neighbourhood.'

'I'm not wandering. I just came to see Lily.'

'Just come home right now, will you? I'm sure that Lily has better things to do.'

'But Mum . . .'

'Don't "But Mum" me. Just do as you're told please.'

Rosie looks at me and rolls her eyes in frustration, then turns abruptly and stomps back through the hedge, past her mother and into the house.

'I'm so sorry, Lily,' Louise addresses me for the first time. 'The doctors say she needs to rest – and I was only on the phone for a minute. She just slipped away.'

She is obviously embarrassed that Rosie has escaped from under her nose again, and clearly she has no idea that I've been involved in a second bombing. In fact I'm not sure that she's even aware that I'd been in the first one. She's pretty wrapped up in her own concerns.

'It's no problem. Have you heard any more about what the . . . umm . . .' I search desperately for the right word, '. . . episode . . . last night may have been about?'

She looks frustrated. 'No, they tried to call it a fainting fit. But they're running some tests.' She shrugs. 'They just say to keep an eye on her.'

I give her a sympathetic look. 'That's not much help, really, is it?'

'No. Look, I'm sorry Lily, I don't really have time to stop and chat. Okay?'

She disappears so quickly I don't get a chance to respond.

I go back inside. I'm awake now. I think about calling Megan and asking her to come over, but decide I can handle it myself. It's too late in the day to call into work and I don't need to, they know where I am – and why. Bobby and I were discharged fairly quickly after being seen at the hospital and then went straight back to the office. I think he stayed but Nikki ushered me out into a taxi soon afterwards, paid the man and gave him my address. I was too numb to be of any use at work and had been on the verge of tears the whole time I was there.

I stand in the lounge feeling sad and lonely. Once again I don't feel up to talking to anyone, but I am starting to feel claustrophobic. I need to get out and clear my head. I need a run. I change quickly, slipping on my battered old trainers and hustling out into the twilight.

Initially I feel heavy and uncoordinated and I struggle along, but after about ten minutes I find my rhythm and start to feel better. Another ten minutes and the stress and horror of the day are starting to melt away. It's been almost a week since I last ran and it feels great. I should have gone out before. Running always helps to blow out the cobwebs.

I'm running along the lakefront, my favorite stretch of footpath, and have just reached the marina when I see Steve Cassidy standing near the café there, talking with someone. He seems a little angry and the other man looks to be trying to calm him down. The other guy is big too, almost as big as Steve, and a little older. I can't hear their conversation and suddenly decide I don't want to. Something about their body language makes me veer away from them, away from the lake, down Wilton Road and back towards home. I don't want them to see me. I'm strangely troubled by a deep sense of danger. Without understanding why I sense firmly that they have done something bad together and I'm convinced that both men are dangerous. I know I should keep away. But where has this 'knowledge' come from?

I glance over my shoulder more than once as I run towards the long expanse of Fraser Park, wondering if someone or something is going to leap out at me. It's stupid, but I can't control the irrational fear that wells up inside me. Steve saved my life. Why would I suddenly consider him to be dangerous? It seems crazy.

I still have no explanation for all the strange, spontaneous and obscure feelings I have been experiencing since the first bombing. Am I somehow picking up on the thoughts of other people – both alive and dead – or am I just going insane.

Then I notice a figure sitting rigid at a picnic table out in the middle of the park. It's gloomy, but darkness hasn't yet fallen completely. The figure is somehow familiar. It's a man, but I can't make out his features.

I'm being watched.

FOURTEEN

The sensible thing would have been to keep running, but I find myself drawn to him. I slow down to a walk, allowing myself to drift towards the picnic table. My fear drains away quickly as I sense that the man is not a threat.

As I draw closer I feel a strong sense of indecision, with an equal helping of sadness. Then I realise that the man isn't watching me, but is gazing blankly at a house across the road. He seems lost in thought and makes no effort to look at me as I move even closer.

My breath catches in my throat as I finally recognise him and stop in my tracks.

'Hey there, Lily. Fancy meeting you here,' he welcomes me softly, without looking over. His gaze remains fixed on the big old house. His eyes are dull and cheerless. I sit on the other side of the picnic table, my back to the house he is staring at so intently.

'Hi Bobby. How's things?' I ask gently.

He says nothing for some time. Eventually he just shrugs. I know why he is here. The house across the road is his parents' home. And there is something special about this picnic table too, but I'm not clear what that might be.

'Come here often?' I ask, trying to lighten the mood.

'Only when the moon is out,' Bobby replies cryptically with a half-smile.

'Oh, okay. So this is some kind of werewolf thing then?'

Finally he looks at me. He considers me carefully at first, and then he gives me a genuine smile. It lights up his face, but his eyes are still sad.

'It might be, Lily. You never know.' He looks up to the sky. 'Good thing it's not a full moon tonight then, isn't it, just in case?'

I shrug and smile back, 'I can run pretty fast. You wouldn't catch me.'

He laughs, 'I don't run any more,' he says. 'Someone told me once that it's better to stand and fight.'

My reply spills out before I give any consideration to what I'm saying. 'Did your father teach you that?'

Bobby blanches visibly. I want to apologise immediately, retract my words, but something stops me. He mulls it over for a long time before finally responding.

'No, actually, it was my big brother,' he says, measuring his words. 'He was always big on standing up for yourself. Facing your fears and all that.'

I know that I'm treading on thin ice, talking about his family, but, for some reason, I once again find myself speaking without really being in control.

'He was very proud of you,' I tell him. 'He misses you.'

He just stares at me now, as the light slowly fades around us. I feel embarrassed again and wish that I could work out whatever it is that's making me say these stupid things – and just switch it off. What am I doing? Where is this coming from?

He opens his mouth to say something, but hesitates, unsure of himself. I'm terrified that he's going to say something to put me in my place, so I leap in first.

'How are your ears now? Are they still ringing? Mine still seem to be humming a little.'

He refocuses and answers slowly.

'They're not too bad, still a bit of a buzz though. It's pretty annoying isn't it?'

'Yeah, but it will fade by tomorrow,' I burble, still trying to lead him away from my comments about his family. 'Trust me, I'm an old hand at this.'

He watches me, still a little unsure, then speaks again.

'I know. I was thinking about that. You seem to be living a very charmed life. Do you carry some kind of lucky talisman around with you?'

'No, just the usual girl-crap in my handbag. You know – purse, lippy, cell-phone . . .'

He nods, a small smile emerging. 'Do you run every day?'

'I try and get out at least two or three times a week. Daily would be a bit much.'

We both go quiet and I catch his gaze drifting across the road again. 'So . . . you probably used to play around here when you were a kid, right?' I ask.

He looks back to me thoughtfully. 'Yes I did. Right here in this park. I have a lot of memories of this place.'

'Good or bad memories?' I find myself asking, wishing immediately that I hadn't.

'Mostly good,' he answers evenly. 'How about you? You grew up near here too, didn't you? Did you visit here a lot, or get out onto the lake much?'

'Yes and yes, I guess,' I respond a little wistfully. 'My mother used to bring me here when I was little, and dad had a friend with a yacht back then who would take us out sailing occasionally. They're all good memories.'

The darkness is almost complete now and I realise I can no longer see his face clearly. The street lights cast a soft glow into the park, but not much reaches us at the table. I get the feeling that neither of us is really keen to delve any deeper into childhood reminiscences and the conversation falters. Bobby starts to stand up.

'It's getting late,' he says. 'My car is over there. Would you like a lift home?'

In the darkness he doesn't see how flustered I am. Images of inviting him in for a coffee, and possibly a little more, flood my mind and I feel my heart beat faster. But I blow it and instead of accepting his offer I find myself saying strange things again.

'You know I'm sure they would love it if you just wandered over and knocked on the door.' The words tumble from me and I can't stop them. 'They'd be thrilled to see you. They really miss you.'

There is silence in the darkness and I know I've overstepped again. I open my mouth to apologise, but this time nothing will come out.

He sighs deeply, a frustrated sound, but he doesn't answer. Finally I find my voice.

'I'm so sorry, Bobby. I should just mind my own business.' I start to move away and stumble a little in the darkness. 'Don't worry about the lift. It's only a couple of streets away. I should finish my run.'

'It's no trouble,' he finally speaks again. I think I hear some regret in his voice but it may just be my wild imagination again. 'It's getting pretty dark now.'

'Thank you but no. I'll be fine, it's really not far.'

'If you're sure . . .'

'Yes . . .' I pause, unsure of myself. 'So I'll see you at work tomorrow then?'

'I'll be there, Lily. You get a good night's sleep, okay?'

'I will. You too. Goodnight,' I say as I turn and start to jog back up to the road.

He doesn't move. He calls 'goodnight' back to me and I'm pretty sure he sits back down at the picnic table as I run away. Resuming his vigil. Still trying to decide what to do.

I feel like an idiot and run home, berating myself the whole way.

I'm day-dreaming as Steve sneaks up behind me the next morning at work and, no surprise here, I jump in shock. I really am a bag of nerves at the moment.

I'm in the photocopy room on level four, running off copies of some statistical work relating to the realignment proposal, when he appears beside me. He only says 'hello'.

He apologises quickly, and I think sincerely, for scaring me and I apologise just as quickly for my reaction. My heart is still racing a little as I await his next move.

'I just wanted to apologise for the other morning, in the lobby,' he says. 'I was preoccupied and may have been a bit rude. I hope you'll forgive me?'

He wants something. One thing I know is that most men only seek forgiveness when they want something. I shrug.

'Sure, but there's nothing to forgive you for . . .' I tail off, unsure what else to say.

'No, I was definitely off. I usually have better manners.'

I shrug. 'Okay.'

He nods back, shuffling his feet. He seems to struggle for words. It's weird. Steve is normally as smooth as silk. I'd never seen him so awkward.

'I heard about yesterday. You did it all again. Are you okay?' he asks gently.

I haven't really talked about it with anyone this morning. Only a few words with Bobby, who appears to have shaken the experience off pretty quickly, but I am expecting Nikki to drop by anytime to get all the details.

'Yes, I'm okay. A bit shaken, but I'm getting better at ducking.' I give him a small smile.

He smiles then too, and it's a bit disarming. He has a roguish smile, sort of naughty but nice. I know a lot of girls have already fallen for that smile. And then I realise, but this time it's just normal female intuition, that he is going to ask me out. Oh no.

'Good on you, Lily,' he tilts his head a bit and keeps flashing that smile. 'I knew you were a feisty one. I like that.'

Good grief, he didn't just call me feisty, did he? My stomach clenches in anticipation of the inevitable.

'You know,' he continues, looking down, feigning coyness. 'I was wondering if you'd let me take you out to dinner tomorrow night? Sort of a celebration of being alive.' He raises his eyebrows to emphasise the question.

I look away, unsure how to answer. He's a good-looking guy, no doubt about that. But everyone knows he's slowly working his way through all the women in the company. God only knows how many have actually succumbed to his charms in the time that I've been working here. Nikki warned me once that he's well into double figures. He probably carves notches in his desk.

I look back up at him. He seems so sincere and caring, but I know it will be a mistake to accept and I struggle for an appropriate answer. Part of me actually feels that I owe him my life – thanks to the urgent meeting request last Friday. I can't just say no. But another part of me is screaming 'Run away Lily, he's trouble!'

'Gosh, umm . . . I don't know, Steve. That would be nice, but . . .'

'Hey come on, no buts,' he leaps in quickly, 'and no strings attached. Just dinner.'

'I'm sorry, it sounds nice, but I'm a bit of a mess at the moment,' I try to look as frail as possible, 'you know, with all the excitement. Perhaps –' I'm about to ask for a rain-check, but I'm cut off.

'Steve, Lily, I'm sorry to interrupt,' It's Nikki, my saviour. She stands in the doorway of the photocopying room, 'but we have the police here again and they're wondering if they might have a word with each of you.'

Then I notice the people behind her. One is the female detective, Natalie Dowd, who came to my place on Sunday, the other a man I don't recognise.

Steve's demeanor changes instantly. He tenses up, the smile evaporates and he folds his arms defensively. He isn't happy to see them. Personally, I'm grateful for the interruption.

There are brief introductions and Steve is asked to go with the man while Natalie stays to ask me a few questions. I find myself unusually nervous. I've done nothing wrong, but can't help wondering if they now consider me a suspect.

'Can you run through yesterday morning for me please, Lily?' she asks first off.

I do so, as best as I can remember it. She interrupts only to confirm details like who was standing where, the exact time, and so on. She asks if I remember seeing anyone else enter or leave the building, like a courier, a janitor, or other employees. Nothing comes to mind. A man in a suit had walked out just as we entered, but I hadn't seen anyone else. She asks if I saw anyone holding a cell-phone, pager or anything similar in size and shape – like a walkman or a small radio. I remember that the receptionist had been texting when we walked in, but that was all. I thought it was an odd question.

Then she asks about my relationship with Steve. Are we more than just work colleagues? Do I associate with him outside work? Do we date? I don't see how it's relevant, but deny anything more than a casual work acquaintance. But she's sharp.

'Didn't he just ask you out on a date?'

'Yes, he did,' I say, a little self-consciously, 'but that was the first time, and he asks out all the women here. You can check with Nikki, he's asked her out dozens of times.' I feel childish as I scramble to prove myself.

'So you've never been out with him?'

'No. Never.'

She pauses, then changes the subject to ask about my other work colleagues. She wants to know if anyone around the office has been acting strangely. Does anyone seem more stressed than usual, or more secretive?

'Everyone is more stressed at the moment,' I tell her, 'we're going through a merger and we had a bomb go off in the building. Everyone's being a bit weird.'

'I understand that,' she concedes, 'but does anyone stand out as seeming significantly more disturbed, unhappy, or acting differently to usual?'

Natalie has an unnerving way of staring intensely into my eyes when she asks her questions and it makes me feel uncomfortable. I tell her no. No one stands out. Then she changes the subject again, making me even more uneasy.

'We talked about this on Sunday, Lily, but I need to ask again whether you have any enemies that you haven't told us about. It is unusual that you've been present during two bombings. Is there anything you're not telling me?'

I feel her eyes bore into me again, searching for the truth. I can't answer, I just shake my head slowly. Why would anyone want to kill me? I've never hurt anyone.

After almost a full minute of silence Natalie leaves me to get back to work. I feel drained. I don't think they are seriously looking at me as a suspect, otherwise I'd surely have been taken down to the police station for further questioning.

As I shuffle out of the photocopying room I watch Natalie join her colleague in the office next to the boardroom. All the offices have glass fronts and I can see some pretty intense discussion going on. Steve doesn't look happy at all.

When I sit down at my workstation in the boardroom I realise I can hear voices seeping through the wall from next door, but not clearly enough to eavesdrop. I wonder what is being said. Claire is seated further away but she catches me trying to hear.

'They've been really going at it in there,' she says.

Lauren nods in agreement. 'Mmm, can't quite make out the words, but there's been some good old desk thumping. Young Mr Cassidy is not a happy boy,' she surmises.

'Methinks he does protest a little too much,' Claire adds, misquoting Shakespeare badly.

I'm surprised. 'You guys don't think he set the bombs, do you?'

They look at each other before Lauren speaks. 'Probably not, but there is something a bit dodgy about him.'

'Nah, he's no bomber,' Claire snorts derisively. 'They're trying to stitch him up and I say good on him for giving them what for. I like a man with a bit of fire. It's hot – and sexy too.'

Lauren contemplates this. 'Hot-headed isn't sexy.'

'He's passionate, you ninny. And that means fiery in the bedroom too.'

'Is that all you ever think about?'

'We all have dreams, sweetie. And if I want to fantasise about that beefy young brute, then I will. He's passionate, fiery, and sexy – all good things. I would.'

Lauren just groans and shakes her head.

Just then both Dave and Reuben pull up outside the boardroom door with their mail trolley. While Dave fusses around trying to look busy Reuben ducks in and drops a bundle of files off to Claire. As he hands them over we hear Steve shout something angrily next door. The sound startles Reuben and he twitches like a frightened bird, accidentally dropping one of the files. As Claire picks it up from the floor she doesn't quite stifle a snort of derision. But before she can ridicule him verbally Bobby walks in with Hector Lawson in tow, allowing poor Reuben to escape relatively unscathed. Dave and Hector glare at each other as they pass. It seems so unnecessary, but they're both such pompous little men. The discussions next door go quiet again.

'Lily, I was hoping I'd catch you,' Bobby says. 'I'm still having issues with Marketing. Brendan is refusing to agree on the overall structure and Hector here is starting to have a few concerns too. Do you have the file with the second draft overview of the Sales and Marketing realignment?'

Hector is glowering at me like I just stole his lunch money, when a sharp and mournful cry suddenly fills my mind:

–he didn't mean it, he's so confused–

I close my eyes to try and shut it out;

–just upset, doesn't understand–

There is another thumping sound from next door, Steve banging the desk again, I assume. I hear raised voices, and then I feel:

–help him, stop him, stop upsetting him–

The words inside my mind again. It feels like the same voice as the one I sensed yesterday, just before the bomb went off at Commonwealth.

Terror instantly courses through me.

FIFTEEN

I open my eyes wide in shock.

Bobby is standing over me, a look of concern on his face. My heart is racing. Hector is just behind him, but he's now staring at the wall between us and the meeting room next door, an odd half-smile on his face. Another angry outburst can be heard and his eyebrows rise in wonder.

'Lily,' asks Bobby, 'are you feeling all right?'

Suddenly there is movement outside the boardroom and Steve, Natalie Dowd and her colleague are walking past. The phrase *'helping them with their enquiries'* obscurely forms in my mind and I know they are taking Steve down to the station.

'Lily?' Bobby is right in front of me.

I struggle to regain focus. The words in my head have slipped away, but the thought of another bomb going off nearby is still terrifying me. I try to make sense of it.

I never actually hear a voice, I just feel the phrases form inside my head, but somehow I know that these words are from an older woman. The bomber's deceased mother, it must be. She's crying out for help, desperate for him to stop the killings.

I try to clear my mind, but it's spinning like a top.

'I'm sorry, Bobby. Just a bit of a headache. I'm okay,' I say. 'You said you want the Sales and Marketing file?'

'Yes please, the second draft.'

It takes me a few moments to lay my hands on it, as my thoughts keep reeling. I can't decide if the mournful words have been a warning or not, but strangely I don't feel any imminent threat. Tentatively I decide it wasn't a warning, just an expression of anguish, of despair.

I finally locate the file and hand it over. Bobby immediately passes it on to Hector who's gone back to glowering at me again. Such a rude and ungrateful man. Then Bobby says something to him quietly and Hector nods and slips out of the room, beginning to examine the files contents as he struts away.

Bobby turns to me, at first hesitantly, and then sits down beside me.

'You know I'm very grateful that you've come in today, but if you need to take a bit more time off I'll understand. You've had a pretty rough time of it.'

I'm still struggling to clear my thoughts and focus on him, but manage to respond coherently. 'No, but thanks. I need to work, it keeps me busy. Keeps my mind off other things.'

'I understand. I feel the same way.' He seems to contemplate something and then speaks again in a lower voice, so Claire and Lauren won't overhear. 'I talked with the police earlier. They seem to think that you being present for both bombings is just a coincidence. I don't think they believe you to be the target, or involved in any way. They just consider you to be very, very unlucky.' He leans in a little closer, looking me firmly in the eye. 'They'll catch this guy. And soon, don't worry.'

I'm not so confident, but I appreciate his sentiments, and it is nice having him so close. 'Thanks,' I murmur.

He looks a little bashful and seems to be considering something before speaking again.

'Have you been sailing recently?' he asks.

'Uh, no. Not for a long time. Why?'

'I was just thinking . . .' he pauses briefly. 'Don has offered to take me out for a bit of a sail around Lake Breckenock on Saturday afternoon. The forecast is good.

Would you like to join us? You know, help to clear away some doom and gloom.'

Suddenly he has my full attention. It sounds fantastic. An afternoon out on the water, sailing with Bobby. A warm feeling flows through me.

'Yes,' I blurt out. 'Yes, thanks. I'd love that.' I think I actually blush.

He beams. 'Great,' his eyes are shining. 'I've got to get back to the good fight right now, but we'll work out more detail later on, okay?'

I nod, smiling from ear to ear, as he turns and leaves.

'There's a cat who's gonna get some cream,' mutters Claire under her breath, but clearly meant for me to hear. I heft my stapler as if I'm about to throw it at her head.

As I stand in the kitchen that evening, wondering what to make myself for dinner, my mood is the lightest it has been for some time. I often cook for Cheryl and Dad but, although I feel better, tonight I'm struggling to find the motivation to create something interesting just for myself. It's easier to put the effort in when there are others to appreciate your work.

It isn't that late and the sun is still an hour from setting. I think about going out for a run, but then something in the back yard catches my eye through the window.

Movement. Someone is out there.

I step away from the window instinctively, and then draw forward again cautiously. My heart has immediately begun racing and I realise I'm holding my breath. Is the bomber at my house? Am I being targeted, here at my home? Is he coming for me?

There is a small figure standing almost in the middle of the yard and I heave a sigh of relief as I recognise Rosie.

She's facing away from me, seeming to survey the garden, and she slowly turns and looks up at the house. She stares straight at me through the window, but I'm not sure she can actually see me. I realise with a jolt that she seems to be having another – what should I call it – another episode. Uncertainty grips me. Should I go to her, or call Louise?

Rosie staggers forward a step, clearly unsteady on her feet. Is she sleepwalking? She almost falls so I move quickly out the back door towards her. Before I get halfway there she drops to her knees and then slumps to an awkward sitting position, holding herself upright with her good arm while her heavily plastered arm lies across her chest. As I get closer I can make out her vacant expression. Her eyes are glazed again, just as they were the last time. Something is badly wrong here. I hurry and drop to my knees beside her, reaching a hand out to her shoulder to steady her.

'Hey Rosie, are you okay?' I ask cautiously.

Her head jerks up and her eyes seem to focus momentarily. She almost seems to smile, but it looks more like a grimace. She tries to speak, her mouth moving as if she is trying to force a bad taste from her tongue. She croaks and then swallows and finally a word emerges.

'Lily.'

My name is all she seems able to say, but the display of recognition is a good thing. It proves she isn't completely lost to this episode, or whatever it is.

'Not easy . . .' she speaks again. Her voice is strained, but the words are clear enough.

'Don't try and talk, Rosie. I think you need help. I should get your mother.'

Her eyes glass over suddenly and she sways against me, almost falling. I lean in closer, putting my arm around her, taking her weight and holding her up.

'No,' she croaks abruptly. She coughs and takes a deep breath. 'No. Need . . . you.'

Then her little body suddenly starts shaking and I'm terrified she is going to have a serious fit of some kind and go into convulsions. But just as quickly she becomes still again and turns her face to mine once more. I hold her tightly so our faces are only centimetres apart. Her glazed eyes clear again and focus on me.

'Need you,' she repeats hoarsely. 'Need . . . to talk to you.' Her eyes gaze into mine intensely. Her body is still and it seems like she has almost recovered.

'It's okay, Rosie,' I tell her gently. 'We can talk anytime. When you're feeling better.'

She lets her head droop forward, leaning in closer.

'You need . . . Grammy,' she speaks more clearly than before, but I don't understand.

'Grammy?' I ask, confused. 'What's Grammy?'

'Up . . . Bluff Creek.' But it's a mumble this time. 'You need . . . go there.'

She isn't making any sense at all. The words seem meaningless. Taking me by surprise she shudders violently and her eyes roll up in her head, showing me nothing but white. I almost scream but hold on and hug her tight until the lurching eases. After the spasm has passed I relax my tight embrace and watch drool running from the corner of her mouth. Her eyes are mercifully closed but she begins talking softly again.

'Grammy . . . Bluff creek . . . you need,' she murmurs softly, but clearly enough, '. . . go there . . . she can help.'

'Okay, Rosie. I'll go there, she can help me,' I reply softly to comfort her. I'm totally confused by everything she's saying but it seems right to agree with her, to soothe her.

'My fault,' she mutters, 'never told . . .' Her voice fades, drifting away. 'Should have . . . told you.'

'It's okay Rosie, its okay. It's not your fault. You're going to be just fine.'

Just as I think the episode is over she suddenly snaps alert, her eyes flying open and head jolting upright. I almost lose my grip and we rock together momentarily. When she speaks again the words are faster – babbling. Her eyes glow feverishly.

'Do you see them, Lily? The faces. Do you hear them? They can't hurt you. They just need help. Go and see Grammy. She'll explain, help you to sleep–'

And then she slumps as if someone has turned off a switch. Her eyes dim and then close as her head flops forward onto my shoulder. She becomes a dead weight in my arms and I almost topple over in surprise.

Struggling to stay upright I manage to push her back, gently laying her onto her back on the grass. Twilight is just beginning to fall and I sit there with long shadows around me wondering what the hell is going on in my life.

I don't understand what I've just heard.

Do I see them? Faces? No. But do I hear them? How could she know that? How could this little girl know that I am hearing things? Hearing voices. Hearing dead people's voices at that. Where the hell did that come from?

I sit there for what must only be moments, but feels like hours, shocked at the final babbling words of my little cousin. Then I snap myself out of it, remembering that she is unconscious beside me. I need to get help.

I check her breathing. It's shallow, but even, like she is simply sleeping. My heart's racing again as I fight off panic. Rosie knew I was hearing things. But how? I need to get her help. Call an ambulance. Get Louise or Evan, her dad. I look down at her again. If we weren't in the middle of my backyard I would swear she is simply sound asleep. But my mind is still reeling. She knew about the voices? How? Finally I drag myself to my feet. First and foremost I need to get help for Rosie. I start to move away but am worried that she won't be there when I come back. But I have no choice –

my cell-phone is inside the house. I look down at her and then turn and run into the house, grab the cordless telephone and sprint back to her side.

She hasn't moved and is still breathing evenly. I dial quickly.

The ambulance crew is the same as two nights previously, but it isn't a joyous reunion. They move quickly and efficiently and take Rosie away, with Louise riding along again, to the hospital for observation. As they load her up I describe the incident as best I can, but without revealing the specifics of our strange conversation. Louise is somewhat wary of me this time, which I find hurtful. Her face is rigid with distrust and she clearly thinks I am to blame for something. Once she reaches Rosie she hovers over her protectively, keeping me at arm's length, warning me off with fierce looks. I don't try to reason with her. She clearly thinks I'm up to something and I hate to think what she may be considering. But she is Rosie's mother and I instinctively understand her primitive urge to protect her child.

As I watch the ambulance pull out of the driveway once again I feel desperately alone. I'm scared and confused. I don't understand what's happening around me. A bomber seems to be targeting me, dead people's words are leaking into my mind and my little cousin is having seizures, but only when I'm around. I begin to seriously doubt my sanity. I need a friend.

Numbly I realise I'm still holding the cordless phone and without thought or hesitation I dial a number I know by heart. She answers on the third ring.

'I think I'm going crazy, Megan,' I say as she answers and then burst out crying immediately. 'I was nearly blown up a second time and my mind is really messed up. I'm losing it here . . .'

She's at my door in less than fifteen minutes.

We sit in the lounge and I tell her about the second bombing. She is furious that I didn't call her yesterday. Of course she'd heard about it, but she had no idea I'd been there as everybody's names are being kept quiet. We were told that the police don't want the media blowing this up into any more of a wild frenzy than it already is.

I don't tell her everything though. For some reason I don't feel comfortable telling her about Rosie's episodes, and the thought of going into detail about the strange words and feelings in my head is just one step too far towards crazy. I want her comfort, her sensible voice, her reassurance. I don't want a trip to the asylum.

'Okay,' she says when I finally stop burbling. 'Okay. So you've now been in two explosions and you think someone's stalking you – trying to kill you, in fact – and because of all this you think you're starting to go a little crazy?'

I stare at her wide-eyed and then nod.

She surprises me by smiling. 'I don't see a problem here. Seriously, it could be a lot worse.' I gape at her. She's trying to make light of it all, once again, but she doesn't know the half of it. 'So where does Greg hide the gin?' she asks, and finally I smile back.

Megan is a breath of fresh air. Just having her there makes me feel that we can work everything out. That I'm going to be fine. We just need a drink. I point at the kitchen, but she is already on her way. She knows perfectly well where the gin is hidden.

She bangs around for a few minutes and comes back with gin, tonic, a bowl of ice, two tall glasses, a sharp knife and a lemon. Better prepared than any boy scout.

'Okay,' she says again as she prepares the drinks. 'So, physically – on the outside – you're fine. No new bumps or bruises or cuts?'

I raise my hands in the air and twist left and right. Nope, no new injuries.

'Good. Excellent. So it's just a few mental problems then?'

'Well yes, that and someone trying to kill me.'

'Aha, so the mental problem is in fact paranoia, to be more specific.' She grins at me, waving the lemon in my face. 'Come on Lily, no one's trying to kill you. You've just had incredibly bad timing this week. The wrong place at the wrong time – twice. That's just really bad luck.'

'But what if it is me they're after. They might try again. Other people could die.'

'It's not you, for crying out loud. You've never even upset a door-to-door salesman. And what would anyone possibly gain by blowing you up? It's not you,' she determines firmly. She moves on quickly, trying to keep me from dwelling in my paranoia.

'I shouldn't say anything, but they're looking pretty closely at a guy from your work. That guy Steve Cassidy. The one who called you just before the first explosion.'

I should be surprised, but the news doesn't shock me at all. There is definitely something a little shady about Steve – as charming to the ladies as he may be.

'I was poking my nose around the ops room at work,' Megan continues, 'and his name seems to come up a fair bit. Did you know he's just been evicted by the City Council?'

I give a small nod and hope she doesn't ask me how I knew that.

'So he had motive for the first bombing too. Do you see?' She's getting quite excited about all this – she's always wanted to play detective. But I don't see her point and shake my head, frowning. How is that a motive to kill someone?

'The first bombing, Lily, at the City Council offices' she exclaims. 'The guy that was killed was in charge of Steve's tenancy termination. He would have signed off on Steve's original eviction notice.'

'Oh come on, Meg. You can't think that someone like Steve Cassidy would blow someone up over being evicted. It's not like he couldn't find somewhere else to live.'

'I'm sure he could, but it's still a motive and it links him to the first bomb,' she pauses, but only for a moment. 'And there's other things. Did you know that the bombs have all been set off by remote control – not by timers, or triggers?'

I didn't know that, and I don't really understand what she means. I frown and shrug.

'Seriously, Lily, don't you watch TV? Usually bombs are detonated by either a timer running down – like an alarm clock going off – or they have triggers, like you turn the key in a car's ignition. You get this?'

I nod, but her knowledge of the subject is starting to turn my stomach.

'Okay, so when they use a remote control they actually have to be reasonably close to the bomb. It's like, uh . . .' She looks around and snatches up the remote control for the TV. 'It's like this. You have to be within so many metres of the TV, or this won't work.'

I nod again, understanding – now feeling even queasier.

'So whoever set off those bombs, all three of them, had to be quite close to them to use the remote control to set them off. Probably not as close as the TV here, but pretty close by.' She pauses, almost breathless with enthusiasm. My insides are knotting up. 'And Steve was right there for your bomb at work, he would have been within range, and –', she stops abruptly, suddenly realising what she is saying. She hesitates, and then continues in a softer voice, less enthusiastically, '– and he called you away from it, just before it went off . . .' she tails off, watching me carefully.

My body cramps and I feel a shiver of horror trickle down my spine as I think about everything I know. In a creaky voice I tell her, 'He asked me out earlier today, on a date, just before the police took him away.'

'Oh my God,' Megan looks horrified. 'You didn't?'

I shake my head. 'I didn't have a chance to answer him. We were interrupted.'

'Oh. My. God!' she repeats, and then she actually brightens and smiles. 'Then you do have a stalker, and a crazy one at that. Wow, you're hotter than I thought.'

I don't know whether to laugh or scream. Usually I enjoy Megan's irreverent sense of humour, but this time I find it tasteless. I slump and go silent, my insides gnawing at me. In an instant she's all over me, apologising profusely. Promising to behave, telling me it's okay, everything is going to be fine. After a few minutes I shake off the haunted feeling and relax a little. She sits back and thrusts a gin and tonic into my hands, telling me to 'get that down you'. I take a long hit. It does help.

Megan now appears contrite. She's even stopped talking, probably so she won't upset me any further. We sit quietly for a minute or two before I finally break the silence.

'Natalie Dowd asked me if I had seen anyone holding a cell-phone, or anything similar. She asked specifically about Steve. I thought it was an odd question at the time.'

Megan nods, 'Yeah, it's a big thing. I really shouldn't have told you. I'm not even supposed to know. They don't want people freaking out every time someone randomly pulls out a cell-phone, or a pager, or anything that could be a remote control. Can you imagine the panic out there?'

I look her in the eye. 'Do you think Steve could be the bomber?'

She hesitates, but holds my gaze. 'It's possible,' she pauses, choosing her words with more care now. 'Apparently he doesn't have an alibi for the first bomb, but the motive does seem a bit lame. And I don't see any motive for blowing up your office. I mean, what has he gained? And it does seem weird that he would call you out,' she starts to grin again, she just can't help herself. 'I mean, you're pretty hot and all that, but you're not that hot. Sure, the guy is definitely keen on you,' she continues, 'but trying to blow you up twice does seem a pretty rank way to get your attention. Sending flowers would probably have been a bit smoother.'

'You're a dickhead, you know that?' I say with a half-smile.

'Yeah, but I'm a lot of fun at parties.' She raises her glass for a toast, 'Here's to Lily's paranoia. May she enjoy the bizarre affections of many more stalkers to come.'

I don't know what to say so I just raise my glass too, and then down it in one. Perhaps drowning my sorrows will be the best idea we have tonight.

SIXTEEN

Sadly the world isn't a brighter place the next morning. My head feels heavy, partially from too many gin and tonics last night, but also from thinking too much about Rosie's strange pronouncements: about the voices in my head and someone called Grammy, at Bluff Creek, who can apparently help me.

Bluff Creek is an actual place, out on the lakefront about twenty minutes drive north of Wilton, where I live. But I've never more than passed through it. I know a little bit about it though, mainly through Claire from work, whose family has a place out there. It's a small settlement, mainly of holiday homes, but with a few permanent residents who inhabit the small, hippie-like township. Claire describes it as a bit of a bohemian backwater, the kind of place you can run away to when your head gets so full of crap that you just want to scream out loud. Her words, not mine, but boy can I empathise at the moment – my head is so seriously full of crap.

Nevertheless, I can't see how ànyone out there could possibly help me with my bizarre mental problems. Rosie's words make no sense so I try to put them out of my mind.

Making things worse today is the atmosphere at work. To call it strained is a serious understatement. Usually our Fridays here are pretty laid-back and cruisy, but today things are tense, especially around the Administration team.

Our letters advising staff that their jobs have been disestablished – and that they will have to reapply for them – all went out first thing. Poor Dave and Reuben were sent out on a special delivery run, tasked with ensuring that everyone personally received their letter. I got one too. Bobby hand-delivered mine, Lauren and Claire's.

And here we sit, just staring at each other. Although we prepared every letter, and we knew they were coming out today, it still feels horrible. Our lawyers had pored over the text to ensure the company's butt was legally covered – making the letters all feel quite formal and stiff, with very little focus on the emotional upheaval they would cause. I read mine again quietly, surprised at how disillusioned it makes me feel.

Our phones have been ringing all morning with people from all around the company seeking answers to a million questions. Almost every caller needs to be reassured that interviews will be fair, that their longevity and productivity will be equally considered, and that any people who are not reappointed will receive fair and reasonable redundancy payouts. It's horrible. Other than being blown up last Friday it's easily the worst day of my short working career. A few callers are upset, many just angry and rude. It's impossible not to get caught up in the swelling tide of cynicism. Lauren ends most of her calls close to tears and Claire needs to take regular breaks to calm herself down. Bobby is out dealing with people face to face and I'm feeling more and more depressed by every call, but trying to console myself that we are doing the right thing. That this is the best and fairest way to handle the situation. But it isn't working very well. Each call makes me feel less certain of myself and of our grand realignment strategy.

And then Steve Cassidy turns up at the boardroom door and I freeze.

Considering all that Megan and I discussed last night I'm shocked to see him here. I guess I thought he would still be at the police station, in custody.

He reaches into his jacket pocket for something.

Oh God. Is it a remote control?

No, I take a deep breath, it's just a letter. He stands in the doorway and holds it up, smiling.

'I got your love letter, Lily. Many thanks.' Only then do I recognise it as his role disestablishment letter.

I don't know what to say, or think. He's smiling, but is he really amused, or is he being sarcastic? My heart's racing. I force a small smile in return, saying nothing.

He slips into the room and quickly pulls a chair up close to mine, sitting himself down. He leans towards me, obviously not wanting Lauren or Claire to share our conversation. He smells of musky cologne. It's quite nice. But I'm bewildered. What does he want?

In a quiet voice he says, 'I'm sorry about yesterday. We never got to finish our chat.' He lets that just hang and I feel compelled to respond. But a small, 'Oh,' is all I can manage. I can't look him in the eye. I wait. He grins mischievously.

'So how about it? Dinner tonight?'

I look at him briefly and then away, trying to find the right words. 'Umm, thanks Steve, but I'm really not up for dinner. Maybe another time . . .'

He isn't fazed at all. Clearly he's done this a few times before.

'No problem, I understand. Look, instead of dinner, how about lunch? No strings.'

I'm torn. I still feel somehow indebted to him for saving my life. But I can't help wondering just how involved in the bombings he is.

'Look Steve, I'm really not sure,' I eventually reply, 'but maybe lunch sometime might be okay, perhaps . . .'

He leaps on it, like a bear on a salmon dancing up river. 'Okay, great. Come on then, it's after twelve. Let's go now, I know a great place.' He stands quickly and takes my hand, gently raising me up out of my seat.

I'm stunned. I didn't meant right now. I look over at Claire and Lauren for support, but find none.

'You go on, Lily. We're okay here,' chirps Claire, leaning back in her chair and grinning.

Steve smiles at them, spreading the charm about. 'I'll be gentle with her, I promise,' he tells them. They both laugh.

I feel sick, but allow myself to be escorted to the lifts and out of the building. He chats amiably as we walk a couple of blocks to what he describes as his favorite 'luncherie'. I'm not even sure if that's a word. Clearly he likes eating there.

As we arrive I'm pleased to note the restaurant is fairly busy. I don't want to end up in some remote, empty place where there would be no witnesses if he tries to abduct me.

We find a quiet booth, order drinks and review the menu. He continues to lay on the charm the whole time. It suddenly occurs to me that I want to clear something up.

'Steve, you know how you called me for that meeting last Friday? Just before the bomb went off?' He nods. 'Why did you need that meeting? You never said.'

He doesn't hesitate. 'I wanted to ask you about the redundancy payouts.'

I'm surprised. Is this the truth or has he been rehearsing this answer, knowing I would be curious? I say nothing, just raise my eyebrows and wait for him to continue. Finally he does with a sigh.

'I've been thinking about taking the redundancy, and not reapplying for my job. But last week it was just a rumour about all staff being laid off and I wanted to know.'

'You wanted to know if Westwood was going to disestablish everyone?'

'Yeah, and to try and work out what the payouts would amount to. But I know that now, thanks to the lovely letter you sent me this morning.'

'But why would you leave? I've heard you're pretty good at your job.'

He takes it as a compliment, puffing up slightly. The great male ego.

'Damn right I am. The best. Top sales every month for the last eight months straight. But my brother's offered me a job. A Sales Manager role with his property construction business. Better pay, company car, a sweet deal.'

'So you're going to leave then?' I find myself actually a little impressed.

'Now that I have your letter – confirming a handsome redundancy payout – well, yes. I'm pretty sure I'm going to get while the getting's good.'

As I'm trying to reconcile this, two men stop beside our table, interrupting us. Both look around thirty and are fairly big. I recognise one of them as the man I'd seen Steve with down by the marina the other night. He looks a lot like an older, more sophisticated version of him. Solid, but not quite as large, with slicked-back black hair. The other guy is more angular, blonde and haughty-looking. Steve stands quickly, a note of deference in his voice.

'Gentlemen, this is a surprise. How are you guys?'

They shake hands and Steve turns to introduce me. 'Lily, this is my brother Richard – who I was just telling you about, soon to be my employer.' He indicates the darker man and the family resemblance becomes obvious. 'And this is James Breckenock, one of our partners in Cassidy Construction. Gents, may I present Miss Lily MacDonald.'

They both nod politely, muttering clipped greetings and I respond with a small waving gesture. We don't shake hands.

'We were just about to order, would you like to join us?' Steve asks them.

They both decline. 'No, we couldn't, but thank you. We've got a lot of business to discuss and we'd just bore you to tears.' Then he fixes Steve with a firm look. 'But perhaps you could slip over for a quick chat before you head back to work, okay?' It's a directive, not a request. Steve nods assent.

They excuse themselves and move over to a table across the room as I feel a wash of apprehension flow over me. I look at their receding backs and feel something inexplicably sinister. I sense somehow that these men have done some horrible things. Illegal acts. I'm convinced of it and have to fight an urge to stand up and point a finger at them, accusing them as criminals. I begin to twitch nervously and wonder. Are they the bombers? Are they working with Steve to kill people? For profit? My nerves tighten and the hair on the back of my neck tingles. The feeling of unease that runs through me is extreme. Something about these men – and Steve too – is disturbing me deeply. I don't understand why, but I want to escape, and urgently.

I also want to tell Steve that he shouldn't associate with them, but I can't do that. It's too late. I somehow know that he has already crossed the line. And worse yet, it doesn't bother him.

'Lily?' Steve is looking at me curiously. 'Are you okay?'

I can feel that the colour has drained from me. I stare at him, suddenly terrified. This man is dangerous, I'm certain of it. I start to stand up.

'I've just remembered . . .' My mind is reeling furiously, 'I was supposed to be doing something . . .' I can't look at him. I feel like I'm falling, spiralling in terror. 'I'm supposed to be meeting my friend, Megan, for lunch . . . right now.' I start to back away from the table. 'I'm sorry, Steve, I have to go. She'll be waiting.'

He stands up, looking frustrated, and then pulls a cell-phone from his pocket.

I freeze. Images of smoke and shattered glass flash through my mind. Is that a remote control? Is there a bomb here too?

'What are you doing?' I ask softly, my voice trembling. I keep backing away.

'Call her,' he says. I don't understand. My mind is like jelly. 'Don't panic, sit down. You can just call her and explain. I'm sure she'll be fine about it.' He offers the phone.

I go numb. I'm so afraid that he has a bomb I can't think. He's dangerous, I sense it. I know it. I close my eyes, trying to focus on his words, trying to push down my rising panic. Finally I stutter, 'I can't, she, umm, her cell-phone is broken. I can't call her.'

He frowns. He's getting angry.

'She'll be okay. Sit down Lily, you're making a scene.'

I feel cornered. I just know that Steve and his brother, and the Breckenock man are corrupt, dangerous, not to be trusted. And I'm starting now to have some confidence in my unusual feelings. I was right about Janet and her baby, and about the kissing thing. Derek confirmed them for me. I don't understand it, but I'm prepared to have some faith in my startling intuition right here and now. These men are dangerous. To me it isn't just a feeling. I am utterly convinced. I need to stay away from them.

'I'm sorry, Steve, I have to go,' I blurt, and I turn and leave the restaurant as quickly as I can without actually running. I hear him curse behind me, but he doesn't follow.

I don't look back. Each step feels like I'm wading through mud, held back by some unseen resistance, as I try to hurry back to the office. Eventually I glance behind to ensure he isn't following me. Part of me rationally understands that there is no real threat creeping up behind me, but that reasonable thought is being blotted out by an absolute blind panic. Megan thinks I'm being paranoid and maybe she's right, but the sinister feelings and vivid sense of danger are very real to me. I'm doing the right thing.

I find myself back in the relative safety of my make-shift workplace in no time at all.

* * *

Nikki slips into the boardroom an hour or so later. Her face wears that 'I-have-gossip-and-I'm-keen-to-share-it' look that we all know so well. Lauren and Claire also sense her enthusiasm and perk up. Nikki quickly takes a seat and offers up the time-honoured line:

'I probably shouldn't share this with you guys . . .'

We all know she's going to tell us anyway, whether we want to hear it or not.

'. . . and apparently the police aren't going to say anything formally, but this will definitely affect the realignment project so I think you should know.' She pauses dramatically as we wait with bated breath. 'You know how two guys were killed in the other bombing, at CCS? Well it turns out that one of them was their Sales Manager.' She makes a bit of a face, pausing again to amplify the moment. 'And the police reckon that he was the target. They think the bombings could have something to do with our merger.'

She looks from me to Claire, to Lauren, as if expecting applause for her investigative efforts but we all just sit there frowning.

It doesn't make sense. How would the death of CCS's Sales Manager affect the merger?

It takes me a moment to recognise that the police are still focusing on Steve. He works in sales. Are they possibly thinking that he has targeted the other Sales Manager for his job?

Nikki looks disappointed. She's bought us what she considers to be fascinating news and no one seems impressed.

'I'm not sure I understand,' I say carefully, 'they think someone's trying to change something about the merger?'

'It's possible, don't you think?' she asks. 'And it does mean that we have one less manager trying to gain an appointment in John's management team.'

There is silence for a moment and then Claire, oozing sarcasm, says, 'So, you think that the bomber is some bloke who's going to the extreme just to secure himself a job?'

Nikki looks suddenly uncertain. 'Maybe.'

'That's crazy stupid, that's what it is.' Claire fires back. 'No one round here is that desperate or outright fanatical enough to go around killing people – not just for a job.'

Nikki flushes and starts to look annoyed.

But Claire is relentless, 'All the guys you're accusing are steady, hard-working, dedicated family men. They're not killers. If they don't get reappointed they'll take their big fat redundancy payouts and their glowing CVs and they'll get hired within days at any other big firm. And anyway, Mike Smith is still alive, isn't he?'

I tend to agree with Claire, but choose to keep quiet. Nikki is a friend and I don't want to offend her. She opens her mouth to retort but then closes it again, starting to look a little more thoughtful.

'Is Mike coming back?' Nikki asks tentatively and they all look at me.

'He hasn't decided either way yet,' I say.

Finally Nikki holds her hands up in surrender. 'Maybe you're right, whatever. But it is strange that the police think the Sales Manager was the target. I'm pretty sure they know a heck of a lot more about this than they're letting on. Anyway, it does have an impact on the senior management realignment,' she says. 'Without Adam and Henry, and now this guy, we're down from fourteen guys trying for eight jobs to only eleven applicants.'

But Claire is still feeling feisty. 'Maybe Head Office has hired a hit-man to take out a few people and save on the redundancy payouts,' she offers up mischievously. 'This will save them a small fortune. Maybe that's really why they sent Bobby here?'

No one laughs. We all just stare at her in horror. She quickly realises she's taken it a step too far and this time she holds her hands up in surrender, casually mocking Nikki.

'What? What did I say?'

No one speaks. We all just shake our heads at her in unison. Claire has a habit of putting her foot in her mouth, but this one's a real clunker. She quickly becomes repentant.

'Oh come on guys, it's just a joke. Bobby's not a hit-man,' she moans, just as Bobby walks into the boardroom.

'I'm not a what?' he asks distractedly.

Luckily for Claire he seems weary and doesn't push it. She turns bright red and suddenly becomes intensely interested in whatever is on her computer screen. It's rare to see Claire blush, and this one's a beauty. Lauren and I catch each other's eyes, both fighting to hold back our laughter.

Bobby's desk is squeezed into a corner. He moves to it, sits down heavily, and starts tapping away intently on his lap-top. Nikki leaves the room without further comment.

Bobby seems drained. There is so much going on today. I know he's just been meeting with the Marketing team, reassuring them about the disestablishments and outlining the process of interviews that will occur over the next few weeks. He looks up and I offer him a small smile of encouragement.

'How did the meeting with Marketing go?' I ask.

'You may find this hard to believe,' he replies, 'but that bastard Armstrong kept throwing his oar in and stirring things up. I just don't get that guy. Nothing we do is good enough for him.' He shakes his head, seemingly exasperated.

'Sorry to hear that,' I reply.

He shrugs wearily. 'Never mind. You can't please everyone.' Then he suddenly sits more upright, clearly remembering something. He looks over at Claire and Lauren and speaks loudly so we all can hear him this time.

'By the way, ladies, I dropped off the letter to Edna earlier. She's going to pop in next week sometime, but she told me she's already made her decision. She won't be reapplying for her job.'

There is a strange silence in the room. I don't know how to react. It's not a surprise, and Edna not reapplying will make it easier for the rest of us to ensure we stay employed. We all look at each other, and it's an awkward moment. We should be sad at losing a co-worker, but no one wants to admit that they're quietly pleased. With an uneasy tension in the air Lauren nods silently and Claire just shrugs. I turn back to Bobby and thank him for telling us, just as Jason Connor appears grim-faced at the door.

I quickly duck under the desk and pretend to search for something on the floor. Jason is a bit pushy for my liking; an ambitious man in his forties who I'm sure was passed over for promotion when Don was appointed IT manager. In my book he's basically a prat, and I'm not in the mood to deal with him. He slides over to Lauren and starts rapid-firing questions about the restructure at her. I immediately feel guilty for dodging him.

When I resurface I turn to refining consultation plans for next week. We need to work through interviewing and appointing over a hundred people and time is going to be a big factor. But first we have to work our way through the layers of employment grading – starting with the Management team. Once the executives are all appointed we can settle in team leaders and supervisors, and then everything else will follow.

John is scheduled to finalise appointments of his team by Monday to enable us to move things along more quickly. I know he's already completed a number of interviews – with both our existing Management, and the men (yes, they're also all men) from Commonwealth. But, as Nikki has pointed out for us, his options are dwindling. Three good men will learn of their employment fate over the weekend. The rest will come together very soon after to finalise the newly merged organisation's structure and assign role responsibilities.

As if reading my mind Bobby looks up. 'Lily, I have an email here from John. He wants the Management team to come together Monday morning, first thing, but he wants to do it on neutral territory. You know, not here and not at their offices. I'd like you to come along too, if you wouldn't mind. Is that okay?'

Once again I am flattered. Going to this meeting will give me an early insight into John's plans and a front-row seat as they negotiate responsibilities and staff numbers.

'Sure. I can make that.'

He smiles. 'Wonderful. He's booked us a private room at the Marina Café in Wilton. It's basically right across from the marina there on Lake Breckenock. Do you know it?'

'That's where we're sailing tomorrow, isn't it?'

'Yep, that's the place. I can pick you up on the way through if you like'

'Sure, yes. That'll be great.' I feel a warm buzz of excitement at the prospect of all this time with Bobby.

But my tingle quickly changes to a blush as I hear Claire failing to stifle a snort across the room and then mutter something about 'flies to a honey trap' under her breath. Jason looks over quizzically, but Bobby doesn't seem to hear her, thank God.

I can't wait to get back to the small semblance of privacy that our normal partitioned-off workspaces will again offer back on level three.

SEVENTEEN

His mood ebbs low again. Things still aren't going as planned.

The day's events have driven him deeper and deeper into his well of fury. He wallowed there for some time, but now he realises that it's time to swing back onto the offensive.

He's aware of some very, very useful information and has formulated a new plan. He always keeps his ears open, learning so much more that way. Listening is such a simple skill, yet so many others seem to have forgotten how to do it. But not him.

As always his plan is as simple as it will be devastating.

He will need two more devices, but that's no problem. He already has one ready to go and can create the second one on Sunday, maybe even a third – just in case. He has plenty of time. He remembers the old saying, 'lightning never strikes twice' and knows that this is what they will think. Not the same place, not so soon after. They will be left reeling, but he needs to ensure his first strike goes smoothly. Then the second will be so much sweeter, so much more meaningful.

His commitment is strong, he's so proud of himself. His mother would be proud too, if only she were here to see what he has made of himself. To see what a man he is now. But she isn't and the guilt returns to burn inside his chest once again. If only, he thinks to himself. If only.

He rouses himself from the funk and concentrates on his new plan. Starts to feel the excitement growing within him again. He is righteous, he is Thor, God-of-Thunder.

He must plan carefully, be ready for any distractions. He must prevail.

EIGHTEEN

The rest of the afternoon is a blur of paperwork and other activity. Sean Peterson drops by to try and renegotiate overall staff numbers for the Finance team with Bobby, and then Brendan Armstrong turns up demanding unreasonably that we increase the number of assistants allocated in his Marketing team's structure. Predictably, it gets ugly.

But Nikki doesn't return, and fortunately neither does Steve.

Both Reuben and Dave stop by to confirm that all the letters have been delivered. Every single staff member has received one. Reuben slips in and out without saying much, as usual, but Dave stops to ask a couple of very odd questions about his own letter. He doesn't seem to understand that he will need to reapply for the job he already has – assuming his job will still exist in the restructure. I'm not yet allowed to tell him that only one Mail Runner role will be available so it makes for a very awkward conversation. He gets frustrated, but finally goes away with a few notes on how to cobble together a CV. I offer to help him format it if he scribbles out the key points. He's not a lot happier when he leaves, but few people I have talked with today are.

By five o'clock I'm grateful to get away. It's Friday night, and I have no plans. Megan is going out on a date, Bobby hasn't asked me out and there is no way I'm going to accept another invitation from Steve. Although, after my performance at the restaurant at lunchtime, I doubt he'll ever ask again.

A quiet night in with a movie sounds perfect, anything to help take my mind off today's depressing events. But it doesn't quite work out that way.

In the end I resist picking up a video and just watch a bit of TV, do a little cleaning and go to bed early with a good book. It's a few minutes after 10 pm when I hear a tap on my bedroom window. I'm still reading, but having trouble focusing on the page as I gradually slip towards sleep. At first I don't fully register the noise and am not concerned. But then it comes again and I sit bolt upright in bed, managing to stifle a scream.

I have no emergency plan. There is no gun, knife or softball bat in my room. I don't have a phone in here either, and my cell-phone is on a charger in the kitchen.

The tapping comes again, more urgently. Someone is at my bedroom window. This is no real achievement on the part of an intruder though. The house features floor to ceiling windows and my room is at ground level. Anyone can walk up and rap on a pane. My head swirls with possibilities. What should I do?

Then a voice emerges. Quiet but insistent, a soft hissing.

'Lily, are you awake? It's me. Lily?'

I slide out of bed, now more confused than terrified. It sounds like Rosie. Surely not.

'Lily, please . . .' the voice persists in a loud whisper. 'Come to the window, Lily.'

I don't have a torch so turn on the main bedroom light and then pull the curtains back quickly, stepping behind them to peer around and out the window.

Rosie is just visible outside in the glow through the glass. She stands there in brightly coloured pyjamas, her white plaster-cast reflecting the light. Initially she seems fine, although as I move closer I notice her sway slightly – like she's only just maintaining her balance. But tonight her eyes are wide and clear and she offers up a small smile.

I frown at her. 'What the hell do you think you're doing out there? You should be in bed.'

'I'm sorry. I didn't mean to scare you, but . . .' she sways a little and the smile drops away. She blinks her eyes as if to refocus and continues. 'I need to . . . sorry, I have to give you this.' She holds out a small piece of paper in her good hand.

I just stare at her. I can't believe she's out there, knocking on my window in the middle of the night, to pass me a note.

'You're kidding, right?' I say incredulously. 'You should be in bed. Your mum will be furious with us both if she catches you here. And what if you faint again?'

'I'm okay, Lily. I think I've . . .' she coughs lightly and continues, '. . . worked this out now.' She pushes the note towards me. 'Please, I can't stay long.' And then she starts to sway again and leans forward, using the house as support.

I don't know what to think, but can't leave her standing around out there all night. I open the window and stretch out my hand. She sort of nods and thrusts the folded piece of paper into my grasp.

'Stay there, Rosie. I'm coming out. I need to get you home.'

Bringing my hand back in, I immediately reach for my bathrobe. I hear her murmur something that sounds like agreement before I dash round to the front door and outside. She is moving slowly back around the house as I reach her. She offers me up another wan smile and I go to support her and begin to guide her back home.

'This is crazy, Rosie. You shouldn't be out of bed,' I admonish her. 'You're not well.'

'Promise me, Lily,' is her obscure reply. 'Promise me you'll go. Right away.'

'What? Go where?'

She's struggling to speak now and I'm terrified that I may need to call Louise and have Rosie removed from my property by ambulance for a third time. She stops walking and grips my arm with a fevered ferocity.

'Bluff Creek . . . Grammy . . . go tomorrow.'

The words are no longer coming easily. I'm desperate to calm her and avoid a full-blown episode that will most likely leave her unconscious on the ground.

'Okay, I'll go,' I say. 'I promise, all right? Just relax, I'll go.'

My promise seems to please her and as I watch she rallies herself to the task of walking on. A hint of a smile emerges, but no more words. We stagger forward a few more steps to reach the gap in the hedge between our houses. Then she tries to push me off. She seems to want to go on alone.

'I can do it,' she murmurs.

'Let me help,' I insist, taking her arm again.

She stops and looks up at me, her expression now unreadable. After a moment's silence she nods slightly.

'Front door is open,' she says more clearly. 'Just to there.'

I nod back and we push through the hedge together and walk slowly to the front door which is, as she'd insisted, standing ajar. There are no lights on though and it is obvious that she has slipped out without being seen. I get her to the door and am desperate to ask her more questions, to understand why she's made such a huge effort when she clearly isn't well. But I bite my tongue. As curious as I am I'm more nervous about being caught outside with Rosie in the middle of the night. Louise would definitely not approve.

At the doorway Rosie only speaks one more time, and her words do nothing but confuse me further.

'Sleeping pills help,' she whispers. 'At night, if the visions are too much.'

I just stare at her, bewildered. Then she squeezes my hand gently and steps into the house, reaching up to pull the door closed softly behind her. I stand there quietly for another few minutes listening for the sound of her falling – or of Louise or Evan finding her out of bed. But no such sounds come so I tiptoe quietly back home.

After I close the window in my bedroom and pull the curtains again I find the note Rosie passed me in the pocket of my bathrobe. I open it carefully and frown as I read the few words that are jotted there.

Bluff Creek. Crystal Heart. Kathryn.

Five words on three lines. All carefully written in neat handwriting with a blue ink pen. And that's it.

Kathryn is obviously a name and I know where Bluff Creek is, but the Crystal Heart reference makes no sense at all. Is Kathryn the person Rosie wants me to go and see? Almost certainly. Why else would she make such a fuss? I try to remember what she said to me yesterday evening. 'You need to see Grammy. She can help.' Or something like that. Is Kathryn actually Grammy, or are they two people? And how can she, or they, help? And what on earth is a Crystal Heart?

I look at the note again and feel deeply frustrated. I can't understand how Rosie could possibly know anything about the voices I've been hearing. She's just a child. How can she be offering me advice? And what was her final comment about? Visions being too much. Sleeping pills will help. What visions?

Finally I lay the note down and go back to bed with my mind all over the place, yet again.

Thankfully, a deep dreamless sleep somehow finds me and I actually feel quite refreshed when I wake up on Saturday morning. It's going to be a big day. While still quite disturbed by Rosie's visit late last night, I'm almost more preoccupied with thoughts of sailing with Bobby in the afternoon. It's a little shameless, but I'm almost shivering in anticipation.

I start the day with a short run, blowing out the cobwebs and helping to get my mind into gear. I shower, dress and then pick up Rosie's note from my bedside table. I read it again and immediately feel that strange pull of obligation that has been bothering me all morning. Last night I promised Rosie that I would go up to Bluff Creek and try to find this Kathryn person. I didn't intend to follow through with it at the time but while I'd been out running, the note, and our strange late-night meeting, had weighed heavily upon me. And, if I'm honest, I'm now more than a little intrigued. Rosie's persistence has been significant. She's clearly ill, and with something possibly quite dreadful, but she continues to drag herself over here to try and guide me towards this person in Bluff Creek. Maybe I should go out there? If I don't she will most likely keep pestering me, and God only knows what damage that may cause.

I reconsider my plans for the day. I have the morning free. I'd been thinking of doing the grocery shopping and some more cleaning, but there is nothing that can't be put off till tomorrow. I check the time, just after 10am. It's only a twenty-minute drive to Bluff Creek and I don't have to be at Wilton Marina to meet Bobby until after lunch. I can easily slot in a trip to Bluff Creek for an hour or so.

Oddly it feels like the right thing to do and, if nothing else, it will be a nice drive out and around the lake. What harm can it do?

It is, without doubt, a beautifully scenic drive.

The road north out of Wilton twists and turns along the shore of the lake. It's almost one lane only in many places but tall trees overhang and the sunlight glistens off the water alongside. It is divine, spectacular, and I'm pleased to feel the weight lifting from my shoulders as I cruise along, humming tunelessly to a song on the radio.

Less than twenty minutes later I arrive in Bluff Creek and have to try and decide what to do next. There isn't much to the place and I cruise along slowly looking for any clue as to what the Crystal Heart reference might mean. I wonder if I might find a monument, or a natural mountain peak shaped like a heart, or some other form of unusual landmark, but it turns out to be something much simpler – and glaringly obvious.

I park across the road from a quiet little row of tatty old shops. From the car I have a spectacular view out over the lake, which is a glorious shade of green and blue sparkling under bright sunlight. I half expect the lady of the lake to emerge and wave to me, such has been the weirdness in my life recently, but she never surfaces. It's hard to tear my eyes away from the shimmering water, the scenery before me is calm and peaceful and I allow myself a deep sigh.

Behind me the little settlement is quiet, with only a gentle breeze disturbing the shady trees I have parked under. I shift in my seat to get a better view of one of the run-down shops in the row across the road. Roughly in the middle of the row is an old shop with heavy curtains lining the windows. I can just make out the name 'Crystal Heart' on a badly weather-beaten sign, but cannot see inside. In stark contrast to the idyllic view out front, the entrance to Crystal Heart looks dark and unwelcoming.

I get out of the car. The street is deserted, just like a ghost town in an old western movie. I look about for tumbleweed, but see none. Although no one else is in sight I make a show of clicking the button to auto-lock my car and set the alarm. As the lights flash once, and the car beeps in confirmation I surprise myself with the realisation of how simple, and how common, a remote control device is. I'm holding one right now. Although it just triggered my car alarm, it could just as easily have triggered a bomb. I try to shake off the creepy feeling that floods through me. I had wanted to put all thoughts of the bombings aside for today. But it isn't that easy.

I gather myself and turn towards the run-down row of shops.

They are all badly neglected. None of them seem to have seen a coat of paint in a hundred years. The creepy feeling is quickly replaced with a nervous anxiety.

What on earth am I doing here?

With no traffic to threaten me I cross the road and reach the door of the old shop with the heavily curtained windows. There is a sign in the window that says 'OPEN', although I note there are no regular hours printed nearby. It's like they only open when they feel like it. I can't see inside at all, as the curtains obscure any view.

My heart is pounding.

The door is unlocked. A chime tinkles as I push it open and step inside. No surprise here, the shop is very dimly lit. There are weak down-lights on the walls, but the curtains keep the room very gloomy. From what little I can make out, the shop is small and filled with crystals, rocks, beads and other things that I would describe loosely as hippie stuff. It fairly quickly explains the unusual name of the shop.

I can smell incense burning. There are books, too, displayed haphazardly among the crystals, and the whole atmosphere is kind of musty. A shiver runs down my spine. Maybe I should just leave?

But instead I take a deep breath and make my way inside. As my eyes adjust to the light a woman seems to appear from nowhere. She glides forward to a counter and leans her hip against it, folding her arms across her chest. She seems to size me up before she speaks.

'Sar shan chai, you come to me early this morning.'

I'm not sure how to respond as I don't understand exactly what she said. I simply opt for a weak attempt at a smile.

'Av adŕe, come in,' she says firmly. 'I won't eat you.'

The woman is probably around sixty, but her hair is black as night. She's a little taller than me and wears a long black dress, right down to her ankles, and is draped in a multi-coloured heavy woven wrap. Quite over-dressed for such a warm day.

Standing ram-rod straight, she is quite stunning in a theatrical sort of way. I'm still hesitant as I step forward, noticing a doorway behind her which she must have entered through, and suddenly I realise I'm not nervous any more. In some strange way I start to feel a small sense of refuge here, not exactly warmth, but I know instinctively that this woman is no threat to me.

Her presence fills the small room, but she is somehow removed from it. Not quite aloof, but definitely remote in a proud and majestic way. It's obvious that she must have been a very beautiful woman in her youth and she is still rather striking. She moves forward to stand directly before me and I have to look slightly upwards into her eyes.

Her remoteness sharply departs and she gives a small start, but recovers quickly and tilts her head slightly to one side, a little wary now. I can see her eyes roving slowly across my face, stopping at my eyes. She reaches out to touch me but suddenly pulls her hand back, clasping it back to her chest. She mutters something under her breath, I can't tell what, and then she shakes her head gently in disbelief.

'You are her spitting image, my chai,' she whispers, 'picture perfect.'

I don't understand what she's talking about. Something in her expression is deeply familiar, but I can't immediately say what. We stare at each other for a full minute before she

speaks again. Her voice is cautious, but the words are almost
an accusation.

'Your name is Lillian.' she states. 'Lillian Grace.'

I step back slightly in surprise, unable to find my voice.
How can she possibly know that? Who is she? But, although
her words have surprised me, I feel no fear. She raises one
finely shaped eyebrow and just gazes at me, like she is
staring right through me. It makes me feel uncomfortable.
She doesn't speak again, she just waits.

Struggling to respond I initially just nod, and then
finally I manage to speak. 'Yes, yes I am.'

'But I will call you Lily, as your friends and family do.'

I nod again, totally bewildered. 'Sure,' is all I can utter.

She reaches out to me again, this time gently clasping
my chin and raising it, and then turns my face left and right.
Like she is checking for markings, or blemishes, or
something like that. I don't like it and pull my head back,
out of her hand.

'Do you mind?' I snap, a little annoyed.

She snorts softly. 'You are the image of your mother,
and your heart bears the same quarrelsome spirit,' she
pauses. 'And you have the gift. I feel it in you.'

This woman is making no sense at all. Has she just
called me quarrelsome? And said that I look like my mother?
In my memories my mother had been an achingly beautiful
woman, I don't believe for a minute that I look anything like
her.

And the gift? What on earth does that mean?

She frowns. 'You have no idea who I am, do you, Lily?'

I look at her carefully. There is something about her that
I recognise, but it doesn't make any sense. I shake my head,
'No, not really . . .' I hesitate, starting to wonder.

But then, in a rush of understanding it comes to me and
I know. Somehow I just know, yet again. I look at the

woman's oddly familiar face and suddenly feel angry, betrayed.

'But you're supposed to be dead,' I accuse her.

She frowns back at me, with just a hint of a smile. 'Passing over to the spirit world is not an exact science, nevertheless I am fairly certain that I have not yet attempted that journey,' she replies.

NINETEEN

'But . . .' I'm desperately confused. 'But they told me you were both dead. Years and years ago. You died before I was born, they said.' I hesitate, not sure if I really want to ask the question, but knowing I must. 'Why? Why would they say that?'

She pauses, considering her words. 'It is complicated chai. But your mamus – your mother – was difficult, and your father is a mere gaujo. He cannot understand.'

I can't believe what is happening here. I feel disoriented as my mind reels in hopeless bewilderment.

My mother's parents are supposed to be long dead and we never talked about them. I never understood why not, but it was always clear that the subject was taboo. The last time I can remember asking my mother about them was when I was about seven. The innocent question had turned into a protracted argument from which I ended up banished to my room. And since Mum died, when I was nine, Dad and I have simply never had cause to discuss them.

And yet here I am, standing before my supposedly long-dead grandmother. A grandmother I have never met. A grandmother whose name, I sharply realise, I had never even been told. Excitement and resentment fight for control inside me.

'I don't understand. Why would they tell me you were dead? Why wouldn't my father understand? And what's a gow-joe? How can you still be alive?'

She frowns and sighs, 'Shookar my chavvi, hush now. Let us not talk of such things at this time. Too many bridges have been burned, too many heartaches to count. We have issues of more importance to talk about, haven't we? I have been wondering when you would come to me. You must have many questions.'

'Many questions' is a significant understatement. I'm utterly dazed; I don't know where to start. But she does.

'It's finally happening to you, isn't it?' she asks knowingly.

I don't fully understand what she's referring to, but feel my stomach immediately knot in reaction to the words as a shiver runs through my bones.

'I don't know, but, well . . .' I hesitate, feeling hopelessly foolish. I'm still deeply shocked and my emotions are running in circles, spiraling furiously. But I finally manage to spit it out. 'Yes, something's happening to me, but I don't know –'

She cuts me off. 'I do know, chai. Don't be afraid, it is not a curse, but a blessing.'

I stare at her. What the hell does she mean?

I can't think what to say next, my thoughts scrambling. This woman is my grandmother, of that I have no doubt. The more I look at her the more I can see my mother in the shape of her face, but mostly in her eyes. We share the same very dark, deep brown eyes. But hers seem shielded somehow, like she is hiding something behind them, which no doubt she is.

She raises her hand in a mildly commanding gesture and signals for me to follow her, leading me through to the back room that she earlier appeared from. Initially I hesitate, but then move after her cautiously. The back room is also dim at first, but she flicks on a light switch and reveals a small space that looks like a movie set.

It's a classic gypsy fortune-teller's den. There is even a crystal ball. The walls are curtained with the same thick and heavy material as the windows out front and the small table has a tasselled blood-red cloth over it. But we keep moving and pass behind a curtain that hides another door, which takes us through into the rear room of the shop. This space is more conventionally decorated with a table, couch, a small kitchenette and even a small television set.

She motions for me to take a seat and busies herself in the kitchen, boiling the electric jug and preparing hot drinks. She doesn't speak, not even to ask what I want or how I have it. I sit on the couch and finally she turns, presenting me with a mug of tea with milk already added – just how I like it – and then sits at the table facing me.

I just sit there, in confusion, and wait. After an eternity she speaks.

'As your mother wished you to believe me dead, then I will assume you know nothing of your heritage, of your bloodline.'

It is a statement, not a question. I don't respond.

'You are Romany, my chavvi. As was your mamus, who chose the life of a gaujo and cast you into the realm of a kennik – a house-dweller.'

There is clear disapproval in her voice and, upon seeing the total incomprehension on my face, she sighs deeply, seeming to be frustrated by my lack of understanding.

'Clearly you understand no Romanes, the language of our people, and for this I feel deep shame. Today I will try to speak only in gaujo English for you.'

She sighs again, rather dramatically, gathering herself.

Then she continues. 'The Romany people have long been known to others as gypsies,' she pauses as I recognise this name. 'Romany are traditionally a nomadic people who the gaujo – the non-gypsy – look upon with envy and mistrust. We are a free-spirited people, steeped in honourable tradition, but misunderstood by almost all outsiders.'

I don't understand. Gypsies are supposed to travel around the countryside, living a simple life in caravans, aren't they? Surely my mother was never a gypsy?

'We are also a blessed people, and this is something you must now understand.'

She takes a long, slow sip of her tea, watching me, deliberately making me wait. She has a certain sense of theatre about her that is starting to bother me.

'In some Romany families there is a hereditary gift, usually passed down from mother to daughter, over and over for all time. This gift enables some Romany women, in true Romany bloodlines, to perform dukkering – which you would know as fortune-telling.'

I start to shake my head in disbelief. This is just crazy talk. I've never been to a gypsy fair, but I've seen plenty of movies with old gypsy crones twittering madly over either crystal balls or tea leaves – or dancing their fingers over someone's open palm. Fortune-telling is a crock. Just like star signs and tarot cards – all nonsense. I start to get discouraged and sit back on the couch, crossing my arms. She continues unperturbed.

'The gift is not always the same, and sometimes it skips a generation, or if there are many daughters not all will receive it. But it always goes on, no matter how the lines of blood are mixed and muddied. Sometimes strong, some-times weak – as the fates provide.'

She looks away, lost in thought for a moment, before letting out another deep sigh and continuing.

'Your mother's gift was weak. It was a massive disappointment,' she pauses, frowning. 'It came early, far too early, when she was only fifteen. Too young to understand, too young to truly appreciate the value of what she had been given.' Her shoulders slump. 'And I was unable to help her to manage it.' She goes quiet, lost in her own thoughts.

My mind is reeling. I try to make sense of what I'm hearing.

'So, if I understand all this,' I begin, unsure of myself, 'then you're saying that I am in fact of gypsy – or Romany – descent, as was my mother. And that she had some kind of gift for fortune-telling?' I stare at her wide-eyed and incredulous.

She looks back at me, snorting this time in some annoyance. 'Yes. This is what I have said, but you must listen more carefully, chai. I have also told you that your mother's gift was weak and it was untrained, so she was not able to use it properly. You must open your ears as well as your mind. You must listen more carefully.'

She shakes her head softly, muttering in Romanes under her breath. I stand up, feeling annoyed at her tone. Newly rediscovered grandmother or not, she is rubbing me up the wrong way.

'I think this might be a mistake,' I say and begin to leave.

She sits upright sharply. 'You must listen,' she demands. 'There is no mistake.'

I'm taken aback by this. The order has been fierce and I stop in my tracks. We frown defiantly at each other. The temperature in the room chills substantially.

'You must sit down,' she continues sternly, rising slowly to her feet. She has a commanding presence in the small room. She points a long finger at me and speaks grimly. 'I have been waiting for this day for twenty years and I will not be denied. You will sit, and you must listen more carefully.'

She stands firm before me, blocking my way out. She has flushed slightly and I begin to wonder if she is altogether mentally stable. But, as I had before, I still feel no fear. I remain certain that this woman is not a threat.

I glare back at her defiantly, and then release a theatrical sigh of my own and sit down again.

'You are so like your mother –' she says quietly. I feel myself begin to soften, and then she adds: '– so disrespectful.'

I stand up again like a shot, surprising myself with this sudden rush of anger as I point my finger back at her. 'How dare you! My mother is dead . . .' I stand there, shaking. 'How could you say something like that?'

She takes in a deep breath and swirls her hands exaggeratedly to blow cool air on her face. She really should be on stage – it's such a dramatic performance.

'All right, calm down. Sit please,' she says. There is little repentance in her voice. 'I will tell you what you need to know. But you should be more grateful.'

I look her in the eye and the understanding overwhelms me. Suddenly I just know that my mother left home because she didn't see eye to eye with my grandmother. There had been a lot of friction. With absolute certainty I know that the relationship had been a major personality clash from day one – where neither of them could agree, and neither would ever back down. Once again I don't know how I can be so completely convinced, but I am. I know this in the same way I had been convinced about Janet's pregnancy, and about Steve's eviction. I just know that I'm right.

And then it strikes me like a thunderbolt.

Perhaps there is something in this woman's incomprehensible tale? Maybe this genetic disposition towards fortune-telling isn't such an insane rambling? How do I know these things? Do I actually have a gift?

Suddenly my legs turn to jelly and I feel faint. I sit down rapidly, snatching a cushion off the couch and hug it tightly.

My grandmother stands over me, not showing concern, but curious. She must have seen the recognition in my eyes and her look now is almost of triumph. It doesn't warm me to her any more than before.

'So maybe we start to understand now, do we?' she shakes her head a little and moves back to her seat. She picks up her tea, once again biding her time pretentiously over an unnecessarily slow sip. Then she says, 'You must learn patience with me. There is much you need to know.'

I glare back at her, not trusting myself to speak.

'You are twenty years old now, I am right?' she asks.

I nod.

'The gift emerges at different times for all, usually the later it comes, the stronger it is. I expected you a year or two ago, as twenty is quite late. Myself, I was nineteen,' she says proudly, 'and my gift is strong. But twenty is not the oldest. Your great-great-aunt Annie got hers at twenty-two. They thought she had missed out.' She looks into the distance as she speaks, remembering. 'But she had amazing powers, she was incredibly gifted. It almost broke her, they said, when she was young.'

Now my heart is starting to race. I force myself to stay calm, and to not interrupt.

'You must tell me,' she instructs, 'how you receive your gift.'

I don't understand. My expression seems to bother her.

'You must describe what you receive,' she commands. 'Do you see images, faces? Are they in the room with you, or just in your head? Do you hear the voices, or is it just suggestions? Tell me what comes to you, chai.'

She seems to actually understand what is happening to me. I feel a rush of relief and an almost equal dose of fear. I have some kind of gift. Perhaps I'm not going crazy. I think desperately about my experiences with Janet, and with Steve and Megan, and Adam and Henry. There have been so many in the last few days, but they have all felt different. Or have they? I try to remember, I want to be clear. I want to understand.

'There have been a couple of occasions recently when I've just known things. I've felt these things with absolute certainty. For one, I knew, without a doubt, that my friend was pregnant. But she hadn't told me, and it was only after she'd died.' A wave of grief washes over me. It's still so hard to think about.

'You must put aside your heartache,' she advises. 'Tell me how it came to you, not what you received. It is the how that is important.'

I bite back on my annoyance, desperately trying not to argue with her again. 'That time, I just knew. I didn't see anything, I didn't hear anything, I just knew.'

'Hmm, yes,' she frowns at me. 'There have been other times, in different ways?'

'Yes. There have been times when I've heard words, short phrases, in my mind.'

'Do you hear this as a spoken word, in someone's voice?'

I think about it, trying to remember each incident. Trying to separate the feelings from the words. 'No, not really,' I decide. 'The words just leap into my head, but I don't hear them. It's not like I'm hearing speech that no one else hears, I don't hear a voice. But I usually know who is providing the words, if that makes sense.'

'And the words, these are from beyond?'

This I don't understand, 'I'm sorry, from where?'

'From beyond. From those who have passed over. From the dead?'

'Oh . . .' I consider it. 'Yes, I think so.' As I think through my experiences I can see this is right, but there is one I can't be certain of. The one I've heard twice now. The woman who is worried about her son doing bad things. I've been thinking of her as the bomber's mother, but can't be sure who she is, or if she is in fact deceased.

'You do not see images with these words?'

'No, I don't see anything.'

'You do not see faces or forms around you?'

'No.'

'Do you sleep well at night?'

This question startles me. I remember Rosie suggesting that I take sleeping pills. I try and reconcile that with this question and get nowhere. *How did Rosie know to send me here?*

'Answer me please. This is important!' she demands.

'No. Yes. I'm sorry, I . . . umm, I sleep just fine.'

She inhales deeply, slowly and rather ominously, and nods.

'Do you ever black out? By this I mean lose yourself and then wake up somewhere and not know how you got there – and find that time has passed?'

That sounds horrible. 'No, that's never happened to me,' I reply thankfully.

'Good, good, this is good.' She pauses. 'I think you have a good gift. If you will take instruction you will do well with it. You are a lucky one.'

'I don't understand. How is having voices in my head lucky?'

She looks annoyed. 'You said you did not receive voices – just words.'

'I don't hear voices, it's just–'

'Then do not say that you do. You must choose your words more carefully.'

I drop my head into my hands, frustrated and confused. Her abrupt manner is upsetting and the weight of this revelation starts to bear down on me. Intuitively so much that this woman, my grandmother, has told me makes perfect sense, but it's also completely crazy. How could I have this gift inside me for all these years and not know? And why hadn't my parents warned me.

I look up abruptly. 'So how do I stop it?'

Once again she makes a show of being shocked, looking first to the heavens and then sighing deeply. Finally she stands up, moves to the couch and sits down beside me, resting her hand on mine.

'Many years ago your mother asked me the same thing, chai,' she pauses, looking deep into my eyes. 'And I had to tell her that there is no stopping your gift. There is no way of turning it off, nor is it possible to ignore it. But with training you can manage it.' Then she smiles, her eyes filled with a zealous passion. 'This gift is a very, very special thing, Lily. It sets you apart from all others, but it promises you a life of rare opportunity. You must embrace the gift. You must accept it as a part of your being and learn to control and focus it. To deny the gift and to try and escape from it will only lead to sorrow.'

I stare at her with a mix of horror and denial and once again I suddenly know something. 'My mother denied the gift, didn't she? She hated it and tried to ignore it, right?'

My grandmother nods slowly, saying nothing.

'Her gift was the main reason you fought. It was why she left you and ran away. She wanted to live a normal life. She didn't want to be a gypsy fortune-teller. She just wanted to be ordinary, and live in a house, with children and a dog. So she ran away.'

She nods again and then asks me, 'Did you receive that in words? Or did you just know it? Can you feel her presence here with us?'

I'm taken aback. There is no denial or acknowledgement. Just curiosity at how I knew. I have to stop and think about it. I hadn't felt any words, I'd just known. But do I feel my mother's presence with us? Is that even possible?

'I don't feel anything unusual,' I tell her. 'I just know. What would it feel like if mum's spirit was here?' Now I'm feeling anxious. 'Would you feel her, or see her?'

'I do not see the dead. That is a rare gift and not one I would wish on anyone.' She stares vacantly for a moment, then focuses back on my eyes. 'I can sometimes feel her here, watching me, but only occasionally. She does not visit often and never in all these years have I been able to directly communicate with her.'

'I don't understand.' I'm intrigued. 'You don't hear words . . .?'

She pauses, seeming to consider her words. 'My gift differs from yours, but only in the style of reception. I am normally able to communicate with the departed.' She stops again, her face an unreadable mask. She looks away from me as she speaks again. 'But I have simply been unable to . . . connect with your mother.'

I want to know more, but her tone is becoming defensive. I decide not to press the subject for the moment.

'So you weren't expecting me today then, were you?'

She says nothing at first, and then finally sighs and admits, 'I was not, but I knew you would one day come. Unless the gift had passed you by.'

A silence falls. It would appear that the gift has not skipped a generation. I wait, expecting her to ask me how I had found her, what had led me to her, but she seems lost in her own thoughts for a moment, as am I.

It is an incredible story and highly unlikely, but I find I actually believe her. This firm belief, as with my other feelings of absolute certainty, suddenly feels natural to me. It's a relief. I'm not going insane. My mind races over all the unusual events of the last week and some parts of it start to make sense. The way I knew about Megan's father's illness, and about Steve's eviction, and of Janet's pregnancy. The words that had been springing unheralded into my mind are some form of communication with the dead. Like I have become some kind of a supernatural radio receiver, or conduit, albeit an unwilling one. The thought is unnerving, but also incredibly fascinating. I'm really not sure how to feel. Is this a good thing, or is this gift going to turn me into a freak-show attraction?

I suddenly realise that my grandmother has stopped day-dreaming and is watching me closely.

'You are confused, chai. This is both a wonderful and a terrible thing,' she says. 'Do not fear the gift or it will eat you up. Accept it and I will teach you how to live with it. You are strong, trust in yourself. Trust in me.'

There are now a million questions careering around my head like a pinball machine. I don't know where to start or what to say when I hear the shop-door chime tinkle clearly.

Someone else has entered the shop. Then I hear the whispered voices of two young women. They sound cautious, but excited. I check the time, as does my grandmother. It's right on 11 am. Only an hour ago I had been at home, oblivious to my new-found heritage.

She continues to watch me intently. 'I have a booking. Will you wait?'

I thought she might have shooed them away and rescheduled the appointment – given that the grandchild she has never met has suddenly appeared in her life – but this doesn't seem to be an option. She wants me to wait.

The world is whirling around me and I suddenly feel that I need to leave. To go home and try to absorb some of this stuff. I look up at her and she can tell my answer from the look on my face.

'You need to go. I understand,' she says simply. 'But you must promise me that you will return very soon. Tomorrow perhaps? I will be here. There is much to discuss.'

Yet again I don't know what to say. I have so many questions, but I realise that I desperately need to clear my head, to try and get some perspective on all this. I nod and start to rise.

'You know,' I hesitate. 'I'm not even sure of your name. Is it Kathryn?'

She nods and draws herself up royally. With an unusual half-smile she extends her hand in introduction. 'Yes, chai. My name is Kathryn and I am your puri dai – or grandmother, but you must call me Grammy, as I used to call my puri dai. This is the way of our people. You understand?'

I take her hand and we shake formally. Her touch is warm and calming and I nod. 'Okay, umm . . . Grammy,' I respond, testing the name out loud. It feels a little strange. 'I'm sorry, I want to stay, and wait for you, but I just can't. I have . . . ahh, other commitments.'

'It is fine,' she replies enigmatically, ushering me back out through the shop. 'I have waited a long time for you, chai. I can wait a little longer.'

As we pass through the fortune-telling room, I drink in my surroundings a bit more thoroughly this time. Everything I see is so foreign, yet somehow also strangely familiar and comfortable. I gesture to the table with the crystal ball.

'You use these things?' I ask her cautiously, 'For fortune-telling?'

She snorts softly, offering a curious smile. 'My customers have expectations. So much here is merely for show.' She winks slyly, 'But understand this, Lily. While our gift is truly inside of us, there is no harm in presenting our services to people as they anticipate.'

That confuses me a little. Is she saying that this is all just here for show? I nod slowly and move on again. The two women fall instantly silent as we emerge into the dimly lit shop, staring at us both openly. Grammy nods at them in acknowledgement and guides me across to the shop's main door.

I turn there, desperately trying to think of something appropriate to say, worried that I am going to wake up soon and discover this has all been some kind of crazy dream.

She beats me to it. 'You have a gift, Lily. Do not be afraid. Trust your instincts. Trust in your intuition,' she pauses. 'Come back to me soon. I will be waiting.'

I nod and smile grimly as I slip out the door. The street is still quiet, my car still out there. Then it strikes me again.

How the hell did Rosie know to send me here?

TWENTY

I drive myself home, lost in thought, struggling to take it all on board. Apparently my mother came from a Romany gypsy blood-line. From a family of fortune-tellers with special gifts. And supposedly I have a gift too, some kind of second-sight. Some kind of ability to communicate with the dead?

Fabulous.

Just what every girl craves – to be able to hear dead people.

My feelings range from bitterness to wonder to horror as the implications roll steadily around and around my mind. Traveling on auto-pilot I'm startled to realise that I remember nothing of the drive as I pull up in my driveway. I look at the house as if I have never seen it before. Nothing makes sense any more. I look over towards Rosie's place. How did she know? I have to find out.

I get out of the car and push through the gap in the hedge. I automatically go around to the back door as that's the usual way we visit. The door is open and I can hear noise and voices from the kitchen. I knock loudly and wait.

Evan comes to the door. He's a nice guy, but seriously under the thumb. In this house it's clear that Louise rules the roost, but Evan seems happy with his position in life.

'Hey there, Lily. How are you?' he inquires amiably.

Before I can answer Louise is abruptly at his shoulder. It's obvious that she isn't pleased to see me.

'I'm good thanks, Evan. Hi Louise. I was just wondering how Rosie is today? Is she feeling better? Have the doctors worked anything out yet?'

Louise edges in front of Evan, blocking the doorway. Clearly she wants to field these questions and doesn't trust Evan to respond appropriately. He looks a little surprised, but says nothing.

'She's doing okay, Lily. Thanks for asking.' Louise's tone is somewhat frosty. 'She's resting now and really shouldn't be disturbed.' Everything about her manner makes it clear that I am being warned off. Louise really must feel I've been doing something to Rosie. That annoys me, but I bite my tongue.

'Okay,' I manage politely. 'That's good. So, no relapses then?'

'No.'

There is silence. Evan looks uncomfortable. Louise looks staunch. She doesn't want me near her child and that's the end of it. I take a step back, starting to feel defensive.

'I'm just worried about her too, Louise. I didn't do anything to her.'

Her face remains rigid, it doesn't match her words.

'Don't be silly. We don't think you did anything to her.'

There is silence again and Evan shifts awkwardly. I don't need any kind of gypsy fortune-telling gift to understand that I'm not welcome here. Louise has already said plenty without any real accusation. She probably thinks that I drugged Rosie somehow. God only knows why I would do something like that. I nod slowly.

'Okay then,' I say cautiously. 'I'll leave you to it then.'

Neither of them reply so I just turn and go back home. There will be no discussion with Rosie today about my Grammy Kathryn – or any other subject.

* * *

It is a little after one when I arrive at the marina, full of anticipation and thankful to have something so pleasant to be offering me distraction. It's been a harrowing morning.

My mind had been reeling with thoughts of my mother, and of my incredible ancestry when I finally made it home earlier. After unsuccessfully trying to curb my anger at Louise's unspoken accusations I spent about an hour digging through the house looking for anything that might shed more light on my mother's past. I went through every cupboard in the house and even climbed up into the attic looking for old boxes of photos or the like. But I found very little. There was an abundance of junk from my father's youth, with albums full of his childhood pictures and certificates and even his rudimentary artwork. But practically nothing of my mother's. There was more of Cheryl's stuff than my mother's and she'd only been in our lives for the last five years. It was depressing.

I did find two old photo albums though, in my Dad's cupboard. One was my Mum and Dad's wedding album, filled with images of the romantic holiday-cum-honeymoon that was their wedding. I vaguely remember being told that they had married on the spur of the moment while on holiday, and that was why no family members were present. Now I realise there was probably a bit more to it. They must have eloped.

They married on a beach, with just a celebrant, some witnesses and a setting sun. The pictures looked beautiful. The album showed them fishing and diving and waterskiing. All smiles and joy, wrapped in each other's embrace in almost every shot. My mother had been exceptionally beautiful, and Dad was looking pretty buff back then too. The images were a bittersweet reminder.

The other album was bigger, but half empty. It tracked them moving into our home, redecorating, birthday celebrations and other parties, and the birth of their only child – me. Clearly Dad was the predominant photographer, as almost all the shots contained my mother. Then there were lots of photos of little Lily, as an infant and then toddler, off to school and more birthday celebrations, again mainly with my mum – and then the album abruptly stopped. When I was nine. The rear half was simply empty. I guess we sort of lost interest in taking photos for a few years at that time and once we remembered how, Dad must have decided to buy a new album to put them in. Clearly this one would remain unfinished forever.

Nothing I found explained why my mother had lied to me though. Nothing helped me understand why she had told me that my grandparents were dead. I find myself wondering whether Dad knew they were alive, or not. Then I realise I had never asked Grammy Kathryn if my grandfather was also alive. I guessed not. She would have said, surely.

So, as I walk towards the piers at the Wilton Marina, I try to find a way to put it all out of my mind. I need distraction. I need something fun to help blow away the horror and despair that I have experienced this last week – and the shocking revelations I have received just this morning.

The thought of the wind and spray whipping at my face as we sail out onto the lake fills me with a pleasant warmth. It's been years since I've been out on the lake. Too many years. It will be fun. And being out with Bobby is yet another exciting tonic. I actually start to smile in anticipation.

I'm a little bit late, but that's deliberate. I don't want to appear too keen. Bobby told me to be at the top of pier B at 1 pm and I already knew that the marina ran its piers from A being closest to the entrance, with its small grouping of cafes and shops, to H being the furthest away. I can see the top of pier B already as I walk casually past the Marina Café. No one is waiting for me there.

I turn my head as I keep walking and quickly scan the faces outside the café, looking for either Bobby or Don. I don't see them, but turn away quickly, embarrassed, when I spot Steve Cassidy sitting alone at a table. He's reading a newspaper and doesn't look up. I'm pretty sure he didn't see me. I haven't seen him since running away from our lunch yesterday and feel a sudden leap of anxiety. My warm anticipation vanishes. Is he stalking me? Did he know I was going to be here? I speed my walk up a little and wish for something to hide behind, but the walk out to pier B is totally exposed. If he looks up he will see me for sure.

I hold my breath as I walk, desperately wanting to remain unnoticed. It's silly really. I try telling myself that I have nothing to fear from Steve, and this is a public place anyway. He's not going to bother me here. Finally I make it to the top of the pier. There is still no sign of Bobby or Don. I try to appear casual as I look back at the café to see if I've been noticed. Steve is still there, but he seems to be absorbed by the newspaper. If he's seen me he isn't showing it. I exhale and try to relax.

I'm not that late and feel sure they won't have gone without me. Would they? I don't know the name of Don's yacht, nor which mooring it is assigned. I only know its on pier B somewhere so I decide to amble along a bit and see if anyone pops up. Perhaps they're already onboard, waiting for me.

Only as I step forth onto the pier do the words:

—this isn't right, my boy—

fly violently into my head. They are desperate words, mournful and distressed;

—leave them be—

and they feel exactly the same as the words I felt just before the bomb went off at the Commonwealth – and while

Steve was being interviewed by the police at work on Thursday. I'm immediately certain they're coming from the bomber's mother.

–it won't help, you'll get caught–

Horrified, I suddenly know that there is another bomb close by. She doesn't want him claiming any further lives.

–you're just confused, so very confused–

Fear rips through me. I feel my legs wobble as I remember Megan telling me that the bomber has been setting the bombs off by remote control, by some form of electronic trigger. I think of my car alarm beeper. It could be anyone, anywhere, but the bomber must be somewhere nearby.

–my baby, my little boy–

I freeze in sheer panic.

Suddenly Bobby is right in front of me.

'Hey, Lily. We were starting to think you weren't coming.'

I didn't see where he came from and I'm so terrified I can't speak. I must be as white as a sheet. He becomes unsure and frowns, eying me carefully.

'Are you okay? You're not feeling seasick already are you?'

–don't go down there, he won't behave–

The words feel insistent. This is the most intense feeling I have experienced to date. Yet different to the swirling bitterness of Adam on level three. Not as angry, more distressed. Anguished. The mother is desperate to stop us, to stop him, to prevent anyone else from being hurt.

Bobby has taken my arm, which is a good thing as I'm trembling with terror and close to tumbling off the pier into the lake. But I can't answer him.

–keep away, keep away–

The words tumble frantically into my head. Then Don appears from behind me, carrying a box under one arm and a chilly bin in the other hand. He stops smiling the moment he sees my face and both men stare at me quizzically.

'Lily, what's the matter?' asks Don.

I don't know what to say, but instinctively start backing up. Away from the boats, desperate to get off the pier.

–get away, the boat, get away–

The words are a clear instruction. The bomb must be on a boat. Probably Don's yacht. Yes, definitely. There is a bomb on Don's yacht and the bomber is waiting for us to get on board.

–stay away, run, run, run–

'Come and sit down, Lily. You look like you're going to faint,' I hear Bobby say as he tries to lead me down the pier.

'No,' I cry out, finally finding my voice. Pulling free of his grip I back up the pier, away from the cluster of yachts and cruisers bobbing in the warm sunlight. The men stand staring in surprise, both wary, concerned. Bobby reaches out to me and steps closer, away from the boats.

'Calm down, Lily. It's okay. There's nothing to be afraid of out here,' he says reassuringly.

I can't think what to say to them. But we have to keep away from the boats, that's all I know. I'm terrified that we'll all be blown to pieces if we aren't back far enough. I back up further and Bobby follows, trying to calm me. The image of another bomb – about to go off any second – is crippling me with terror. I want desperately to just turn and run, but I can't leave the men out there. Don still hasn't moved. He looks very uncomfortable. I can tell he is trying to decide whether to join Bobby in trying to calm me, or just leave him to it. He takes a half-step further down the pier and I panic.

'No, please,' I hear myself say. 'Don't go out there. There's a bomb on the yacht.'

This stops Don dead in his tracks.

Now both men openly gape at me in disbelief. Bombs simply are not a joking matter any more. Too many people have died. Too many others hurt. It's obvious they're both incredibly shocked. Don's face says it all. How can she know that? He keeps looking from me to a blue and white yacht – about halfway down the pier on the right – and back again.

Bobby carefully voices the question that hangs between us. 'Why would you say that?'

They stare at me, awaiting a response but my heart is pounding so furiously I just can't think what to say. I want to run. Now that I can see how close the yacht is, I desperately want to be further away. Much, much further away. I glance over my shoulder and see Steve Cassidy standing just outside the café, watching us. He's frowning. My blood runs cold.

'I just know,' I tell them quickly. 'Don't ask me how, I just know. Please, don't go down there. Come away. Please.' I begin backing up again, slowly putting more distance between myself and the yacht. Then I see the woman.

Her dark hair catches my eye first as it suddenly pops up on the deck of the blue and white yacht. She looks over and smiles brightly at us, waving hello. Oh God, this must be Don's wife Sue. Already on board the yacht. She stops smiling and looks puzzled as the three of us on the pier stand frozen, grim-faced, not returning her wave.

The men look at each other, silently trying to agree on their next move – both bewildered but cautious. Bobby turns to the boat and then back to me. 'What's going on, Lily?'

– *get them away, get them away, please* –

Don's face is ashen and he slowly lowers the box and chilly bin to the pier. 'You really think there's a bomb here?'

I look at him desperately, still unable to speak. I nod.

'You think there's a bomb here, on my yacht?' he asks again, glancing towards his wife.

I nod again. I can feel that my eyes are wide with terror. I must look crazy. Don looks at Bobby.

Bobby shrugs. 'Maybe we should all go get a coffee before setting out?'

Don nods slowly. Clearly they both think that I've finally lost the plot. 'Sure, why not?' he says and starts to walk cautiously down the pier, towards his yacht.

– don't go, don't go on the boat –

'No, wait,' I suddenly cry out. Don stops again, half turning. 'He's watching us.'

There is absolute silence. Neither man can decide what to make of this unbelievable information. Don seems a little angry, while Bobby appears cautious.

'Who's watching us, Lily?' he asks gently.

I feel like an idiot, like Chicken Little hysterically screaming that the sky is falling, but I know I'm right. I sense that he's watching, from somewhere nearby. Then Grammy's recent words flood into my mind: Trust your instincts, trust your intuition. I still don't really understand how my supposed gift lets me know this, but I'm certain we're in extreme danger.

'The bomber is watching us, Bobby, and he uses a remote control thing for setting off his bombs. He can see us and he's waiting for us to get on. Then he'll blow it up.'

Don takes another step down the pier, looking sceptical. 'I'll go and get Sue and we'll go grab that coffee, eh?'

'No, wait,' Bobby says quickly, stopping Don yet again. He turns to the yacht, where Sue is watching us, wondering what is going on. He waves his arms in a big 'come here' gesture, but doesn't call out. She looks surprised and gives an exaggerated shrug, raising her hands in a 'what?' motion, looking to Don for clarification.

Don sighs loudly. His shoulders slump and then he copies Bobby's beckoning wave. Sue starts to climb over the yacht's railing and I feel a surge of relief, but it's short-lived.

TWENTY-ONE

Something is wrong.

His frustration is mounting. The girl seems to be messing things up. Damn it. Just get on the bloody boat.

This time his observation post is good, but not as good as the parking building. He'd been comfortable looking down upon his targets last time, but this will have to do.

He is committed. He needs this to go well, so then it will go even better the next time.

He can't understand what she is doing. Why is she holding them up? He's close, but not enough to hear their words clearly. His device is ready, he is ready, and the small plastic box is warm in his hand. His targets are right there, so tantalisingly near, but his excitement is turning to anger.

One of the men starts to move forward and his excitement intensifies, but then the man stops. The bloody girl has called out to him, stopping him. He wishes he could hear her. He glares at them, filling with fury as the man takes another step but stops again. The girl seems to know, but how can that be possible? Then they wave towards the boat and he watches in abject horror as the woman starts to climb off the boat too.

No! No, no, no! They're ruining the plan. Why aren't they getting on the boat? They can't possibly know.

Anger rears up inside him and he throws the small plastic box to his feet.

As it smashes open the detonation of the device surprises even him.

TWENTY-TWO

Sue has only taken two steps towards us on the pier when the words inside my mind cry plaintively:

–noooooo, baby, no, no–

It's too late.

The yacht erupts in a ball of white light.

As the yacht explodes behind her, the shockwave lifts Sue off her feet and flings her up and over a large cruiser berthed opposite their yacht.

For a brief moment I watch as she tumbles through the air before I feel myself being driven backwards, off the pier also, as Bobby slams into me in a crushing bear-hug.

We crash into the water together, Bobby landing on top of me like a sack of potatoes. His body is limp and heavy and I struggle beneath him. The water is murky and surprisingly deep, even though we are so close to the shore. Thrashing about in terror I fight my way out from under him, pushing away from his inert form, and finally break the surface in a desperate struggle for air.

My mind swirls with shock and horror; I can't take it all in. Another bomb, my God – I *am* being stalked. Someone is trying to kill me. I look wildly about. I'm bobbing about two metres from the pier, right beside the hull of some kind of medium-sized boat – a large jet boat possibly – and only a few metres from the rocks that line the bank along the marina.

I hear shouting, but it is muffled, lost in the hum that is roaring in my ears yet again. I hear a second, smaller, explosion and something sails over my head, landing with a splash well beyond me. Oh God, what's happening?

Then I remember Bobby. I spin around in the water, he'd been right here with me. Where is he? I can't see him. And then a flash of blue catches my eye beneath the surface. Bobby was wearing a blue polo shirt. Oh God, no.

I duck-dive quickly towards the blue thing I've just seen. He isn't down very deep, only about a metre, but he isn't moving. I get both hands under his armpits and spin around, kicking out wildly, desperately trying to pull him to the surface. I kick frantically, pulling, heaving. Our heads break the surface together, but he is completely limp and impossibly heavy and we both start to sink under again.

I can't do it. I can't save him. I'm not strong enough.

Then the water beside me splashes and shakes. Someone is suddenly there beside me, in the water. I feel Bobby being pulled back up, dragged towards the rocks. I release him and gulp in more air, then follow. A man is pulling Bobby to the shore. A big man. Oh, thank you, God. Thank you. He reaches the rocks and pulls himself up, turning to grip Bobby more firmly and pull him up too. I finally see his face.

It's Steve Cassidy.

I freeze in the water, staring incredulously.

Then another man appears, and then another, and a woman. I don't know these people, but they are here to help. As I bob uncertainly in the water the three men work together to manhandle the unconscious Bobby up the rocks and onto the ground above. Then one of them begins mouth to mouth as Steve comes back down the rocks to offer me his hand. I just stare back at him in shock.

'Are you hurt?' he asks, his voice faint in my ringing ears. 'Can you swim over?'

I can't speak, but suddenly I want out of the water and I lurch forward, thrashing across to reach up and take his hand. He hoists me up almost effortlessly and puts an arm around my waist to steady me. I don't fight him; my mind is too numb. I start to clamber up the rocks and, as I see Bobby cough and open his eyes, I remember the others.

'Don, Sue. Are they okay?' I shout at no one in particular.

The woman points back over my shoulder, towards the pier and the burning yacht. I spin too quickly, making myself dizzy and see the third man pulling someone up onto the pier. It's Sue. Don is still in the water, pushing her up as the man drags her onto the floating wooden pier. Steve looks at me, calm and decisive, and must consider that I am now safe enough. He releases me and skips over the rocks and pulls himself up onto the pier. He helps the man pull Don from the water and together they carry Sue's motionless figure up to the higher ground where Bobby and I lie. Sue doesn't look good.

Bobby is alive – I can see he is now breathing on his own – but he has made no effort to rise. His eyes are closed and he holds his head in his hands as he lies flat on his back. I can't seem to move myself. I feel certain nothing is broken, once again, but I'm too deeply stunned to rouse myself. I shift my gaze back to Don and Sue. She still hasn't moved and Don is kneeling over her, weeping openly.

As I watch the scene, everything becomes slightly surreal around me. Colours blur as my head spins faintly and the roaring in my ears changes to that familiar hum. It's like time has slowed and I'm not actually here, but am observing everything, like I'm watching a movie.

I can't believe it. I just can't take it all in. My third explosion. Why me?

Suddenly I feel sick and I turn away from the people around me and throw up on the rocks. I heave until nothing more comes, and then I dry heave some more.

When I turn back a small crowd has gathered to watch the burning boat. I don't recognise any of the faces, only

Steve's. I hear sirens approaching and see Steve's expression change. He looks as if he's trying to decide whether to stay or to slip away quickly. He catches me watching him and our eyes lock. I can't read his expression any more, nor can I feel anything in my mind. Had the words I heard before come from his mother? Is Steve's mum alive or dead? I don't know.

Then he walks towards me. I instinctively recoil a little, but force myself to stay calm. He crouches in front of me, resting his weight on one knee. We're both dripping wet.

'Are you okay?' he asks softly, but loud enough to penetrate the hum.

I don't know what to say at first, but eventually answer as honestly as I can manage, 'Not really, but I think I'll live.'

He nods, watching my eyes. His expression unreadable.

'You think I'm doing all this, don't you?' he asks flatly, surprising me.

I find myself instinctively denying the accusation, but only through a small shake of my head.

'You're wrong. I'm not the bomber.'

I try to shake my head a little more firmly. I just don't know any more. I open my mouth and shut it again when nothing comes out.

He glances over his shoulder. An ambulance has arrived and the police are now turning into the marina carpark.

'I'm going to go. Change into some dry clothes. The police are going to want to talk to me again and I don't want to sit around dripping all afternoon.' He watches me for a reaction. 'They think I'm doing this too, but they're wrong as well. I'm not the bomber.'

He drifts away quietly, threading his way through the crowd, heading back towards the small group of shops near the café I'd seen him at earlier.

I sit there dripping in the warm sun, my mind spinning. The fire from the yacht has almost burned itself out. People are milling around, trying to see all the action. I just sit there numbly, waiting for someone to once again come and drag me off to hospital in an ambulance.

Then I hear Don's wailing pierce the buzz of the crowd and the hum in my ears. The cry is tortured and soul-destroying. He's calling his wife's name, over and over and then crying simply 'No, no, no' in denial.

Even before I sense the words I know she is gone.

–it doesn't hurt, Donny, it's all right, there's no pain–

Some of the people around Sue and Don back up a little. The man who has been trying to resuscitate her is now sitting back, a sorry look on his face. The paramedics arrive and one of them firmly demands that Don move away so they can do their thing, but he clings to her.

–I thought we'd have longer, but I'm sorry, I can't stay–

The paramedics begin unpacking their life-saving equipment and one man gently moves Don aside. But it's too late, I feel sure of that. I shiver involuntarily and then burst out crying. Sue has died. I never even met her and now she is dead, and it's all my fault. I even heard her leave. I felt her pass over. It felt like she moved right through me, leaving a vague impression of her essence with me as she went. Obviously the bomber is trying to get me and Sue has become yet another innocent casualty of his twisted obsession.

I weep uncontrollably until someone eventually helps me into the back of an ambulance, and then I weep some more. Someone decides that I need a sedative and I vaguely feel a small sharp pain and then nothing more.

I wake in a hospital bed early in the evening, with a policewoman camped at the foot of my bed. She looks bored. She perks up a little when she sees I'm awake and stands, stretches, and then leaves out of the room without saying anything.

I'm in a single room. The sun is setting through the windows and I feel pretty drowsy. The after-effects from the sedative I guess. And I'm hungry. I lie quietly for less than a minute before images start flashing into my mind's eye: Sue's smile as she raised her head on the yacht; Bobby's shocked face as I tell him there is a bomb on board; Splashing about in the water with Bobby weighing me down; Steve offering me his hand; Sue's lifeless form being carried up the pier; Don's wails of anguish. A feeling of helplessness overcomes me.

A female doctor comes in and drags me from my haunting reverie. She informs me in a matter-of-fact tone that I am essentially okay, with no broken bones or any suspected internal injuries. She tells me I have been very lucky, with most of the blast being absorbed by the man who was with me acting as an inadvertent shield.

An image of Bobby coughing and coming alive flashes before me and I ask her if he is all right. I'm informed that he's doing okay too. He took a blow to the head – probably from flying debris – and inhaled a little water but is otherwise fine. He will recover fully. I ask if I can see him and I'm told that this will be okay tomorrow, but he needs to rest tonight. I ask if I can go home now, but she is insistent that I stay in overnight for observation this time. She asks if there is someone she should contact for me. I think briefly about Megan, or Nikki, or even my Aunt Louise, but in the end I decline. I don't want my friends seeing me like this. She asks if I feel up to talking with the police, who have a few questions for me. I agree to talk with them, but only after eating something, as I'm feeling very weak. She nods and quietly leaves to make arrangements.

I lie still and let the images flood through my head once again. So much has happened in such a short period of time.

I see a blackened human form wrapped in pink; Steve with blood running down his face; Bobby sprawled on the reception area floor after the explosion at CCS; Rosie inert in my back garden; a thunderous blast at the pier – white and hot and blinding; and then Sue's face once again. Her smile had seemed so welcoming, so open and warm.

I'm on the verge of tears when a nurse with a food trolley arrives. The food is basic, but good enough, and it helps me to refocus.

The police turn up soon after I've eaten. It's Detective Natalie Dowd once again, accompanied by the bored policewoman who had been sitting with me earlier. Natalie makes me run through the sequence of events and this time it is much, much harder to explain. The last two bombings were a complete surprise to me, but this time I have to try and explain my prior knowledge. Both Bobby and Don would surely tell them how I had tried to stop them getting on the yacht. But how do I explain this without sounding like a complete freak? Frankly, I struggle.

'So let me just confirm that I've understood you here, Lily,' Natalie Dowd says, addressing me but glancing quickly at the policewoman alongside her as she speaks. 'You arrived at the pier and simply had a very bad feeling about the yacht. Like a premonition. That something terrible was about to happen. That a bomb was about to go off. Is that correct?'

I take a deep breath and sigh deeply. They're both staring at me suspiciously. I nod, feeling desperately self-conscious. 'Yes, that's right.'

'So you did *not* see anyone place the bomb on the yacht?'

'No.'

'And you did *not* receive any kind of tip-off about the bomb?'

I hesitate. Does a supernatural warning in my head, from the bomber's deceased mother count as a tip-off?

Surely it does, but I just can't admit to it. 'No,' I reply simply.

They both watch me intently. I can't meet their eyes. They know I am lying.

'No phone call. No text, or note on your car?'

'No. No tip-off. Just a kind of . . . premonition.'

'I see,' she says, although it's clear from her tone that she doesn't see at all. 'You appreciate that this is a little difficult for us to work with, Ms MacDonald, don't you?'

I duly note that my first name is no longer appropriate. 'I'm sorry, but it's the truth.'

Natalie Dowd sighs then rapidly changes direction. 'Can you describe for us, please, your movements since leaving work yesterday afternoon.'

I pause to think, where had I been? 'I went home after work and just had a quiet night in alone, um . . .' I pause again and she interrupts.

'You had no visitors and didn't leave the house at all?'

Oh God, I am a suspect. My stomach clenches. 'No, I didn't leave the house, and I didn't have any visitors. I'm sorry.' I think about Rosie's late night visit to my window, but I can't tell them about that. Again it's clear to all present that I'm lying.

'I see. And Saturday morning? Were you home alone also?'

This is getting worse by the second. 'No, I went out for a run about 8 am. After that I went for a drive up to Bluff Creek. I . . . um, I visited a crystal shop up there.'

'I see. Did you buy anything there? Do you have any receipts?'

'No, I'm sorry. I didn't buy anything.'

The questions continue on for another twenty minutes with little further being established. I tell them that I only went to the crystal shop, no others. I didn't stop anywhere for petrol, or anything to eat, so can offer no evidence of my whereabouts. Other than a brief visit to catch up with my Uncle and Aunt next door I was home alone all the rest of the time. No, again, I didn't see anyone planting the bomb. No, I didn't plant the bomb. Yes, Steve Cassidy was there. He pulled Bobby out of the water. He helped Don too. He told me he was going to change into dry clothes and left. No, he didn't appear to have a cell-phone or anything similar.

By the time they finish and leave me alone even I'm beginning to feel that I may actually be guilty of something. I must now be significantly higher on their suspect list, either that or close to being certified as crazy. Silently I wish I'd refused to speak with them.

The policewoman stays in my room and eventually the doctor comes back. Although I am well enough to be released and go home we agree that I will stay the night – for observation – and she offers me a sedative to help me sleep. Having the policewoman here is distracting me somewhat from my worries, but my mind still swirls with doubt and anguish and shame. The images are clearly all memories, not visions or premonitions, but I feel sure that I will not be able to find sleep naturally so I accept the offer.

As I drift away I vaguely remember Rosie's words about sleeping pills helping. She is right. Sometimes the promise of a dreamless oblivion can be hugely appealing.

TWENTY-THREE

Finding Bobby's room the next morning is pretty easy. It's only two doors down from my own, and also a single. I've been discharged and I'm ready to leave but want to stop in and check on him first. I've been told he's recovering well and will be discharged himself later this afternoon.

I'm wearing the same clothes from yesterday. They have been dried off by the hospital staff, but feel uncomfortable today. I've already decided to throw the whole outfit away once I get home. I can never wear it again.

Bobby is sitting up in bed and smiles as I enter the room. But it isn't the same flashing grin I received yesterday as I arrived at the marina. It is somehow strained, like he isn't too sure about me now. This is what I have been dreading.

I stand near the end of his bed awkwardly, mutter a small 'hello' and have difficulty meeting his gaze. I feel like a freak. What must he be thinking?

I stand there, shifting my weight nervously from one foot to the other, and try to think of something appropriate to say, but can't. Maybe I should just leave? Finally he breaks the silence and I'm very grateful.

'You were in overnight too then?' he asks softly.

'Yes, they wanted to observe me . . . I don't know why.'

'Me too. Apparently I caught a bit of a bump to the head and inhaled a wee bit of water,' he says, giving another uncertain smile. 'I understand you helped to fish me out of the lake. Thank you.'

'I didn't do much.' I force a small smile in return. 'You're pretty damn heavy.'

'Sorry about that.'

'Don't be.'

There is a few moments silence, and then I ask, 'Have you seen Don since . . .?'

'No.' More silence. 'No, I haven't.'

'Have the police been by? To talk about it?'

'Yes,' he says carefully. 'Yes, they have.'

We fall into an awkward silence again. I feel compelled to explain, but I just don't know where to start, what to say, how to say it. How do you explain that you hear voices to a man you're attracted to?

'How did you know?'

I just stare at him. My mind reels, searching for some kind of plausible explanation. I take a deep breath and steady myself. The truth. I have to tell him the truth.

'I sometimes get premonitions,' I finally blurt out.

He raises his eyebrows slightly, but doesn't say anything. He just waits. I take another deep breath and exhale slowly.

'I get these premonitions every now and then, and I just know something is about to happen. Or sometimes I just know what someone is feeling. Not thinking, or anything like that – I can't read minds.' The words come in a rush, cascading from me suddenly like a waterfall. 'It's pretty scary, and I don't understand it, but yesterday I just knew. I knew he was watching us, and that he'd put a bomb on the yacht.' Then just as suddenly I falter, the words drying up. 'I just knew,' I mumble and stop.

Bobby watches me silently, but I can literally see the cogs turning as he thinks it over. He frowns, shakes his head a little and then asks, 'Like a psychic?'

A psychic. Possibly. I'm not sure it's the correct description but it sounds much better than a gypsy fortune-teller. Aren't psychics able to read minds and bend spoons?

'Yes, sort of like that, I guess.'

He mulls on this for a minute. 'Wow,' he says. 'So that would mean that you also had a premonition at the Commonwealth bombing, right? You looked really pale and freaked out there too, just before it went off.'

I can't believe it. He actually seems to believe me. He doesn't think I'm crazy. I nod. He nods back. We stare at each other.

'You, umm . . .' I say hesitantly. 'You're okay with that?'

He smiles, more genuinely this time. 'Sure, why not? Either you're a pretty damn good psychic or you're in cahoots with the bomber. I prefer the former.' He hesitates. 'Unless you were at the pier before us and saw him going onto the yacht?'

'No,' I shake my head. 'I didn't even know which one was Don's yacht. I'd just arrived when you met me.'

He nods again. 'So, a psychic ability then. How's that working out for you?'

I try on another small smile. 'Well, I haven't worked out the lottery numbers yet.'

'Maybe with a bit more practice, eh?'

'Maybe.'

We fall into silence once more. Bobby breaks it yet again.

'So I'm guessing the police were a little less under-standing.'

'I don't really understand it myself, so why should they accept such a crazy explanation? They probably think I'm in with the bomber. I don't know. They haven't arrested me at least.'

'He does seem to be following you around a bit though, doesn't he?'

A shiver runs down my spine. I don't answer.

'I'm sorry,' he says quickly. 'You must be terrified. Look, I should be out of here soon. Do you want me to come home with you?'

I feel a warm, deep colour run quickly up my face. Bobby suddenly realises what he's said and tries to backtrack.

'Oh, hell, I'm sorry, that came out all wrong. I meant to keep you company. I wasn't coming on to you,' he hesitates, putting his head in his hands and peering out between his fingers in embarrassment. It's kind of cute. 'Sorry,' he mumbles through his fingers.

I forgive him immediately, but I still decline the proposal. I tell him that I really just want to go home and shower and change. But that I do appreciate his offer. He nods in agreement and we talk briefly about the meeting tomorrow morning. We will have to go back to the marina for Jonathon Green's new executive management structure gathering. All of a sudden the choice of venue seems horribly inappropriate, but it would be a major hassle to change it at this short notice.

I still strongly suspect that the bomber is stalking me, so I suggest that I shouldn't go, but Bobby won't have it. He tells me he needs me there and goes to pains to reassure me that he doesn't think anyone is targeting me. He isn't going to keep his distance. In fact, after surviving three bombing attempts, he says that he thinks I am probably the safest person to be with under the circumstances. He's going to stay close.

That makes me feel a little better, but I still insist that I drive myself to the marina tomorrow. We can meet there, rather than him having to pick me up. He just shrugs.

As I start to leave I'm suddenly compelled to appeal to him once again about going to visit his parents. I know they live nearby and, while I vaguely understand his reasons for avoiding them, I have a really strong feeling that they'd be glad to see him and I tell him so.

He stiffens immediately, frowning at me.

'You don't know when to leave something alone, do you Lily?' His voice is measured, but there is a clear under-current of annoyance. 'Is this a psychic thing?'

'I guess it is. I'm sorry, I don't mean to upset you, but sometimes I just feel obligated to share things like this. They really would love to hear from you. Both of them.'

'So you say,' he replies flatly.

I don't want to push it. It's obvious he is unhappy discussing the subject. I sense that he won't go and see them. He has been deeply hurt and it's left him heavily scarred. Maybe one day he'll go back, but I don't think it will be soon.

'I'm sorry,' I say again, wishing I'd kept my mouth closed. 'I'll see you tomorrow.' I turn to leave.

'Lily, wait . . .' he calls after me. He hesitates and then motions me forward, to come and sit on the side of his bed. 'I'm sorry, I'm being rude. I think after all we've been through in the last few days I probably owe you more of an explanation.'

Oddly I find that I don't agree. 'You don't need to explain to me. It's private. I get it.' I move to the bedside but remain standing.

'You don't want me to explain?'

'You don't have to. I think I already know.'

'Is this a psychic thing again?'

I hesitate. It seems clear in my head, but I might be completely wrong. I realise that part of me needs to know if I am right or not. What do I really know?

'You think they don't love you,' I start cautiously, 'because you grew up feeling like a spare part, an unwanted accessory. Your father ignored you your entire life and you resent the way he distanced himself from you while he was showering love on your big brother. You hate your father for that. You left them without even saying goodbye.'

The room goes silent once again and he just stares at me. I watch him absorb my words. He looks away, struggling for a minute and then turns to face me again.

'You should think about having another crack at those lotto numbers.'

Peversely, I feel a small glow of self-satisfaction. I really must have a gift, some kind of crazy psychic gift. Still, while I realise that I'm a bit proud of myself, I'm frightened at the same time.

'I'm sorry Bobby.'

He shrugs softly. 'It's petty. I'm all grown up now. I should just get over it.'

'You're too hard on yourself. To grow up feeling unloved and unwanted by your own family, that's not an easy thing.'

He can't meet my eye. I should stop talking, but a new compulsion drives me.

'I don't think it's healthy to hold onto that sort of pain, but if you endured twenty years of heartache, then maybe you need twenty years away from them to heal. It's not easy to just let it go. It takes time. Living with that sort of pain isn't petty.'

I try to consider how I would feel if I'd endured long-term emotional neglect as a child. But I can't. Losing my mother was a terrible thing, but it brought my father and me much closer. He has doted on me – all my life. I can't imagine Bobby's pain.

'I'm so sorry,' I tell him again.

'Don't be, it's not your fault. Shit just happens, doesn't it?'

I can't argue with that.

Before I leave the hospital I manage a quick visit with Mike Smith, our injured Sales Manager at HBS. He looks grey and washed out, but he manages to smile. His head and arms are heavily bandaged and he can't move much, but he can talk without pain. That's good, because Mike loves to talk. He's a natural salesman.

We chat mainly about work and I update him on the restructure. Not so surprisingly he doesn't seem to care. He's in his fifties and financially comfortable. He enjoys his work, but it isn't his whole life. Even without my psychic gift I know he has no plans to return to the merged company. He's happy to take the payout and move on with his life. Try something new, slow down a little. It sounds nice to me and I'm only twenty.

I don't stay long and promise to visit again soon. Then Megan picks me up from the hospital and drives me home. I'd called her earlier, when I first woke up. This is now the second Sunday in a row I've messed up our normal Sunday morning run. She's beside herself with worry when we get out to her car.

'How could you possibly be at a third explosion? And still be basically in one piece? What are you, some kind of Wonder Woman? And why haven't the bloody police stopped this guy yet? It's outrageous.'

I have no answers for her and just sit there becoming more deflated and confused as she rails sporadically during the drive home. She feels guilty because her beloved police department hasn't yet caught the bomber, and she is frustrated because she hasn't been with me to offer assistance at any of the explosions. And for some reason she seems angry that my Dad isn't home to protect me.

'He should be here. He's your father – for crying out loud. He should be home, you should call him. It's not right that you have to deal with all this without him.'

'It's not Dad's fault, Meg. And even if he was here there's nothing he could be doing.'

She fumes over this, but we both know she's just venting her frustrations. I'm more inclined to bottle up my feelings, but Meg will always let it all out. If she's angry, or frustrated, then someone has to be blamed. Eventually she lapses into silence.

Once we arrive home she sits me down in the lounge and goes to make us both a coffee. I sit there yet again feeling miserable and depressed.

I think about the bombs, each one so very, very loud and frightening and about how I have been only just out of the destructive range of all three. How does that happen? My mind whirls and spins, driving itself to dark places.

I think about work, and about all the redundancy letters that went out on Friday. It strikes me suddenly that I am technically unemployed right now, thanks to those letters. And I helped to write them. How must all the other people from work be feeling this weekend?

Then I begin to think about the weird psychic things that have been going on inside my head. They're scary, abnormal. And there's nothing rational about it either. How can someone that is supposedly dead communicate with me – from inside my head? I feel a little queasy as a shiver runs through me. What had Grammy Kathryn said? It was a curse, but also a blessing.

I think about yesterday, down at the pier. Without this gift, this curse or blessing, I would have clambered happily onto that yacht and Bobby, Don and I would also now be dead.

Megan walks back into the room bearing two large mugs of coffee. She immediately starts to sound off again, this time continuing her rant about the ineffectiveness of the police. I decide that I have to tell her. She's my best friend and I need to come clean with her. I felt better after telling Bobby. She deserves to know too. I hold up my hand in a firm 'stop' gesture and speak quietly.

'You need to listen. I need to tell you something.'

She frowns, not used to being cut off like that, especially by me. But she stops talking and sits down, intrigued. She says nothing, just shrugs curiously and waits.

I take a deep breath, steady myself and start talking.

'Yesterday morning, before I went to the marina, I met my maternal grandmother for the first time ever. My mum's mother. I thought she was dead, but it turns out she isn't.'

I pause, trying to frame the words carefully. Megan is quickly wide-eyed and listening intently. I can tell she is already bursting with questions but she's restraining herself uncharacteristically. I continue.

'She lives up at Bluff Creek and she's some kind of a gypsy fortune-teller. A psychic, I think. I'm not sure. And apparently this psychic thing runs in the family.'

As she stares at me in fascination I tell her everything. I tell her about the words I've recently started feeling. I try to explain that I don't actually hear the words, not like someone is talking, but that the words just form in my mind.

I tell her how I'd known about Janet's unborn baby, and her infidelity. I tell her about Adam's family – his team – and his anger, and about my experiences on level three. I tell her about feeling things about people I am with – like Bobby's issues with his father, and about Steve's eviction problems.

This last revelation seems to strike a chord with her and I hesitate, expecting her to want to ask about my comments on her father's illness, but she waves me on. Her eyes are like saucers and I can tell that while she is struggling to take it all in, she's totally fascinated. Optimistically I begin to feel that she really does want to understand and believe me.

So I tell her about the unidentified woman that wants me to help her son. I tell her that I'm certain that this woman is the bomber's deceased mother and that she forewarned me about the bomb on the yacht yesterday. That she saved my life.

Megan's mouth hangs wide open now. Literally gaping at me.

Then I tell her about visiting Grammy Kathryn, but I hold back on how I found her. I still don't understand how Rosie knew and I don't want to add that complication into the mix. I tell her about how Grammy said it was normal in my family for the gift to emerge in your late teens, or early twenties. I explain that my mother rejected her gift and the family ways when she married my father. I tell her that my mother lied to me about Grammy being dead.

'So, apparently,' I finally wrap up, 'I am of gypsy descent and have a psychic gift – as well as having a mad bomber stalking me. Crazy, huh?'

She nods slowly, still trying to absorb everything I've just said.

'So, do you see dead people? Like the kid in that *Sixth Sense* movie?'

I remember the movie clearly. The boy had actually seen dead people, mangled and bloodied, and they'd spoken to him face to face. It was horrific.

'No, not like that at all. I just sort of hear the words inside my head, or I just know things. Like intuition, but multiplied ten-fold. It's really hard to explain clearly.'

'So is it more like flashes of something? Scenes or images, like in that Kevin Bacon movie? What was it, something about echoes . . .'

I remember this movie too: *Stirs of Echoes*. Not really my kind of thing, but Megan loves thrillers and we'd seen it together. Kevin Bacon had premonitions of things, shown to him by a murdered woman's ghost. His premonitions had been flashes of things that were going to happen, short snippets like in a movie trailer. It wasn't a fun movie. I enjoyed him in *Footloose* a lot more.

'No,' I say again. 'Not like that either. I don't see anything. I just feel things.' I try to think of a movie or a TV show that mirrors my experiences, but can't.

'So this is like being clairvoyant, seeing the future?'

'No, I . . . umm, I can't see the future.' Or can I? Isn't that what a premonition is? Seeing the future. I'm not sure and fall silent. Megan watches me thoughtfully, and then moves on to other aspects of my psychic gift.

'So were you able to verify anything else? I mean, other than the bomb on the boat?'

It's a good question and I think about it. 'Yes. Janet really was pregnant. Her husband, Derek, confirmed that for me. And he knew what I was burbling about when I went off about her kissing another guy.'

Megan nods, a little impressed.

'And I think I was pretty close with Bobby's parental issues. But I don't really know about anything else.' I pause. 'Unless, umm, that thing about your Dad? You know, being ill?' I wait cautiously, unsure how she'll answer.

She looks at me uncertainly, and then finally sighs. 'He found a lump. He didn't want anyone to know. But the tests came back a few days ago, and it's benign.' She pauses. 'You said to me that it can be fixed, and it can. It was a bit of a scare, but he's going to be fine. So that's four things correct,' Megan says. She offers a crooked smile. 'Well done. The force is strong in you, little one.'

I try smiling back at her but it doesn't feel right, and then I feel a clear shift in the atmosphere. Megan is jealous. She's trying hard not to show it, but she is actually envious of my gift. I sense that she would desperately love to have some unique talent like this, to be able to do something special that no one else can do. I'm mortified. I don't want this but she would bend over backwards for it. I try to find something to say, but can think of nothing appropriate. Megan speaks first.

'So what are we gonna do about all this? Do you think you can use this psychic gift to identify the bomber?' I can hear excitement creeping into her voice. 'Maybe we can track him down before he blows anyone else up? Catch this bastard.'

And there she goes again. My friend Megan, the crime fighter. The frustrated super-sleuth. Desperate to play detective and solve the crime. But I have no such ambition.

'No way, Meg, no thanks. I am not a detective and we are not the police.'

'But think about it, Lily. If you have this clairvoyance thing then surely you can identify him. Just call up his mother on your psychic telephone and ask her his name.'

'I can't do that, Meg. I don't know how. I'm not in control of it.'

We lapse into an uncomfortable silence. I take a sip of my coffee. She drums her fingers on the table, and then lets out a loud exasperated sigh. It reminds me of Grammy. Then Megan suddenly sits up and looks at me, raising both her hands in question.

'What?' I say.

'You just had some kind of idea. I could see it.'

'I thought I was the psychic.'

'Don't play games with me. When I sighed just then your face screwed up, and I could see some idea ticking over in there. You've got no poker-face at all. What was it?'

This time I sigh heavily. 'You reminded me of my Grammy Kathryn.'

'So?'

'So . . . she's apparently a real psychic.'

Megan understands immediately and brightens in a flash. 'All right then, excellent. So she can help us find this crazy bastard. Come on then, let's go. Shift your bum.' She stands quickly and motions to the door. 'Bluff Creek, here we come.'

I groan inwardly. 'No, Meg. I don't think so. Let's just think about it, okay? I'm just out of hospital and I feel lousy, there's a mad bomber out there stalking me, and I only met this woman yesterday for the first time. I can't just bowl in there and ask her to help us try and find some nut-job who keeps trying to blow me up.'

'Oh come on, harden up. Do you want to just sit around waiting for this guy to actually get you with one of these bombs? Or to get some other people that you know? If you can do something about this, don't you think you owe it to those people he's already killed to get off your arse and do something? To at least try?'

Her speech gets me a little angry, but it also makes me feel guilty, which I know was her intention. Damn it. I feel certain that this isn't a good idea but I stand anyway, shaking my head in disbelief that I could let her talk me into it.

'You're a pain in the ass, you know that?'

'Yeah, but I'm the best pain in the ass you've got.'

I sigh again, resignedly. She's already at the door.

TWENTY-FOUR

As we arrive in Bluff Creek I'm both nervous and confused. Nervous about meeting my grandmother once again, especially with Megan alongside, and confused about why we are doing this. Megan seems to think we're going to enlist my grandmother on her crime-fighting crusade. I find this highly unlikely.

Megan drives and, after we quickly grab some take-aways for lunch, she spends the entire trip updating me on who the police believe might be the bomber. I think she wants to make sure that we're on the same page before we enlist Grammy's help. She talks constantly, while I only murmur occasionally, as we zoom along.

Apparently they now have several suspects, but Steve Cassidy is top of the list. The case against him is quite detailed, but I'm not convinced. Neither is Megan actually, and nor are the police apparently, which is why he has not yet been arrested.

The facts, as Megan outlines them, are that Steve has no alibi for either the first bombing in the City Council carpark building, or for the third one at Commonwealth's offices. He claims to have been home alone at the time of the carpark bombing and was supposedly in traffic, on his way to work, when the Commonwealth one went off. And, of course, he was present at both the second bombing, my first one at the HBS offices, and at the marina bombing just yesterday. So it's possible that he could have triggered all four bombs.

Establishing motive is a bit harder. One theory the police are considering, in line with Nikki's suggestion the other day, is that the bombings might be part of some crazy scheme to gain advancement within the restructure of the two building supply companies. They're aware of Steve's plans to go and work with his brother so that would count him out. Add to this the fact that they've searched his flat and his car and found no physical evidence of bomb-making. Megan admits Steve could still be a possibility though. He might simply have a hideaway somewhere containing all his bomb-building gear.

They also have quite a few other theories. They think it's feasible that someone at either HBS or CCS may have some motive for targeting our managers. They think some of the deaths have just been collateral damage, intended to throw the investigation off track. The idea sickens me. Whoever is doing this must be a very, very disturbed person.

Megan reminds me that Sue worked for the council. Apparently she was just promoted to a supervisory role within the Councils Property Management division. She moved up to replace the man who replaced the guy who died in the first bombing. A sort of tragic domino-effect appointment. So Sue had just become a more senior part of the council division responsible for managing housing assets in northern Hawthorne. The same team that Steve was evicted by – supposedly linking her death back to the first bombing.

The more she talks the more confused I get. It's like a massive puzzle and it makes my head spin. I have no doubt that Megan could talk for hours on the subject but I eventually interject. There is one question I have a niggling need to ask.

'What about me, Meg? Am I a suspect?'

She goes quiet and the silence is deafening. Then she responds slowly, measuring her words more carefully than usual.

'Your name is in there, but not in the primary list–'

'But it's there, on a list? Which list?'

More hesitation – and then, 'They're not really . . .'

'Am I on the target list?' There's a faint quiver in my voice.

'Yeah, but that doesn't mean anything . . .' She tails off again. Megan going quiet is a rarity. There's obviously something she's not telling me. 'I'm also a suspect, aren't I?'

She becomes very focused on her driving and chews her lip a little. 'Sort of . . . your name is actually on the associate list too. They think you may be helping him somehow. But they're really not sure. Your involvement is confusing.'

It's not the first time I can't think of anything to say and Megan desperately fills the space between us, almost babbling in her efforts to console me.

I'm grateful when we finally arrive at Bluff Creek. I'm starting to worry about what will happen now. Megan seems convinced that I, or my grandmother, can somehow get ourselves inside the bomber's head – in some psychic way. And by some means get his name and an address for his bomb-building hideaway. Can you believe it? Maybe I'm not the only one who's a little bit crazy here.

As we cruise along slowly, Megan gets all hyped up again. We pull up in the parking area across the road from the line of decrepit old shops and she practically bounces out of the car.

'Wow, nice outlook,' she says, admiring the beautiful lake-front scene before us. Then she spins abruptly, dismissing the tranquility and surveying the scruffy shops. She wrinkles her nose in distaste. 'Eew. Your grandma's here somewhere?'

'Mmm,' I reply, pointing to the shop with the heavy curtains filling the windows, 'in that one. The Crystal Heart.'

'Oh . . . charming.'

'You wait till you see inside.'

Early on a Sunday afternoon the place isn't as deserted as it had been yesterday morning, but it's close. We don't have to dodge any traffic as we cross the road and only see the odd person ambling along up and down the line of shops. But when we reach the door we find that the Crystal Heart is closed.

I'm not sure how to feel. All the way up here I've been thinking that this is a mistake. That Megan might embarrass me, or Grammy might think me rude to have brought her along. Maybe just turning around and heading back home will be the best result.

But Megan isn't so easily deterred and tries the door. It's locked. There is no information in the windows. No opening hours and no telephone number. Just the small cardboard sign that currently displays the word 'CLOSED'. Megan steps back and looks up and down the line of shops. They're all closed, almost. There is a dreary looking café a little way down the road, which appears to be open.

'Come on,' she says, moving purposefully towards it. I follow reluctantly.

The small café is very tired and old-fashioned. There are no customers and a bearded old man sits quietly behind the counter reading. I hang back just outside the doorway as Megan bustles in and starts asking questions about the lady who owns the crystal shop. The man is polite at first and says he can't help her – if the shop is closed, it's closed. She asks him for a phone number and he just shrugs. She'd started her interrogation all sugar and spice, but swiftly moves to a more confrontational manner when she realises that he isn't going to tell her anything. You can tell that she's just dying to pull out a badge to try and force him to cooperate, but I'm pretty sure even that wouldn't help. In a small community like this I guess that everyone is fairly protective of each other. I'm just about to walk in and drag

Megan out of the café when a voice behind me makes me jump.

'Your friend is too pushy, chai. Is this always her way?'

I spin around to find my grandmother peering over my shoulder. I didn't hear her approach. She looks very different from yesterday. Gone are the flowing black dress and the multi-coloured wrap. Today she wears a simple, matching two-piece tracksuit and sneakers, as if she is going for a run. She notices me taking in her outfit and smiles.

'You don't think I dress like a gypsy all the time, do you?' she says wryly. 'One must keep oneself in shape to live a long and healthy life, mustn't one? But you know this already, my chai, do you not?

I just nod, still a little out of stride. She scowls past me.

'You need to rein in your friend, Lily. She is upsetting Harold.'

I turn and can see that Harold is indeed becoming upset. The old man's face has started to blanch and Megan is gesturing wildly. I call her, but she just flicks a hand in my direction to wave off the interruption. I call her again in a firmer tone of voice. This stops her and she turns, frowning. I point silently at the woman standing behind me. Her face registers surprise and then frustration as she turns back to Harold and gives him a searing 'thanks-but-no-thanks' look. Then, without another word, she turns and strides over to where we are standing in the doorway. She stops before me and gazes at my grandmother intently.

'So you must be Lily's Grammy Kathryn,' she says.

'And you must be Lily's ill-mannered friend,' Grammy responds evenly. 'Do you not think that an apology is due to the good man back there?'

Megan looks like she's just been slapped. I groan inwardly.

'You're kidding. That man couldn't have been less helpful.'

'Perhaps he would have been if you had displayed slightly better manners?'

'How dare you? I wasn't rude. All I asked him was–'

I cut them off there, raising both hands in open-handed stop signs between them. 'Let's not argue, please. Can we just let it go and leave the poor guy alone?' Fortunately they both clam up and start to move outside. I go in quickly and apologise to Harold on Megan's behalf. He just nods in acknowledgment and goes thankfully back to his book.

Outside the two women are regarding each other suspiciously, but mercifully in silence.

'Grammy, this is my best friend Megan. Megan, this is my grandmother, Kathryn,' I say. They both nod at each other warily and I turn to Grammy Kathryn. 'I told Megan all about our meeting yesterday and she was . . . umm . . .' I search for the right word, '. . . intrigued, and wanted to come with me today and meet you too. You know, provide a little moral support. I hope that's okay?' Grammy just raises one eyebrow and says nothing, so I press on. 'We both want to learn more from you about my . . . umm . . . gift. There's much about it that is troubling me.'

Grammy returns her focus to me, fixing me with her deep and piercing brown eyes. She takes her time to respond, milking the moment. She turns her gaze slowly to Megan and then back to me before she replies.

'Walk with me,' is all she says, taking off down the road towards her shop before I have the chance to respond. Megan and I quickly gather ourselves and follow.

She moves quickly for a woman I believe to be well into her sixties and, surprisingly, she doesn't stop at the crystal shop. We scurry to keep up and are still a step behind her when she turns at the end of the row of shops and starts up a short bush-laden side street. About halfway up she crosses the road and leads us up a path, through overgrown bushes to the front door of a small cottage. It isn't locked and we follow her up a short hallway and into a reasonably sized lounge area. The windows open out towards the lake, but the bush and trees are so overgrown you can barely make out glimpses of the sparkling water through them. The cottage is clean and uncluttered; nothing like the shop at all, but it does have that slightly musty old-person feel to it. Grammy stops and turns, motioning us both to a couch on the left wall, facing the windows. Then she takes a seat in a large, overstuffed armchair across from us. Her throne, I can't help thinking.

'You live here?' Megan says. It's part question, part statement.

Grammy frowns at her, 'Yes, obviously. Perhaps you will make it to detective one day, with such observational powers.'

The unnecessary sarcasm grates on us both, but the message she delivers sends a small thrill of surprise through me. Megan picks it up too and somehow doesn't react to the jibe. How had she known that Megan so desperately wants to be a detective?

'You live here alone?' I ask gently.

This softens her a little, as she knows what I am really asking.

'Yes, my chai, I have been alone here for many, many years. Your grandfather passed on before you were even born. I have never remarried.'

'I'm sorry,' is all I can think to say.

There is silence in the room. Thankfully Megan is holding herself back and I feel that Grammy wants me to lead the way. I take a deep breath and fire away.

'I'm trying to come to grips with the gift, Grammy. I'm trying to understand what it is, and how I can . . .' I pause, '. . . manage it. You know, control it.'

She nods slowly, acknowledging me but saying nothing. I continue.

'It's been suggested to me that this gift might be a psychic ability, or possibly clairvoyance. What do you call it?'

She stays silent for a minute, moving her gaze onto Megan thoughtfully and then back to me. I get the feeling that she isn't comfortable that Megan is with us.

'Whatever you tell me I'll just repeat straight to her after I leave. I don't mean that horribly, but she's my best friend. She's helping me. I really need her at the moment.'

Grammy mulls on my words for a while, taking her time and I start to feel as if she is performing for the audience again. Finally she speaks.

'There are many gaujo words for the gifts our people bear. They call some psychics, others mediums or even fortune-tellers. Your gifts, as you describe them, are more akin to clairaudience, but this is never strictly the case. You may develop clairvoyance with time, or become a fine healer, or you may be a natural vessel for channeling, but none of this is clear as yet. We still have much to discuss, much to try out.'

I consider her words. Something about these names resonates with me. Clairaudience is quite a mouthful, while psychic feels the most comfortable, whether it's strictly right or wrong, I don't know. Grammy is watching Megan, silently daring her to say something. Megan stays quiet.

'Okay, so how do you know that I am clairaudient and not a clairvoyant or a medium? What's the difference?'

She leans forward a little. 'A medium is able to let a spirit make use of her body, to speak and pass on messages, while a clairvoyant generally sees more with the inner eye. They experience images mostly, whereas you described a gift of only words. Clear and sharp words and phrases, yes?'

'Yes,' I agree. 'I see nothing at all, no images, no faces. I just get words in my mind.'

'This is clairaudience and it is good and bad. Bad because you may have more difficulty identifying who is sending the messages. Do you understand; if you see nothing then there is nothing to describe. But it is good because you will sleep better at night. Some clairvoyants are unable to close their minds off at night, as they receive images while they try to sleep. This can be harrowing as occasionally these images are intense, sometimes tragic.'

I consider this for a moment, suddenly remembering her words from yesterday. 'Was my mother clairvoyant? You said she had trouble sleeping. Is that why?'

She hesitates, frowning once again at Megan who now seems utterly fascinated. Clearly she isn't comfortable discussing my mother in company. I appeal to her once again.

'Please Grammy, it would help me understand.'

She turns back to me and exhales another deeply exaggerated sigh. 'Yes, your mother received images. And they came mostly at night, almost never in the day.' She hesitates, carefully considering her next words. 'As I understand it she used sleeping pills to block the images and allow her to sleep at night. I tried to discourage this, but she would not be told. She was difficult, your mother.'

I feel Megan shift a little beside me as I try to absorb this. I can't help thinking about the Kevin Bacon movie again. That poor guy was almost driven insane by images in his mind. Maybe he should have tried sleeping pills too, like my mother had. But it probably would have spoiled the movie.

'So what else should I be able to do then?'

She rolls her eyes at me. 'My chai, you do not understand this, do you? There is no rulebook. There are no set parameters. There is no can-do-this, but can't-do-that,' she pauses. 'Your gift will be unique to you, as all of our people's gifts are unique to each individual. You are clearly able to receive messages from those who have passed, and you clearly are able to sense issues of strong emotional value to others. But whether you have the second-sight, or if you are able to heal, or if you can allow the departed to speak through you we will only know if we try these things. There is no easy answer today, I'm afraid.'

I don't know what to say to that and take a moment to contemplate it all when beside me Megan finally breaks her silence. Staying quiet for so long must have been killing her.

'I'm sorry for upsetting that man before, and I'm sorry if I've upset you in some way, but I would love to know how Lily knew about my father's illness. Can you explain that?'

I don't think Grammy wants to answer the question, but surely she has to concede that Megan is making an effort. I'm quietly impressed. I've never heard Meg so deferential before.

Finally Grammy tilts her head and responds, her voice touched with annoyance. 'I have already explained. This is essentially one form of clairvoyance. The ability to sense issues of strong emotional value to others. The concern for your father was high within your subconscious mind and Lily merely sensed it.'

'So, she read my mind,' Megan asks.

'Not your conscious mind, but she was able to draw the feelings from your subconscious. It is quite a different thing.'

'Okay, but then, how did she know that he was going to be all right? When she first mentioned it I didn't know he would be fine. We were still awaiting the results. She couldn't have read that from my mind.'

Grammy smiles in an enigmatic way, seeming to enjoy Megan's confusion. 'This is not a science, girl, it is a spiritual journey. How she knew that his prognosis would be clear is not something the gift reveals, even to its owner. It is merely one part of the gift that we just accept and use where it is appropriate.' She fixes Megan with a frosty gaze. 'Just as you should accept that a married man's bed is no place for you.'

Megan freezes, her eyes becoming saucers. Her mouth falls open and she closes it again rapidly, drawing herself back onto the couch. Her eyes fall to the floor. Grammy allows herself a mocking smile, clearly pleased that she has made a direct hit on a tender issue. I just sit there in bewilderment, and then feel a mild disgust overcoming me.

'Meg?' I ask softly. 'You haven't. Have you?'

She can't meet my eye and shifts uncomfortably where she sits. Then she rallies, determined not to have her dirty laundry so publicly aired, and turns on Grammy.

'Okay, well done. So you have a bloody gift. Good on you,' she snaps. 'So tell me, Grammy, how come you've just sat around out here and said nothing while your granddaughter has almost been blown to bits by a mad-fucking bomber three times recently. Did you not see that coming?'

'Megan!' I cry out. 'Don't!'

Grammy flinches as if she's been physically struck, but Megan has been stung by the adultery accusation and continues on relentlessly.

'Three bloody times!' she barks, standing up. 'If you're so god-damn insightful, why haven't you warned her? And why haven't you tracked down the freak that's doing this? What kind of a bloody psychic are you, you mean-spirited old bitch!'

'Stop it,' I shout as I leap up too. 'That's not fair, just stop it.' I grab her by the shoulders, positioning myself between them. I can see the anger burning in Megan's eyes. She's furious at being exposed like this. I glare back at her. Bringing her here was a mistake. I should have trusted my instincts more.

After a tense few seconds she seems to sag, her anger spent. She lets out a deep sigh and apologises.

'I'm sorry, Lily. I shouldn't have said all that,' she mumbles forlornly.

'Maybe you should give me a couple of minutes here on my own,' I suggest quickly.

She nods, then mutters another meek apology and slips out quietly. I try to gather myself and turn around slowly, ready to begin trying to smooth things over again, but Grammy is gone.

TWENTY-FIVE

'Shit,' I say out loud to nobody in particular. I head further into the house. There is a small dining area at the end of the lounge and I find a kitchen just around a corner, to the left. Grammy is standing there with arms folded, waiting for a kettle to boil..She has two cups laid out, presumably waiting for me to join her.

'Megan's gone for a walk,' I tell her quietly.

She says nothing in response. She just pours boiling water into the teacups. I wait patiently while she completes the little ritual and finally presents me with a cup of tea. We move silently back into the lounge, returning to the seats we had previously occupied. I sip my tea and wait.

'You're friend is very loyal and that is good. But she is desperately ill-mannered, which is not so good. I think it best that you leave her at home when you next visit.'

'Yes,' I agree. 'That would probably be best.'

We sit in silence for another minute with the strain of Megan's discord heavy in the atmosphere. I wonder if she will respond to the accusations or change the subject. She chooses to respond, in her own unique manner.

'There are many dangers in the world, Lily, and we can never know them all. Nor can we always predict them. Nor would we want to.' She pauses, probably more for effect than to gather her thoughts. 'Our gifts do not pass us the secrets of the world with ease, you must understand this. If any Romany could use their gift for locating buried treasure, or to make a fortune on the stock market, then where would the excitement be in life? Where would there be challenges to overcome?' She leans forward in her seat, fixing me with that hypnotically intense gaze. 'I will not pretend that I knew of your predicament, for I did not. Nor will I now offer you guidance in the way forward, for I sense that whatever is to come is meant to be. But I know that you will prevail, and that you will return to me again and again. This is a challenge that you have been chosen for. It will not destroy you, but it will help to shape you.'

She sits back, leaning into the armchair, closes her eyes and draws in a long, deep breath. She exhales slowly and then sits upright, taking a sip of her tea. Finally, she speaks again. 'You must face the fear, and when you do you can set things right once again. Do you understand this?' she asks. I shake my head. No. I don't understand a thing. She half-smiles and then nods, 'but you will, my chai. You will.'

We sit in silence for another minute and then I speak.

'I'm sorry about Megan's attitude, Grammy. She was out of line.'

'Yes she was, but you should not apologise for her. It was not your fault.'

I want to call her out on the rude way that she treated Megan, but I just can't. Meg had gotten herself off to a bad start and with two strong personalities there is always going to be a rather nasty clash. I shouldn't have bought her here.

'Next time I will come alone, but for now I think we should call it a day, don't you?'

'You are always welcome here, chai. Anytime, day or night.'

'Thank you,' I say, pausing. 'See you again, then.'

'Kushti Bok, my chai.'

I give her a perplexed look and she smiles. 'It means "good luck",' she advises in translation.

I nod my thanks and turn away. I know that I will be back, probably many times. And I also know that it will be a complicated relationship as Grammy is clearly a difficult and contrary woman. But there is still much I need to know about my gift, and about myself. As I leave I actually start to feel that I may one day enjoy my ability, not fear it as I have so far. If I can learn to control it and not let it control me, I may be able to use it positively and help people. But I'm not really sure, it still seems so frightening, so crazy and unpredictable. But perhaps I can tame it?

I wander out through the bushy path, looking back over my shoulder as I walk away. Her cottage is a reasonable size and looks solid but, as with the line of shops, is badly in need of a spruce-up. And the gardens simply need blow-torching.

I find Megan sitting on a large rock by the waterfront, not too far from the car.

'It's beautiful out here, isn't it, Lily?' she offers as I approach.

'Yes it is, just as long as you face this way and don't look back at the crusty old shops behind us.'

'It's a shame, isn't it? Someone should clean this place up a bit.'

I nod in agreement and shiver a little as a cool breeze bites through my clothes. 'Come on, we can compare notes on my delightful Grammy Kathryn on the drive home.'

We sit in the car in my driveway after a moderately uncomfortable trip home. Along the way Megan has confessed to the indiscretion that Grammy accused her of and we are trying not to dwell on it. She's embarrassed. She knows it's wrong. The guy in question is one of the police officers at work, no one that I have ever met. He's apparently good-looking, rugged, and has quite a dry sense of humour. When he told her that his wife didn't really understand him she'd fallen for the cliché and allowed herself to slip up, twice.

She promises me that she will break it off immediately and never allow it to happen again. I'm disappointed because we've talked about married men many times before. I've run out of fingers and toes trying to count the number of times that we've been hit on by married men in bars and nightclubs. But we'd made a pact with each other that we would never be the 'other' woman. No matter how hot they were, or what they promised.

Now Megan has betrayed that promise and I'm very disappointed. She never lied to me about it, but I still feel as if she has gone behind my back.

As I sit in the car, trying to convince us both that I have already forgiven her, I get a sudden and very strong feeling that her married man is also playing the field with someone else. I just know it, and it makes me angry. This time I decide to trust my intuition, because I somehow know that it is an absolute fact. I turn to face Megan.

'This guy is more of a cheating scumbag than you know. You're not the only bit on the side he's playing at the moment.'

She looks stunned. 'Are you sure?'

'Yes,' I answer. 'I'm positive. In fact, that slimy toad is shagging around all over the place. You should keep well away, he's bad news.'

'Who is the other one, Lily? Can you tell me that?'

I barely have to think about it and find myself saying, 'She's blonde and skinny. She's married too. He met her on a call out, for work . . .' I pause, trying for more. 'That's all I know.'

'Wow.' Megan whistles softly. 'I'm impressed. You can't give me a name?'

I try. I concentrate and search and search inside my head, but get nowhere. Nothing else comes to me. I shake my head gently. 'No,' I tell her, 'that's all I've got.'

'Okay, cool. No worries,' she pauses. 'So what's the bomber guy doing right now? Can you tune in on his mum?'

I look at her and frown. Then I think, why not? Try it. You never know. I look away from her and then close my eyes to see if that will help. I try to remember what the words sounded like as I heard them, but struggle. It wasn't a voice I heard, just the words. Sharp and clear, coming through in staccato bursts. I screw up my face and try to send a message out. Try to call out to the mother figure. But nothing happens.

I open my eyes, feeling a little silly. Megan is staring at me, holding her breath. She raises her eyebrows in question and I simply shrug in response. Then she points out the front windscreen of the car. 'Your little fan club is here.'

Rosie is standing further down the driveway, watching us and waiting. I groan. What now?

'I should get going,' Megan says. 'I need to drop into the office and have a little chat with someone about a skinny blonde chick he may also know.'

I almost feel sorry for the guy, but not quite. He has it coming and, by God, he's going to get it. Then she apologises again, for about the millionth time since we left Bluff Creek. We hug and I get out of the car.

'Hey look,' she quickly calls out at me, 'how about I come back afterwards and make you dinner? My way of really saying sorry. How does that sound?'

'That'd be great. Good plan.'

'You call me if anything else happens, won't you?' she says before I close the door.

'Of course I will. You go, give that bastard hell.'

'Don't worry, he's toast,' she smiles wickedly, and then she drives away.

I turn to see that Rosie hasn't moved. She's still watching and waiting so I take a deep breath and make my way up the driveway to say hello.

'My mum said I'm not allowed to visit you any more,' Rosie announces as I reach her. I realise that she is standing in a spot that is screened from view of her own home. She's hiding so that her mother can't see us talking.

She seems different again, but this time different in a more ordinary way. She stands without swaying and watches me through clear and bright eyes.

'Really? And did she tell you why not?'

'She thinks you made me sick somehow. Did you?'

'No Rosie, of course not. I would never do anything to make you sick.'

'So are we still friends then?' she asks.

'Of course we are. We'll always be friends, you and me.'

She gives me a toothy grin. I smile back.

'Okay, good,' she says, seeming relieved. 'I'd better go. If Mum catches me over here she's gonna be really mad.'

'Don't worry, Rosie. She'll come around. She's just been very worried about you. You just be a good girl and do what she tells you, okay?'

She nods and turns to go, but I stop her with a quick outstretched hand.

'Hey, just a quick question before you go.' She looks up at me with big curious eyes. 'How did you know about Grammy?'

She looks blank. 'Who?'

I repeat the question. She continues to look blank and shakes her head. 'I don't know Grammy. Who is she?'

I ignore the question, now even more perplexed. 'Do you know where Bluff Creek is?'

She makes a face, clearly trying to think if this means anything to her. 'No. Where is it?'

'How about the Crystal Heart?'

She shakes her head immediately, 'Is that some kind of computer game?'

I don't answer her. As I look into her eyes I strongly sense that she's telling me the truth. These names and places mean nothing to her. I probe further, cautiously.

'You wrote me a note, and you delivered it to me.'

She looks puzzled and shakes her head. 'No I didn't.'

We stare at each other for another long moment. Finally I speak, 'You should get going. We don't want your mum getting upset with us, do we?'

She seems startled as she remembers her mother's current mood and looks around quickly to ensure we aren't being observed. As she turns back to me I wave her towards the gap in the hedge. She shrugs and gives me a little finger wave with her good hand as she leaves.

I'm mystified. She clearly remembers nothing of her late-night visit. How did she know where to send me?

TWENTY-SIX

Megan is in fine form when she returns. When I finally open the door to her persistent knocking she is grinning hopefully, a bag of groceries in her hands.

'Mexican, baby!' she announces cheerfully, raising the bag. 'Tacos tonight!'

It sounds fantastic.

She heads straight to the kitchen and I follow her. This time I dig around in Dad's cupboard, finding a half-empty bottle of tequila before procuring a knife and lemons to prepare the drinks. A cup of coffee just isn't going to cut it tonight.

We eat, we drink, and we talk. Or, rather, Megan talks. It's one of the things that she does best. Besides making great tacos, that is. But she doesn't want to talk about the guy from work or the blonde 'other' woman. All she will tell me is that 'he's been dealt with' wearing an expression of grim smugness. I actually start to feel sorry for him.

Instead she babbles away about the ongoing investingation, covering and recovering everything we already know, yet again. I'm tiring of it all, but listen anyway.

Steve Cassidy remains top of the list and she's just learned that they're widening the scope of the investigation to look more deeply at all his friends and associates. But the idea of this bomber working with an accomplice doesn't feel right to me. Everything I've felt about the bomber screams 'solo'. Especially as the mother's words make it sound like its just one man. Just one 'bad boy' – her son alone – not a partnership.

After a while she seems to tire of the subject herself and I'm relieved. It feels like we've been going over and over all this stuff endlessly and getting nowhere. It's draining and frustrating.

'So anyway,' she says by way of changing the subject, 'your lovely new Grammy.'

'Mmm?'

'I was thinking about her before and, you know, I don't remember how it was that you said that you found her.'

That was because I hadn't said.

'Lily?'

I think hard, ideas scrambling around my mind. The whole episode with Rosie really has me bothered. Nothing about it makes sense and I'm still not sure that I'm ready to share it with anyone. But I don't want to lie to Megan. She already knows so much and she has more than proven herself as a good friend, especially in the way she has so readily accepted my sudden weirdness.

'How did you know?' she persists. 'Was it voices in your head? Did a spirit . . . I don't know, guide you there?'

I shrug and finally sigh in resignation.

'No. Nothing that simple.' I roll my eyes and shake my head, not sure how to phrase the words. 'You're not going to believe me.'

'Seriously. After everything else, why wouldn't I? Come on, just tell me.'

So I do. I walk her through each of Rosie's weird visits and fainting episodes, or seizures, or whatever they were. I tell her about the note and how Rosie subsequently seemed to have no idea what I was talking about when I mentioned Grammy or Bluff Creek.

She sits and stares at me in stunned silence for a moment. She's met Rosie quite a few times and is clearly shocked by this new information.

'So, do you think she wrote the note?' Megan finally asks.

I feel relieved. Once again she seems to believe my explanation without question. It would have been a mistake to lie to her. And she has typically focused in on trying to solve the mystery.

I give her question some thought. The handwriting was definitely childish and I think it's likely that Rosie did write it herself. I have no proof, but it feels right.

I nod. 'Yeah, I'm pretty sure she did.'

'But how could *she* possibly know?'

'I don't know. That's what really troubles me.'

'Do you think Louise knew about your mum? Did Greg know? He must have, surely?'

I shake my head softly. 'I'm pretty sure that Mum didn't tell anyone. She kept it a secret. Even from Dad. So I doubt if Louise could possibly have known.'

'Maybe, but if Louise did know, then she may have had it written down somewhere. You know, in an old diary or something. Rosie might have found it and read it.'

This is a stretch, yet somehow it seems vaguely plausible. How else could Rosie have known? I try to imagine my mother sharing her secret with my Dad's sister. It doesn't add up. I'm not sure they were all that close, and Louise only moved into the house next door after my mum died – to help Dad cope through the hard times that followed. She'd been really great back then.

'I don't know, Meg. I'm pretty sure Dad doesn't know. If he did, surely he would have said something. You know, warned me about all this in advance.' She frowns and chews her lip as she thinks about it. 'And I can't see how Louise would know. If Mum hadn't told Dad, why would she share that sort of thing with Louise?' The more I think about it the more certain I become. 'No, neither of them knew.'

She looks thoughtful for a moment and then brightens suddenly. 'Okay, so maybe Rosie was doing some kind of family tree research and found out that way?'

'Is that possible?' I ask. 'She's only ten.'

'Anything's possible. She could have googled it.'

I'm not so sure though. 'But why would she say she doesn't remember giving me the note?' I ask. 'And what's with all the fainting fits? If she'd been doing family tree stuff, why not just say so?'

Megan frowns again and doesn't respond for a moment. Then she lets fly in an entirely new direction, surprising me yet again.

'What about . . . hang on . . . maybe she has the gift too. It's a family thing right? Maybe she's been getting messages from beyond and then sharing them with you?'

'Hold on,' I say, trying to sort it all out in my head first. 'Rosie is my cousin, but she's on my Dad's side of the family. The gift is from my Mum's side. She couldn't possibly have it too, so that theory doesn't work.'

We're not getting anywhere. It's time to move on.

'I think I need another shot,' I pick up my empty tequila glass and wave it at her.

'Me too,' she agrees. 'Maybe more than one.'

'You know, it's getting late, Meg,' I suggest. 'Maybe one more and then we call it a night.'

She looks up at me quickly, trying to mask her disappointment. 'I'm sorry. This isn't really helping, is it?'

I shrug. 'I don't know. You've definitely thrown out some new possibilities. More to consider.'

She snorts. 'You're such a diplomat.'

I wave my empty shot glass again and smile. 'So where's that drink?'

She quickly refills both our little glasses and we raise them together in a toast. 'Here's to a new world of mysterious depths and supernatural abilities,' she says.

'And to all of us who sail in her,' I reply, tossing the fiery liquid down my throat and banging the empty glass onto the table. The tequila warms me and as I blink to clear the tears that have welled up in my eyes, I can just make out Megan studiously refilling both our glasses once again.

There will be nothing more, sensible or not, decided upon tonight.

It's quite late when I eventually pour Megan into a taxi. Neither of us is in a fit state to drive her home. Especially after I accidentally let slip about how nice I think my new boss at work is. Megan grilled me like a seasoned investigator over that admission, not letting up until I told her absolutely everything I know about Bobby. By the time she left the tequila bottle was well and truly empty. I'll definitely have to restock Dad's kitchen cupboard before he gets home.

Thankfully, my head is only mildly fuzzy as I rise to an early morning start. It's Monday, and it's going to be a big day at work. I'm due at the breakfast meeting at the Marina Café by 7.30 am, along with all the newly appointed executive managers. The eight men gathering at the café would all have received a call from Jonathon over the weekend, confirming their appointments. The other three will probably be staying at home, preparing their CVs, and readying themselves for the new job search ahead.

I dress quite formally, as seems appropriate for an occasion such as this. I also make sure I have a bite to eat first as I don't think I'll be comfortable digging into a proper breakfast in front of the new management team. It's hard to sound knowledgeable and businesslike with a mouth full of scrambled egg.

I get there early, just a few minutes after 7 am, but that's deliberate. Having survived yet another horrible and tragic event, right here at the marina only two days ago, I feel it's important that I revisit the pier. Grammy advised me yesterday that I should face my fears and I have taken that to heart. Visiting level three at work had been awful after the explosion there, but I knew it needed to be done. I'm not sure if I will be able to go back and work on that floor again, but a part of me is determined to try. And that same part of me is driving me to visit pier B again. Don's wife Sue died there and I felt her pass on. At least I'm pretty sure that's what I felt. In part, again, I want to see if her spirit is still lingering there, like Adam's and Henry's seem to be on level three. Or if she has in fact passed over to wherever it is a person's soul goes when they die.

I also feel that I need to visit there before I go into the meeting, to get the worry out of my mind. To ensure I don't spend the entire morning glancing out the window, to the place where my last traumatic experience occurred.

So, I park my car in the same place in the carpark I did on Saturday and, taking a deep breath, I stride out towards the entrance of pier B.

TWENTY-SEVEN

The excitement is coursing through him once again.

It's addictive.

He is still feeling disappointed that Saturday's effort didn't go exactly to plan, but he's calmer about it now. It wasn't the end of the world. He still feels an immense swelling of pride at the end result. At the beauty of his handiwork. The exploding boat was impressive, without a doubt. Better than impressive, it had been awesome. Simply awesome. Thunderous, in fact.

The accidental nature of the detonation doesn't worry him either. These things happen. He was able to repair the simple, but effective, transmission device that he uses as a trigger. He's even worked out why the device went off. He considered reworking the trigger when he rebuilt it but decided against it. Simple is best and he doesn't plan on throwing the damn thing around again. So he merely repaired it to work exactly as it had before.

His new device is already in place and it's the biggest he's ever built. It's going to be extraordinary. It'll be at least twice as devastating as the one on the boat, but it needs to be as he wants to express himself over a much larger area this time. To really create an impression.

He surveys his current domain. He's comfortable and perfectly positioned. Higher up than the last place, with an excellent view across the entire area. He considers sitting up more leisurely in one of the leather seats, but then he would be visible and that won't do. He decides to stay where he is. To keep low and not risk giving away his position.

The excitement rushes and tingles through him once again as he shakes his hands in readiness. The butterflies in his stomach tremble and quiver. He hasn't felt so alive since the last time.

'Oh Mama, if only you could see me now,' he says aloud, but softly. 'You'd be so proud.'

TWENTY-EIGHT

As I make my way out to the piers I pass by the Marina Café. This morning no one sits at the outside tables – it's still a little early and possibly too cool for outdoor dining.

Walking with grim determination, I feel my stomach knot up a little as I pass by pier A. I can see the top of pier B just ahead and start to really tense up.

I stop at the point between the first two piers where Steve Cassidy dragged both Bobby and me out of the water. My legs feel slightly shaky. About ten metres ahead is the spot where they attempted to resuscitate Sue. A leaden feeling fills my stomach and a small tear forms in one eye. I wipe it away quickly and take another deep breath. I try to open my mind to let Sue in, but there is nothing. I feel nothing of Sue here at all and I become immediately confident that Sue has passed over. She accepted her fate and moved on with dignity.

In a small way I'm disappointed that I'm not able to feel her here, but I also understand that it's better that she has gone. It's better that she isn't suffering here, unable to make sense of what happened to her. I start to relax and then . . .

–he's at it again, such a bad boy–

The bomber's mother is inside my head once again. A wave of terror washes over me and my knees go weak. Only once before have I received her words and not been involved in an explosion. The bomber must be somewhere nearby. But where is he, and where is the bomb?

I realise that I'm standing out in the open, in full view of the line of shops and clearly visible from the carpark and from many of the hundreds of boats docked quietly within the marina. I'm totally and completely exposed. He must be able to see me. I catch my breath at the terrifying realisation. Oh God, what will he do?

– he's not himself,. he doesn't mean to hurt anyone –

I stand stock still for what feels like forever, rigid with terror, completely clueless as to what I should do next. If I run he will see me, and he'll know that I'm on to him. But where is the bomb? If I run, will I be heading away from it or straight towards it? I force myself to move, my heart pounding furiously while my mouth is bone dry. I start to turn a very, very slow circle, standing exactly where I am, just a few steps away from the top of pier B. I see first the other piers running away from me in a long line around the edge of the lake.

–please help him, he's being such a bad boy–

I keep turning slowly, till I can see the carpark. Nikki is just climbing out of her car. She's wearing a sleeveless blue sundress. She hasn't seen me and starts to move towards the café. Brendan, our Marketing Manager, is standing near the café door with another man, someone I don't know, and then they go inside together. My heart nearly bursts out of my chest when the location of the bomb suddenly becomes very, very obvious. The Marina Café. It has to be. In only a few more minutes it will be crammed full of Westwood Building & Construction's entire new executive team.

–just talk to him, please . . . you can help him–

I want to run. The desire to flee, to get as far away as possible, is overwhelming. But I can't leave all those people to die. I know without a doubt that there's a bomb. I can warn them. But how, without walking into the café? I desperately rack my brain. My cell-phone! But I've left my handbag in my car. Why did I do that?

–please, he's going to be bad again, help him–

The mother is desperate, but I'm frozen with fear and shock. I don't know what to do. I still just want to run away. But instead I find myself turning again, spinning slowly further around, looking past the line of shops to face the piers again. Abruptly I realise that I am looking for Steve Cassidy. He has to be here. I can hear the mother in my head, so he must be here now. Mustn't he? But where? Dammit Lily, you're supposed to have a gift. Why don't you damn well use it? Talk to the mother, find him.

But how?

I screw my eyes shut tight, desperately trying to focus in on the mother. I think hard to myself, where is he? But no words come. Then I open my eyes and I suddenly just know. He's right in front of me. Straight ahead. I've already spun myself subconsciously to look directly at him. Straight in my line of vision is a motor cruiser moored almost at the top of pier A. It's partially obscured by the mast and foredeck of a yacht closer to me, but I know with absolute certainty that the bomber is on that cruiser, watching the café, watching me.

—you can stop him, please help, just talk to him—

I force myself to take a step forward, and then another, as I start to walk towards pier A and the motor cruiser moored there. I have no real plan in mind when a sudden movement to my left suddenly draws my attention.

Bobby is in the carpark, talking with Nikki. They're both looking in my direction. It stops me in my tracks. I look back at the cruiser. Did I see someone move in the cockpit? I turn back to Bobby and Nikki. He's gesturing that she should go to the café. She looks across at me and says something. I can't make out their words, but it's clear they are debating who should come over and get me.

—oh no, don't make him angry, he can be so naughty—

Eventually Nikki begins making her way towards the café. I want to shout out and tell her not to go in there, but the bomber will surely hear me. Somehow I sense that I made him angry here the other day and that he set off the bomb in frustration. I don't want that to happen again. I don't know how many people are already inside the café. I don't want anyone else to die because of me.

Bobby watches Nikki move away for a moment and then begins to stride purposefully towards me. He's moving stiffly, clearly not fully recovered from Saturday's explosion. I force myself to stand still, terrified that the bomber is watching us. He may get angry and set off the bomb. I can't live with that on my conscience. I force myself to watch Bobby, rather than look around at the cruiser again. My heart hammers away, my stomach knotting in turmoil, but I stand my ground. Then I suddenly know what I have to do.

TWENTY-NINE

He watched the girl arrive, park her car, and then drift out to the top of pier B. He continues to watch her silently, becoming angrier. It's the same damn stupid girl that messed everything up for him here on Saturday. He doesn't understand why she doesn't just go inside. Why the hell is she out here now wandering aimlessly around the carpark?

Then he notices another car arrive and another. His targets are starting to appear. This calms him a little. When he looks back at the girl he is surprised to find her staring directly at him. Just standing there with a funny look on her face, staring straight at the place where he is hidden. A ripple of anxiety courses through him.

There is more activity in the carpark. That bastard from Auckland is here now too, talking to the blonde bimbo who thinks she is so god-damn perfect. He feels the excitement return. He wants them both in there. He wants them all.

His anger flares when he realises that the stupid bastard from Auckland isn't going into the café with the blonde bitch. He's coming out to the girl.

Damn him. Damn the girl too. Why can't they just stick to the damn script and go to their bloody meeting?

He shifts his weight to make himself more comfortable again and carefully draws the small plastic box out of his sweatshirt pocket. He caresses it, slowly warming it in his hand as he watches the man close in on the girl.

He glances over at the café, and then back at the couple, trying to decide what to do.

THIRTY

It seems like an eternity waiting for Bobby to reach me, but he eventually does. I shift my position slightly as he draws closer and as he finally reaches me I have my back to the bomber. He stops right in front of me as I hoped he would.

I take him by surprise, launching myself forward into an all-encompassing embrace, hugging him to me with a vengeance. I whisper quickly into his ear.

'Hug me back. Don't speak. Don't let me go,' I murmur quietly. 'Turn your head so that you're facing me and don't look away.' I can tell that I have taken him completely off guard, but he complies instantly with my demands.

'Now listen carefully. You have to believe me – the bomber is here again. Don't let me go and don't look away, he can see us.' I feel him stiffen, then he is still for a second, and then he gives me a small squeeze and I can feel him nod ever-so-slightly against me. Our faces are practically touching – his breath is fresh on my neck.

'Do you have your cell-phone on you? I ask in a whisper. He nods almost imperceptibly once again and I feel a huge wave of relief wash over me. Thank God.

'Okay, keep holding me. I have an idea.' His eyes are bright and alive, but I can sense the fear behind them. Mine must look the same.

–he's just a baby, doesn't understand what he's doing–

I try to block the mother's words from my thoughts, but it's impossible. I look up into Bobby's eyes and quietly and quickly tell him what I want him to do. He whispers back his understanding and tells me what I need to know. Then we both take a deep breath and separate, but only back to arms length before he draws me in again, to tuck me under his arm this time.

I'm pleased to find that our bodies fit together comfortably. I feel protected and I snake my right arm around his waist as his left arm draws me in to his chest. He lays his head at an angle on top of mine. Then, with my left hand, I reach into the jacket pocket of his suit and carefully extract his cell-phone. As I hold the phone close to his chest and click away through its list of memory-saved numbers we start a very, very slow walk back through the carpark, and towards the Marina Café.

—no, please, don't turn away, my boy needs help—

I find the number I need and make the call. The conversation is brief and to the point. I tell her what she has to do. She doesn't believe me at first so I demand that she let me speak to someone else and she is offended. Then she comes around, realising finally that I'm serious and agrees to do what I'm asking. I can only pray that the others will take her seriously.

'It's done,' I tell Bobby and he hugs me a little tighter. Now we just need to complete our part, to give them enough time. I quickly realise that we've covered almost half the distance back to the café while I was talking on the phone. The café isn't large, but it seems to loom up before us like a caged lion. I'm terrified. I don't want to go any further, but I force myself onwards.

'Let's just stop here a moment, shall we?' Bobby whispers cautiously. 'He can't hear us here, surely?'

He stops and gently releases me from the embrace. Then he drops to his knee and for a split-second I think he is going to suddenly produce a ring from his pocket and propose marriage. Silly really. But instead he starts fumbling with his shoe and I realise he is pretending to tie his shoelace just to use up a little more time. It's a simple but brilliant strategy.

If I wasn't so terrified I might have actually applauded his quick thinking. It gives me another idea.

'Didn't you leave your briefcase in your car?' I ask softly. 'We should probably get that, don't you think?'

He looks up at me grinning broadly. 'Of course we should. How could we possibly go to the meeting without all our files?'

—please help him, you can stop him, don't walk away—

The mother's voice is persistent. I desperately want to respond to her, to communicate with her in some way, but don't know how. I squeeze my eyes shut and try to speak with her through my mind, but I can't feel anything happening.

When I open my eyes and look up I freeze in horror, yet again. Jonathon Green has just arrived and is weaving his way through the tables outside the café. A small squeal of dismay escapes me. Bobby looks up, curses quietly, and then bounces to his feet, breaking into a half-trot and calling out John's name. John stops and turns, only a few metres from the café's main door. Bobby slows down well short of the tables and gives John a 'come here' wave, calling out that he needs to catch up with him about a private matter before the meeting. John looks annoyed and glances at his watch, obviously trying to communicate that the meeting is due to start soon. He's expected inside and clearly doesn't want to keep everyone waiting. The mother's words tumble into my head again;

—don't let them go in, you must stop them—

Bobby has stopped moving now and is standing at the edge of the tabled area. He tells John that he won't keep him long, but that he really needs to discuss the matter in private. He gestures again, this time towards his car, telling John that he needs to show him something. I'm too terrified to move, silently praying that John will do what Bobby asks. I wonder what the bomber will be making of this. Will he have realised that we're onto him, or is he waiting until we are all inside the building?

—get them away, get them away, oh please—

I suck in a deep breath and begin to stride purposefully towards Bobby and the line of shops. I know it's important to give the illusion that we are all going to end up inside, eventually. As I move closer I see John look at his watch again and frown, clearly signalling that he isn't happy. Bobby is standing his ground though, just outside the perimeter of the tables.

Please, John. Don't go inside.

THIRTY-ONE

What the hell is going on? What are they doing?

He wasn't surprised when the girl boldly embraced the bastard from Auckland a few moments ago. He'd seen her flirting with him before; knew they were getting it together. He wouldn't be surprised if they'd already done the nasty.

He lightly caresses the small plastic box and bides his time. The stupid girl seems upset about something, probably about the wondrous display that he engineered here only two days ago. He'd thought then that this girl seemed to know about his bomb, but that simply isn't feasible. She can't possibly know anything. He still doesn't understand why she insisted they move away from the boat. It must have been some sort of coincidence. He can't think of any other possible explanation. But he's annoyed that she's out here today, wandering around, stuffing up his plans again. It fills him with rage.

Then the couple start heading back to the café and he relaxes, enjoying the rising tingle of excitement inside him. But they hug each other like limpets, moving ponderously.

It's so pathetic – a snail would beat them back.

But he is a relatively patient man and he waits, certain that he will soon be savouring the satisfaction of yet another perfect storm. Then they stop so the man can tie up his shoelace and, just as he is starting to get frustrated again, his heart flips with joy when he spots a late arrival. He thought that Green was already inside – although he hadn't seen him enter because the girl had distracted him. But this is better.

Now he knows for certain. He feels the rush again as he watches Green moving through the tables towards the door.

But then the bloody Aucklander calls out and stops him. Damn it. Surely they can just chat inside? Something's wrong, the girl isn't moving. She's just standing there.

He raises the small plastic box, ready to release the device he so lovingly prepared yesterday. He smoothes his thumb over the blue plastic button and steadies himself.

The girl starts forward again and he lowers the box. It looks like they're all going to go inside and that will be better. Much more certain within the confines of the building. Once they are inside everything will be in place and he will unleash hell.

THIRTY-TWO

As I make my way towards the men outside the café John finally huffs out a deep breath and begins to wend his way back through the tables towards Bobby. I force myself to keep walking, but slow my pace, carefully inching a little further to the left with each step, moving now more towards the carpark than the café. John reaches Bobby who immediately takes him by the arm and guides him away, towards his car. John seems uncomfortable with the intimacy of the touch but doesn't shake him off. I alter my direction more noticeably and speed up to reach Bobby's car at the same time as they do.

'What the hell are you two up to?' John demands.

'There's another bomb,' Bobby responds quickly, 'in the café. You can't go in there. Just jump in the car and we'll explain further.'

John's face pales. He has already experienced one explosion and was very, very lucky to survive relatively unscathed.

'How do you know? Did someone get a tip-off?' he asks quickly. 'Shit, what about the others? Who's in there?'

Bobby assures him that everyone else should be all right. Hopefully they are all out by now and the police should be on their way.

—please don't let him do this, he isn't a bad boy—

The mother's words are inside my head yet again and I quickly forget about Bobby and John. The bomber is still out there, and I hope fervently that Nikki has got everyone out. Suddenly I realise that I should be terrified, but I inexplicably now feel quite relaxed. I'm sure I have beaten him; my plan seems to have worked. No one is going to be killed today.

All of a sudden I'm overcome with the need to try and talk with him. To explain to him how upset he is making his mother, no matter how odd that seems. To try and get him to surrender to the police when they arrive. I don't understand why, but talking to him suddenly feels like the right thing to do.

I turn away from Bobby and John and begin to walk evenly, but decisively, back towards the piers. I'm going to confront him and persuade him to stop these attacks.

—you can help him, he'll listen to you—

I'm well on my way before I hear Bobby cry out to me to stop, it's not safe. I keep walking and I don't look back. The bomber must see me. I can feel it, but I suddenly feel comfortable that he is powerless to hurt me, or to hurt anyone today. I simply can't explain why I feel that, but I do. I keep on walking.

I hear running feet behind me and in a moment Bobby is there beside me, reaching out, laying a hand on my shoulder, trying to stop me. I hear him speaking but the words seem to just fall away around me. I gently brush his hand away and keep moving. So he rounds in front on me, blocking my way. I have to stop as he puts a hand on each of my shoulders, holding me back, talking rapidly at me from arm's length. I ignore his pleas and smile at him. All of a sudden I feel extremely confident, but I couldn't explain why if I tried.

'I'm okay, Bobby,' I say. 'I have to do this. I have to try and reach him.'

'But what if he's got a gun, or a knife, or another bloody bomb? What then? How will your psychic ability help you then?'

'He doesn't have any of those things,' I tell him emphatically. 'His bomb has failed this time and now he's confused. If I can just talk to him I think I can get him to surrender. You have to trust me.'

Frankly I've no idea where that little speech just came from, nor do I understand how I can be so damn certain that he's no longer a threat to me. But I just know, and I'm starting to accept that I should use my intuition, that I must trust my feelings. Grammy told me to face my fear and if this doesn't qualify then I don't know what will.

–he's just confused, talk to him, please–

I gently push Bobby's hands off my shoulders and start walking purposefully towards the top of pier A once again. After a few steps I can hear Bobby pursuing me again, but this time he falls in alongside and doesn't try and stop me.

'So where exactly is he, Lily?'

I don't point because I don't want to scare him off. 'He's in the cockpit of a motor cruiser that's tied up near the top of pier A. The one with the dark green stripe, straight ahead.'

'I see it.'

But then we both hear it. An engine springing into life. The throaty rumble of a motor cruiser starting up. We glance at each other briefly and start to run. We can see that the cruiser is already free from the pier. He must have cast off before starting the engine.

THIRTY-THREE

He doesn't understand what has gone wrong.

His beautiful, extraordinary device seems to have failed. He's devastated, almost overwhelmed with shock as he struggles to conceive how this could be.

He knew something was up when Green stepped away from the café. It made him furious. In an instant he reached his decision, swung his arm up and pressed firmly down on the big blue button.

But nothing happened. Nothing at all.

He jammed his thumb down again and again, not understanding. Not believing that the device wasn't going off. He knows he's not too far away. He'd tested the distance and is certain that he's well within range. He could be at least another ten metres away and the signal would still transmit. He wonders if they could be blocking it somehow. But it's inconceivable. They'd need to know exactly where the device is located – it's not just lying around obviously. And the signal would still broadcast through anything they could use to improvise a barrier.

He must have made a mistake. The thought deflates him and he slumps. But he never makes mistakes. He's brilliant with electronics – it can't possibly be an error on his part.

He sits up, onto his knees, and aims the transmitter out through the cockpit window, pushing the button again, shaking the small plastic box. Nothing. He throws it to the deck, half in disgust, half hoping that it will trigger the device as it had the other day – but still nothing happens.

Then he notices the girl. She's now beside the car with the two men, but she's staring straight at him. Directly at the boat he is on. How is she doing that?

Suddenly she starts walking straight towards him. His heart begins to race. She's going to lead the bastards straight to him, and he swiftly moves into survival mode. He has to get out of here. He can't return to the pier and escape through the carpark. They're all out there and without the chaos of the explosion they will notice him leaving. They'll see him, recognise him.

But he is too clever for them. He has a plan B.

He scrambles to the stern and quickly unties the single rope that still holds the boat to the pier. He'd already untied the others and released them earlier. He's prepared. It had made the boat bob about a little more than was desirable, but it will now save him precious time.

He slips quickly back up into the cockpit and reaches into the open space on the motor cruiser's dashboard that he had also created earlier, using a chisel and a crowbar. He finds the wires that he needs, that he has already pared back and exposed, and he twists them together, igniting the boat's big diesel engine. It rumbles into life and settles into a satisfyingly throaty purr.

He stays low in the cockpit, trying to hide behind the big leather seats, but knowing he will have to expose himself as he steers the boat out of the marina and onto the lake. He flips the hood up on his sweatshirt and raises himself just enough to see over the cockpit windscreen.

Then, without looking back, he opens up the big engine and the boat surges forward.

THIRTY-FOUR

Bobby curses loudly as the cruiser leaps forward and sharply turns away from us, pointing itself out into the vastness of Lake Breckenock. We stop running. I can see the dark shape of a man crouched over the wheel, trying to hide behind the big leather chairs. He is wearing a hoodie and he doesn't look back.

I turn to face Bobby, silently asking the question.

'No, I didn't see his face either,' he says. 'But he wasn't a big man. In fact it could just as easily have been a woman. What do you think?'

'It was a man, I'm certain of that. Not a woman.'

The cruiser speeds out onto the lake and then veers right, heading south towards Garston, the next suburb of Hawthorne around the lake from Wilton.

'He'll be heading for Bristow Bay,' says Bobby angrily. 'It'll be deserted this time of the day. That's where I'd go.'

I gape at him. 'Do you think? Why go there?'

'Because the banks of the lake are deep there and, assuming he doesn't own that cruiser and isn't worried about damaging it, he could easily run it right up into shore and just jump off the bow, straight on to dry land. The area is all parkland so it would be easy to have hidden a car there. He could get out onto the main roads in no time.'

'You seem to have a natural instinct for this.'

He blushes, bless him. 'Not really, I'm just a natural problem solver. That's what I'd do. But who knows where he's heading.'

'We should tell the police, get them to go there now.'

He nods in agreement. 'Yeah, we should, but they're not here yet.

We look around. The marina is quiet and almost deserted. I can see Jonathon Green watching us from the relative safety of Bobby's car and a large man ambling along in front of the line of shops. I recognise him immediately and shake my head in amazement. Steve Cassidy seems to have a knack for being in the wrong place at the wrong time.

'So what do we do now, All-Seeing One?' Bobby asks me with a crooked smile.

I can't believe it. The bomber is getting away, right now, as we speak, and he is teasing me. I shake my head at him and sigh.

'I'm damned if I know. Maybe we should steal a boat too and give chase?'

He laughs at first, and then cuts himself off, looking at me carefully. 'You aren't serious about that, are you?'

Before I'm able to answer him a police car arrives. I grab him by the hand and run towards it, dragging him along behind me.

'Come on, maybe there's still time to get roadblocks up around Bristow parklands.'

'I doubt it,' he calls back as we jog along, 'by the time we finish explaining all this he could be halfway to the moon.'

Instinctively I know he's right and that I'm going to have some pretty tough explaining to do for the police. How did I know about the bomb? Or where the bomber was? They aren't going to believe me just like that. It might be hours before they move to set up road-blocks anywhere.

But we keep running anyway. We have to try.

It's just before 8 am when the police first arrive on the scene. Thankfully they quickly accept that the bomber is getting away across the lake and they call it in, using the description that Bobby and I provide, sending cars to every conceivable place he could dock.

Then they start in with the questions. The bomb squad arrives and begins the slow process of clearing the scene. While I feel certain that there is only one bomb, I understand that they can't just accept my word and they search high and low.

Bobby and I are separated from the others, and from each other. The uniformed officers make us sit in separate cars and wait until the detectives arrive, clearly to ensure we're unable to collaborate on our accounts of what happened. Eventually Detective Dowd comes to sit with me in one of the cars.

She manages to keep a relatively straight face as I tell her about receiving another of my premonitions and I describe the series of events pretty much exactly as they occurred. I see no point in trying to disguise anything as I'm sure Bobby will be telling her the same story and if our tales don't match we will be here all day. Natalie is obviously sceptical, but she's heard me describe a premonition before so she doesn't seem totally surprised. She fires off all sorts of questions, making me go over and over the unlikely saga, clearly looking for inaccuracies. Trying to find holes. I don't think she finds any, but I wait uneasily for what seems like a lifetime while she interrogates Bobby afterwards.

I pass the time trying to keep tabs on the executive management team as they mill around an area of the carpark they have obviously been confined to. I can't see them all and I wonder if any of them are missing. But Nikki is with them and she's sobbing almost perpetually. When I'd called her on Bobby's cell-phone she got angry at first, thinking I was pulling some kind of sick stunt. But I'd been pretty blunt with her and she'd quickly come around, relaying the message to the rest of the team in alarm: 'There's a bomb. We have to get out, and we have to get out through the back

228

or the bomber will see us leave.' I imagine there will have been much disbelief, even some panic. It must have been terrifying – the bomb could have gone off at any moment.

Natalie tells me little, but she does clarify one thing I hadn't understood.

Apparently the restaurant owner searched quickly and found the bomb, knowing instantly what was out of place in his restaurant. I still don't know what it was disguised as, but this crazy guy – desperate to save his business from being destroyed – picked the damn thing up and ran out the back, tossing it into a big steel rubbish bin. This is probably why the bomb didn't go off – because it was moved too far from the bomber's remote control or perhaps the steel walls of the bin deflected the signal? Natalie wasn't really clear and wouldn't offer any detail on how the remote triggering should work.

Everyone else just got out and ran away, out the back door and down to the far end of the shops. They stayed hidden until the police arrived.

But then Steve wandered into the middle of it all. Seeming to register that something was going on he watched quietly as the police arrived and we ran over to them. Then he simply sat down at one of the tables outside the café and waited for them. It only took a few minutes for one of the uniforms to recognise him, then they ushered him over and sat him down inside a third car. He's still there, looking bored and frustrated. I'm sure they will interview him soon, before they decide to take us all down to the station to make more formal statements. I actually feel sorry for Steve. I'm quite certain now that he isn't the bomber, but the police can't be so sure. They just see that he is here yet again, at the scene, and they aren't going to ease up on him in a hurry.

An hour or so later Bobby and I are reunited at the station, but Steve remains isolated.

After providing our separate statements again, in more detail, we are made to wait in a small interview room. We ask repeatedly if they have found the cruiser, if they have caught the bomber. But they won't tell us anything. So we just sit around, becoming more and more bored and frustrated, before I have an idea.

Remembering that Megan is working today, I fish out my cell-phone and call her.

'Don't tell me,' Megan answers in a low voice. 'You're at Wilton Marina, aren't you?'

I smile involuntarily, 'I thought I was the psychic here?'

'Oh. My. God. You're not?'

'Actually, not any more. We were earlier, but right now we're in one of your interview rooms, here at the station. It feels like we've been here all damn morning.'

'We? Who are you with?'

I tell her.

'Okay. Wow,' she says softly. I can tell she is dying to slip through to check Bobby out, but probably would get in trouble if she did. 'So, did you see him?' she asks.

'The bomber? Yeah, sort of. Just his back. He was wearing a hoodie.'

'And everyone's okay? I heard that it didn't go off.'

'All okay. It didn't go off.'

'No way, that's amazing.'

'Hey Meg,' I speak quietly, conspiratorially, 'Do you know if they found the cruiser?'

She hesitates, but only for a second. She must be checking to ensure no one can overhear her. She could lose her job for telling me this.

'Yep, hours ago. He was long gone though.'

'Where?'

'Would you believe he just tied it up at Garston Wharf and walked away? Pretty casual huh? They reckon he either had a car waiting or he simply jumped on a bus, or just walked into town. One witness, an old guy, saw a short man in a grey hoodie climb off the boat and walk away about fifteen minutes before our car arrived.'

'Damn it,' I say, feeling angry. We could have driven to Garston Wharf in less than ten minutes from Wilton Marina. If we hadn't stopped to talk with the police we could have been there as he was tying up the boat and walking away. Damn – that's so frustrating.

'They've got forensics all over it right now. We're calling round all the taxi companies and the uniforms are out there chasing down any bus drivers that went through that way this morning. Hopefully we'll get something soon.' Megan pauses, 'You all right there?'

'Yeah, I'm fine,' I reply, not feeling it at all. 'I'm just hacked off. We almost caught this guy, but he got away yet again. How does he do that?'

'I don't know, maybe he's just lucky? Who knows?' She pauses again, 'Hey look, Lily. I have to go now, work stuff here to do, okay? I'll call you later, this evening. Okay?'

'Sounds great, talk to you then,' I say and hang up.

Bobby is waiting patiently as I put the phone away. I tell him quickly what I've discovered from Meg. He's surprised.

'So much for my wild theory about ditching the boat at Bristow Bay. But that's pretty damn bold, to just pull up and park it at the wharf there.'

I agree. It's hard to comprehend.

About half an hour later they finally let us leave. This is even more frustrating as they don't even ask us any more questions. I wonder if they simply forgot we were there, but I don't ask.

We don't see Megan as we're ushered out. I'm not even sure where her desk is.

'So what now, Boss?' I ask. 'I guess it's back to work?'

'Uh, I guess so,' he sounds as disappointed as I feel. 'But not quite yet, eh? I'm starving, haven't eaten all day. Can I buy you lunch first?'

I smile. 'Best offer I've had in a while.'

The lunch is nice, but what's best is that we manage to find so much to talk about. We've spent most of the morning at the police station sitting together in silence. I guess there's something about being in a place like that that makes you want to say as little as possible. Like they may have the room bugged, or they're watching you through a one-way mirror system. Maybe I've been watching too much TV.

We hardly talk about work, brush right over our frightening experiences that very morning, and I even manage to avoid pestering him about visiting his parents. We just chat about random things, like you do on a date. It feels good. It's nice.

Somehow we get to talking about movies. Doesn't everyone? Bobby mentions that movie *The Sixth Sense* and I half expect him to ask me if I see dead people too, just like Megan had. But he doesn't. Instead he comments on how it was such a change for Bruce Willis, from all his *Die Hard* action-type roles. Then he makes an odd comment.

'You know, it makes me wonder about *our* bad guy. This crazy-arse bomber that's chasing us around. Why the hell is he doing it? Motive, I mean. You know, when you think about the bad guys in movies, they all have clear reasons for their actions. Understandable objectives. Mind you – their motives weren't always clear until the end of the movie – but you knew that the bad guys wanted something specific, didn't you?'

I nod. At the table behind me a small boy suddenly let's fly with a minor tantrum. Something about wanting another fizzy drink. We're distracted for a moment, but then Bobby carries on.

'But, for the life of me, I don't get our guy. Is he just crazy, or is he actually trying to prove something. I can't imagine what he's gaining by doing these things.'

I think about the words I've received from the bombers mother but can't recall anything that might suggest his motive. His mother doesn't think he's a bad boy, but he's definitely doing some very bad things. It makes me wonder.

'Something must have set him off. I mean, people don't just go crazy overnight,' I offer, immediately realising the irony in my words. Only days ago I thought that I was suddenly going mad. But I push this aside quickly as Bobby continues.

'Yes, but what was it, I wonder?' he agrees. 'What could have happened to him that would make him flip out and go around blowing people up? It's just so extreme. I can't imagine being that crazed, that possessed, that full of hate. Can you?'

Actually I think I can but I don't respond immediately. I still have bad memories of losing the plot myself when my mother died. I'd felt such a terrible, gnawing pain inside for months afterwards. I remember being hellishly angry at everything then and I know I'd been quite a handful for Dad – and when he was grieving so deeply himself. But to be so full of hate that you'd actually go out and murder other people? That I don't understand. Not at all.

But then I recall the intense feelings that flattened me on level three only last week. The depth of anger and raw despair that I sensed from Adam Mitchell's spirit as he railed against the injustice and senselessness of his tragedy. Adam's fury had been so concentrated it seemed to have physically manifested itself and caused a vase of flowers to topple over. I feel myself shiver at the memory.

'Are you okay, Lily?' Bobby asks, interrupting my reflection. I realise I haven't answered his question and now really don't want to. I actually can imagine something possessing a person with enough venom to make them want to kill. I felt that intensity from Adam.

As I open my mouth to try and respond the little boy at the table behind us erupts into another tantrum, this time knocking a vacant chair over beside me. His mother looks mortified and is trying to calm him. Everyone is staring. Abruptly she gathers him up and drags him, literally kicking and screaming, from the restaurant. Another chair topples as they leave, then it's finally quiet again. Bobby mutters something under his breath.

'What did you say?' I'm curious.

'Full of the devil, that one,' he repeats, looking a little sheepish. 'Just a silly old saying . . . for naughty children. I feel sorry for her, that poor woman.'

'Maybe you should go after her and offer your services as a problem-solving fix-it man?'

'I don't know Lily,' his smile is contagious. 'Ridding children of demonic possession is a little outside my usual areas of expertise. Do you think there's a market for it?'

I smile, but don't respond. He continues.

'Maybe that's what's wrong with our crazy bomber. Maybe he's possessed by the devil?'

I'm not sure if he's joking or not. I frown at him.

'Something's definitely getting under his skin, but I don't think it's the devil.' As I say the words I get a strange feeling – like a light has been switched on inside me, but the feeling isn't as clear as others I've had recently.

I have to shake my head to get back to the here and now as I momentarily lose track of the conversation, trying to – unsuccessfully – explore that faint glimmer of light.

'No, probably not,' Bobby says. 'Who knows? I guess I'm getting a bit off-track. I've had my eyes opened to so many supernatural things lately.'

'Hmm, you really have turned to the dark side, haven't you?'

He reddens then, just a little. It's very cute. Thankfully we seem to mutually decide to let the subject drop and we are both quiet for the first time during our lunch date. Whatever the illuminating idea might have been is now lost.

I feel oddly frustrated.

THIRTY-FIVE

The waiter is suddenly hovering and Bobby waves dismissively to decline the offer of more drinks. I check the time – it's a little after 2 pm. The thought of going into the office depresses me.

We established earlier that this morning's aborted management meeting would be rescheduled for first thing tomorrow and I know there isn't much we can progress at work until that meeting is completed. Having the new executive team appointed is a good step forward, but we now need their buy-in to our realignment plans before going further. I decide quickly that a little time out might be better.

'Bobby, would you mind terribly if I don't go back to work?'

'No, of course not,' he responds quickly, making no effort to talk me around. 'You've had a pretty harrowing morning. Go put your feet up. We can catch up again tomorrow.'

He seems to have abruptly reverted to a manager-employee tone and I immediately regret asking and ruining the moment. Most of the discussion over lunch had been light and cheery and, I think, we both really enjoyed each other's company. However, I'm pretty sure he's as disappointed as I am to have our 'date' come to an end.

Bobby looks at his watch. 'We should get going. I'll get the bill. You go and grab us a taxi. Then we can both pick up our cars from the marina and be on our way. Sound like a plan?'

I nod and stand, thanking him for the meal and the good company. He offers me a warm smile that briefly causes butterfly tingles in my chest.

I find us a taxi and we're back at the marina in no time. Just as we pull up in the carpark I take a deep breath, lean over and plant a small kiss on his cheek. He seems surprised.

'What was that for?'

'Just a thank you, again. For everything today. For believing me.' I become embarrassed as I say it and hastily bail out of the taxi, just turning to give him a small wave as I reach my car. Clambering in quickly, I lower my head and begin digging around in my handbag, making a show of looking for something. As I peek sideways out the window I see Bobby reach his car and I duck my head again as he gets it started and drives away. Only then do I stop fluffing around and sit back in my seat.

It's been such a huge day. So much has happened and I need to try and get my head around it all. So I just sit there, looking out into the carpark. The Marina Café is closed and there are very few people around. The police seem to have done everything they need to do and have left the area already. I wonder if they're having any luck tracking the bomber down. I hope so.

I think about what happened here earlier. How I was able to receive messages from the bomber's mother, but unable to return them. Unable to reassure her that we were doing all we could, that we were trying to help him. The one-way nature of this psychic thing frustrates me. But I think about how I had been able to thwart his plans and I allow myself a small smile of self-congratulation. It feels good. Well done, me.

I start thinking about Grammy, and then Rosie. I still haven't figured out how she knew to send me out to Bluff Creek. Suddenly the strange feeling I had at lunch returns. My illumination in the darkness. I'm pretty sure the answer is within my grasp, only I just can't pin it down. I rack my brain to try and understand. What the heck was it?

Looking around for inspiration it suddenly occurs to me that I never heard from the bomber's mother again after he fled the scene on the cruiser. Why is that? Does she follow him around? I think about the other bombings. It's suddenly very clear to me that I've only heard her words when the bomber is close by. Does that mean that a spirit can follow someone around? Is that possible? Is that how it works? There's so much I just don't know.

I realise that Steve has often been nearby when the bomber's mother has spoken to me. Is she following him around too or could he be working with the bomber? But it doesn't feel right. Why would he help pull Bobby out of the water? And he saved my life too. Perhaps he did those things to deflect attention?

I don't think this is it though – it's not the answer that's nagging at me. I think back to lunch with Bobby, trying to relive how pleasant the date-like lunch had been – and then suddenly it hits me, crashing through like a ton of bricks, and I have the answer.

I struggle frantically to line up all the facts with what little I know of the subject. I can't make it work, but the idea grabs hold of me so firmly that I become certain I am right. But what should I do now? How can I prove it? Perhaps I should just leave it alone?

I begin scrambling in my handbag for my cell-phone, but stop dead as soon as I pull it out. It's no use to me, I don't have her number. Damn it. So stupid. I'll have to go out to see her again.

I start the engine quickly and drive out of the carpark. I need to know if my theory on this is right. I need to talk to Grammy.

The sign in the door of the Crystal Heart reads 'CLOSED' so I keep driving and pull up outside Grammy's bush-enclosed cottage. I practically leap from the car and bound to her door, knocking feverishly as soon as I reach it. After an interminable wait the door eases open.

'Sar shan, my chai,' she greets me pleasantly enough. 'This is a surprise.' Grammy is clearly not used to being disturbed on a Monday afternoon and I notice her look past me to ensure I haven't dragged another friend along this time. But she is safe, I'm alone today. She's dressed once again in a comfortable tracksuit, with no hint of the gypsy flamboyance of her working get-up.

'Hello Grammy,' I reply, a little breathlessly. I'm filled with a desperate urgency to pick her brains. 'I have a question. May I come in?'

She seems a little bemused but steps back, opening the door wider, and gestures that I should enter. I make my way through to the cosy lounge. I hover nervously as she drifts past me, heading for the kitchen.

'I will put the kettle on,' Grammy announces. She watches me curiously as she fills the kettle with water and flicks the switch. 'You seem a little agitated.'

'I'm not sure how to put this,' I say hesitantly. 'I was wondering if . . . well . . . if you would be able to tell me about being possessed. You know . . . spiritually.'

She raises an eyebrow quizzically. 'You think you are possessed?'

'No Grammy, not me. Someone I know.'

She stares at me for a long time without saying anything and I begin to wonder if I have made a mistake in coming back here. Her moods seem to vary wildly and I can't be sure if she has any desire to help me. She might just as easily mock me and belittle my idea. I feel small under her gaze and begin to doubt myself. Maybe I have this all wrong? Then she finally speaks.

'It is a very rare and difficult thing for a spirit to possess a living being. It is not one of my areas of expertise.'

She takes another long pause and I have a small moment of déjà vu. Bobby used a very similar phrase in relation to this same subject during our lunch together. Except then we had been joking about being possessed by the devil.

My theory is a little different to that.

Grammy folds her arms across her chest and continues, 'Is this "someone that you know" not passing themselves over willingly?'

'What do you mean?'

'You know so little, chai,' she shakes her head as she berates me gently. 'It is like facing a blank page and having to fill every line from scratch.'

I try to ignore the unnecessary dig. 'That's why I'm here. I need your help. Will you share what you know with me or should I go and look it up on the internet?'

'Ha,' she snorts. 'Your mother's looks and her temper to boot. Be calm, chai, of course I will help you.' She turns away and busies herself making two cups of tea – again without asking me what I want or how I like it. I can't decide if she somehow knows what I would like, or if she just doesn't care and would do it her way anyway.

As she splashes a little milk into both cups, she asks, 'Is the person that you believe to be possessed aware that he or she is being used in this manner?'

'No, I'm pretty sure not.' My curiosity is off the scale now. I wait again.

'Then that is a very unusual situation. Do you know who the spirit is that is taking liberties with this person?'

I nod slowly. 'I think I do, but I can't be sure.'

My answer clearly intrigues her. 'Tell me more,' she demands, and so I do.

My tea is quite cool by the time I finish outlining my theory. Grammy has listened attentively, barely interrupting, and only to clarify certain points, but never – in sharp contrast to her usual manner - deriding my guesswork.

When I finish she has an unfathomable expression on her face as she sits in deep thought. I sit silently and wait. After some time she announces that she knows what to do and, surprisingly, produces a small cell-phone from her pocket.

She makes a call and talks very quickly, using a lot of Romany words that I do not understand. Clearly whoever she is talking with does and the conversation seems heated. Then she suddenly flips the phone shut and looks at me.

'My cousin Anna is on her way,' she says. 'We will get to the bottom of this soon.'

Anna arrives in less than ten minutes – she must live nearby.

Grammy disappears into the kitchen and potters around, eventually returning with a large tray of cake and biscuits and three fresh cups of tea. It seems that Anna is not going to be asked how she likes her tea either. This actually comforts me somewhat.

Anna turns out to be a short and slim woman, and younger than I expected. I had pictured someone closer to my grandmother's age, but she can't be any more than thirty at the most. She has bland, dull brown hair, which frames a friendly, if rather plain, face. Grammy introduces me and clarifies that Anna is her uncle's youngest daughter, and a distant cousin to me. I sharply realise that there are probably many more relations out there that I have no idea about and I feel a small stab of resentment at my mother for her life decisions.

Anna takes a seat and quickly helps herself to the cake and tea as Grammy turns to me to finally explain why she has bought Anna here.

'Anna has the gift of mediumship,' Grammy announces bluntly. 'She has agreed to submit herself and help us to confirm your suspicions.'

I turn wide-eyed towards Anna, who half-smiles back with a little shrug. She seems resigned and calm and continues eating her piece of cake. I have a vague idea of what a medium can do, but have never met one. She seems so normal.

'Oh my God,' I finally manage to say. 'Anna, I can't ask you to do this . . .'

She shrugs again. 'It's not a biggie. Mum's done a deal with Kath.'

'What?' I turn to Grammy, unclear of what this means.

'It is nothing, chai. We have agreed to an exchange of services, that is all.'

'I don't understand.'

She rolls her eyes and then explains. 'The process can be draining – when Anna uses her gift. She was supposed to work tonight but will instead help us out here today. So I will compensate her with a return reading. It is merely an exchange of services, a barter arrangement.'

I must look bewildered, so she continues. 'Anna is family. We cannot pay her for her efforts, but we cannot leave her out of pocket, obviously.'

For some reason I never really imagined Grammy's shop as being her primary source of income. I don't know why, but it seems more like a hobby. And clearly Anna makes a living from her gift too. I'm deeply touched. Grammy has believed in me enough to have effectively paid for someone to help to prove me right – or wrong as the case may yet be. I stumble over my words.

'I can pay . . .' I begin, and then stop, unsure if that would be appropriate.

'No,' says Anna softly. 'That wouldn't be right.'

Grammy frowns at me and I instantly feel that I've crossed some unseen line.

'I'm sorry . . . and thank you,' I say to Grammy, with great feeling. I then turn to Anna and repeat my thanks to her also. I have no idea if this will actually work, or what to expect, but the realisation that I have an entire extended family that I have never previously met – and that they are prepared to help me out so readily – is very touching. I'm humbled.

'Enough,' Grammy snorts a little derisively, but this time I don't mind. 'Anna must prepare herself, so we will need to be patient, and quiet. You understand?'

I don't really, but I say nothing and nod.

Anna then produces a CD from her handbag and passes it to Grammy without comment. Grammy loads it into her CD player and starts it up. The instrumental music is low, gentle and rhythmic – quite soothing and relaxing. Grammy then draws the curtains and switches on a small table lamp that dims the room considerably. Then she sits down and quietly sips at her tea, becoming quite still.

I sit rigidly, unsure what I am supposed to do, if anything. My eyes dart back and forth between Anna and Grammy, waiting for something to happen. For what seems a very long time nothing does. Anna closes her eyes and relaxes back into the chair, occasionally adjusting herself to be more comfortable, as if she is settling in for a nap. Grammy just cradles her teacup and stares off into space, looking at neither Anna nor me. I watch Anna's breathing settling, getting slower and more even until it seems she has actually fallen asleep. Still nothing happens.

I turn back to look at Grammy, expecting her to begin chanting or to wave a magic wand or something. But she just sits quietly, as still as a statue.

THIRTY-SIX

The wait is endless. I want to fidget and develop a desperate need to scratch my nose but fight it off, remaining as still and quiet as I can. Only my eyes move as they dart between the two women. I try looking away, staring into space as Grammy is doing and then quickly look back at one of them, expecting to see some form of radical change, but none comes. I begin to feel disappointed and frustrated.

Then Anna twitches.

Just once and her head lolls back and forward slightly and stops. I see Grammy move slightly, adjusting her gaze towards her much younger cousin.

Anna twitches again, this time more pronounced, and she seems to shiver as she leans forward slightly with her back beginning to arch. Grammy is alert again, watching carefully.

Lurching slightly Anna's head lolls fully forward. I'm too freaked out to move, I think I may have stopped breathing for a few seconds.

Abruptly Anna's head rises up again and her eyes are open. They seem glazed at first but they slowly clear, revealing heavily dilated pupils. She seems to find her focus and gazes for a minute across at Grammy, and then she turns and stares unblinkingly at me. When she speaks her voice seems deeper than it was before.

'Lily. My little Lily,' her words are clear, but throaty. 'Hello again.'

I can't speak. I stare at Anna in disbelief, completely forgetting everything that I had so convincingly told my grandmother. My mind goes blank and I know my mouth must be gaping open like a fish out of water.

My theory was right.

Before I can respond Anna turns her face to Grammy and speaks again. 'Hello mother,' she says, pausing to lick her lips. 'It's been a while.'

'Yes it has, Evelyn. Too long,' Grammy replies evenly.

'I couldn't get through. I doubt you'll believe me, but I tried and I just couldn't get through.'

'Sometimes it is harder when the bond is closer. You might have known this if you'd taken more interest when I tried to counsel you,' Grammy tells her righteously.

Anna's face goes blank and her eyes glaze again, her head lolling slightly. But then she rallies and the eyes focus once more. 'Please don't lecture me, mother. This is not an easy thing – and Anna will wear more quickly if we argue.'

Grammy gives her a dark look. She is not one to back down easily. But she acknowledges the rebuke with a gesture and relents, settling back into the couch. Then Anna turns to face me. My heart almost stops. Her unblinking eyes watch me intently. Her lips now carry the faintest of smiles.

'Mum?' I ask tentatively, finally finding my voice.

Her smile broadens and, although I am still looking at Anna's bland and open face, I can see her there. I can somehow see my mother's beautiful eyes and perfect features. Tears begin to trickle down my cheeks.

'You're all grown up, my little princess. You're so beautiful.'

Oh God, how I've missed her. I want to hug her but I don't know the rules. I don't know what is allowed or how long she can be with us. My voice cracks.

'I miss you so much, Mum, so very much. It wasn't fair that you had to leave us.'

There are no tears in Anna's eyes, but I can hear the sorrow in my mother's voice.

'I would do anything to be with you now, Lily, you must know that. There is so much that I didn't tell you. I was so selfish. Can you ever forgive me?'

'Of course I forgive you, of course I do,' I say with as much force as I can muster between the sobs that now wrack my body. I'm reeling in shock and my emotions are turning themselves inside out.

Eleven years after her death I'm talking with my mother. I was just a child, only nine years old. My heart is literally exploding with joy and sorrow all at once.

I realise that I am now, finally, able to have the conversation that I've dreamed about almost every night since she was torn from my life, but I'm still not really prepared for it. I felt certain that I was right, but I never expected to have her come through like this – and so clearly this time. Collecting myself, I want to confirm what I already know.

'It was you, wasn't it? Guiding Rosie?' I ask quietly.

'Yes Lily that was me.' She pauses, gathering herself. 'I couldn't get through to you either. I tried and I tried, just as I have been trying to get through to your grandmother, but nothing worked. I just couldn't get a message through at all.'

Suddenly Grammy chimes in, clearly intrigued. 'How did you do it, Evelyn?'

Anna sits back in the chair, turning slightly to better address us both. Her eyes remain focused and wide, but the expression on her face stays oddly subdued.

'Trial and error mainly,' she says clearly, 'out of desperation. I have been watching you, Lily. I felt certain that something was finally happening to you, but I felt so helpless, and so guilty. I should have warned you. I thought I had more time.'

I nod supportively, wanting to hear everything, desperate to understand.

'But I couldn't get through in the usual ways, no matter how hard I tried. So I tried entering people, to try and communicate with you, but they all blocked me.'

I have so many questions already. What are the usual ways? How does a spirit enter someone? But I hold my tongue and nod encouragement for her to continue.

'Then poor little Rosie had that accident and broke her arm, and knocked herself out. It seemed providential somehow. So I tried entering her while she was unconscious and actually made a little progress. I got in, but I couldn't make it work.'

'How do you mean, make it work?' I ask, unable to help myself.

Anna's head lolls slightly and the eyes glaze and refocus before she answers. 'We don't have much time, I'm sorry.' She pauses again momentarily, seemingly to reassert her presence within Anna. 'I couldn't work it. I mean, I couldn't move or talk.' She plunges on. 'So I tried a couple more times and found that I could finally get a fair connection when Rosie was asleep and less guarded. That was when I wrote the note and knocked on your window. Rosie had been fast asleep, exhausted and an easier . . . um, target, I guess.'

I'm stunned. My mother had taken possession of my poor little cousin and had been controlling her each time that she had come over to my house and had one of her strange fainting spells. My Aunt Louise is never going to believe this, not that I'll ever tell her.

'But it worked,' she continues. 'It worked and you made it here, and now you know. This is such a huge relief for me, Lily. You can never fully understand how hard it has been for me, watching you and not being able to be there and help you. To guide you.'

My heart wrenches again at these words, the despair in her voice so plain to hear, while Anna's face remains relatively impassive. It's such a bewildering feeling. I'm both wildly overjoyed yet desperately struggling to understand how this can be happening.

'You don't get the images at night. Do you, Lily?' my mother asks.

'No, no images at all, at least not so far. Just words in my head.'

Anna barely moves, but I sense an exhalation – like a sigh of relief.

'That's good. I hated my curse, or gift, whatever you want to call it. I received images, many frightening, and I tried to block them.' She pauses in reflection and then continues. 'I took sleeping pills at night to keep the images at bay. I didn't tell your father. I didn't want him to think of me as some kind of circus freak. I didn't want you to worry either, so I didn't warn you. I thought I had more time. I'm so sorry, Lily. I never meant to leave you like that.' Anna's upper body rocks ever so slightly. I don't know what to say. It wasn't her fault she died – it was an accident.

Then my mother, via Anna, speaks again.

'Greg seems happy now . . .' she breaks off and Anna's eyes glaze over again. She mutters something unintelligible and then her eyes clear, once again wide and unblinking. '. . . with Cheryl,' she finishes with some effort. 'Are you happy, Lily?'

My mind reels, desperately trying to find the right answer. 'I cried myself to sleep every night for years after you . . . left us. It was . . . horrible. But Cheryl is nice. And she cares about us both, but she's not you. She never could be.'

Anna's head lolls a little more and then turns towards Grammy.

'You will help her, won't you, mother?'

Grammy does not hesitate, 'Of course I will, Evelyn. As I would have helped you if you had let me.' I frown at her –

she still seems hell-bent on stirring up a fight – but she ignores me.

My mother tries not to bite though, instead pleading with her. 'Don't force her to use her gift, please. Let her find her own way. Please just be there for her, in my place.'

Grammy appears irritated. 'You think I have not learned patience in all my years? Dordi, chai, I will not push her. She is as headstrong as you ever were, if not more so.'

Anna sinks back in her chair, her head falling backwards and eyes closing. I feel a flash of anger and despair.

'Mum, are you still there? Don't go.' I rise from my seat.

Anna's head jolts up again and her eyes snap open –they are still dilated. My mother appears to still be with us. She faces me once again.

'I am almost out of time,' she tells us. 'I can feel Anna trying to re-exert control. I must go very soon.' She pauses only momentarily. 'Lily, your Grammy can be difficult, but there is much she can teach you. Please persevere. Be thick-skinned. You need to understand so much about the spirit word to help you manage your gift.'

I sense Grammy stiffen, but I do not look across and she mercifully stays quiet.

'I cannot seem to reach you as others can, but I will always be there, watching over you. Believe this, please. We can talk again another day.'

My heart is swelling in my chest and tears once again begin streaming down my face. There is something hard blocking my throat. Anna slumps back in the chair and a few, final words slip out as her eyes close again.

'Trust in yourself, Lily, and remember . . . I will always love you.'

And then she is gone. Anna slumps and her head slips to one side. She is breathing evenly and seems once again to simply be sound asleep. There's a brief moment where I think I feel my mother before me, around me, within me. But then the feeling is gone too and I lower my head into my hands and weep softly.

Grammy makes more tea.

She leaves me sitting there and slips into the kitchen, pottering around once more. Anna remains sleeping deeply in her chair. I slowly recover myself, stunned at this incredible turn of events. Of all the things that have happened to me in the last few days, this has had the most extraordinary effect on me. I can scarcely believe it. I have just had a conversation with my mother, who has been dead for more than half my lifetime. I struggle to comprehend how this is possible. I stare at the sleeping woman across from me. How did she do it?

And then I think about poor little Rosie, who had allowed my mother in also, but because she had been weak, not willing.

Grammy returns and places a fresh cup of tea before me. She hasn't made one for Anna. She sits back down and gazes across at Anna before turning back to me.

'You would not have believed it if you hadn't seen it with your own eyes, would you?'

I shake my head, still unsure if I believe.

'She has an incredible gift, our Anna. And she understands its value,' she says. 'By this I mean her uniqueness, and what she can give to others, not the monetary value.'

She watches me to ensure I understand the difference. I do and I nod.

'She could gain substantial financial rewards with her gift if she chose to,' Grammy continues. 'But she chooses not to. You see, her gift is quite draining. She will sleep now for two or three hours. When she awakens she will remember nothing of the conversation we had with your mother, as she was not there. She had given herself over. Do you understand?'

This time I think that I do actually understand, if only vaguely, and I nod again. My mind is still reeling with questions, but Grammy seems to anticipate them.

'You do not understand what she meant by "not being able to reach you as other's do", do you Lily?' I shake my head. 'You receive words from the dead, do you not?'

'Yes . . . I do.'

'But your mother could not get words through to you, as others seem able to.'

'No,' I admit.

'If your mother had shown more interest in her heritage, in our unique Romany roots, she would have known that this is quite common. Often those in our family with gifts are unable to communicate with close family members and other loved ones who have passed. Especially where the bond was strong during life.'

'Why not? It seems so unfair.'

Grammy snorts and shakes her head, 'Life is not fair, chai. Why would you expect the afterlife to be any fairer?'

'So that's why you can't communicate with her either? Because you were so close in life?' I shoot back at her.

She purses her lips and looks away. There is silence for almost a full minute, only broken by Anna's soft sleep breathing. Then she rolls her eyes and sighs dramatically.

'Do not confuse the depth of our relationship with closeness, or lack of it. Evelyn was my daughter and I loved her immensely, even when we disagreed. I will always love her.' Her tone softens, 'I was never able to provide a reading for her in life and neither could she reciprocate. After she passed I tried many times to reach her, but I could not.' She clears her throat, fixing me with a meaningful glare, 'In Romany lore it is believed that this blockage exists to protect those with gifts from losing themselves when a loved one passes. Just imagine how easy it would be to slip away from the world of the living if we were able to converse freely with those spirits who meant so much to us during our lives. The emotional turmoil would be enormous. It would be wrong. It would lead to madness.'

Her eyes glaze over at that and I suddenly understand. She cannot communicate with my mother, or with my dead grandfather for that matter. I know immediately that his passing still causes her great sorrow. She would give anything to still be able to communicate with him. It torments her daily.

'I'm sorry, Grammy. I didn't mean . . .' I tail off, embarrassed now. Then I remember Anna, asleep, right there with us. 'But surely, couldn't Anna, or someone else –'

She shakes her head fervently. 'No, my chai. What we have done here today is a very special thing. Anna did not know Evelyn very well, as there was a big age difference and they lived miles apart as they grew up. Anna's mother was not happy. To bring Evelyn through like this stretches our family laws and traditions greatly. I have never asked of them this way before, nor will I again.'

I don't know what to say. I feel terrible, but incredibly thankful. But I have to be honest with myself. If I had known that Grammy was drawing such a big family favour I would still have wanted to go ahead. It may be selfish, but I'm still very glad we had done it.

'Thank you,' I finally say again quietly.

She dismisses me with a wave of her hand. 'It was necessary. This needs to be very clear for you, chai. If I had simply tried to explain you would still have been full of doubts.' She hesitates, 'And I was not certain myself. What Evelyn managed to achieve through this little girl is rare. You should be very proud of your mother, to have accomplished this thing – this full possession of an unwilling living being. Her love for you must be very strong indeed.'

There is pride in her voice and a lump forms in my throat. I am again humbled.

'Will Rosie be all right?'

'The child was not injured during the possessions?'

'No, not physically.'

'Then she just needs sleep, as Anna is doing now, and she will be fine. The only ill effects of passing yourself over to a spirit are exhaustion and the blackout. Anna will remember nothing of the time she was gone, and neither will your little cousin.'

I feel enormous relief. If Rosie had been hurt, or damaged mentally in some way because of me I would not have been able to live with it.

'So, does that mean we can talk to Mum again sometime, when Anna's recovered?'

Grammy frowns and looks exasperated. 'You must listen more closely, Lily. We have already spoken of this. Anna's efforts today were a very, very special thing. This will never be repeated. It would not be right.'

I did already know this, but her words crush me once again. The brief interlude could only ever be a one-off. I close my eyes to hold in the tears and think back over every word my mother shared with me in those magical few minutes. She will always be with me, watching me, loving me. The lump forms in my throat again and I hug myself fiercely. I understand why it has to be this way, but it doesn't make it any easier.

An arm gently encircles me and I realise that Grammy has moved to kneel in front of my seat and is wrapping me in her arms. It seems so out-of-character for her; she's always been so standoffish in our previous meetings, so aloof.

I lean in and hug her back intensely.

THIRTY-SEVEN

The next morning, a little before 7.30 am, I arrive at the Mt Wallace Hotel. It's looking a little more tired than I last remember it. While everything about it still gives an impression of solidity, the grandeur has faded. Not with neglect, just age. Still, the lobby is open and pleasantly warm regardless, but it's no longer majestic.

I stayed on at Grammy's for a while last night and she cooked dinner. Anna eventually came around and, after a strong cup of tea and something to eat, she slipped away quietly. It was a strange situation as, by some unwritten mutual understanding, we spoke very little afterwards and did not discuss the channeling at all. I don't think the subject is considered taboo, just private.

Grammy was actually quite pleasant during the evening and proved to be a fine cook too. After Anna left we chatted a little about channeling, a little about clairvoyance, but mainly about my life growing up with my mum and Greg – and then with Cheryl. I surprised myself and opened up to her quite a bit and she surprised me by maintaining a pleasant tone almost throughout. I had expected some sharp comments aimed at Dad, but she seemed to be holding herself back. Perhaps my mother's plea for her to help me had touched a nerve, or maybe she was just lonely and enjoyed the company. Either way it was a nice evening and I actually slept quite well last night. I feel pretty good today, a warmth deep inside from knowing that my mother is still with me, watching over me.

As I enter the hotel I immediately spot Brendan Armstrong blustering away ferociously into his cell-phone. It's like the thing is glued to his ear. I feel sorry for whoever is on the receiving end of his call as Brendan is almost spitting with contempt. Someone's getting a bollocking. I veer away and head towards the reception desk, but quickly see the sign and veer again. A small blackboard is situated just outside a pair of closed ornate double doors. It reads simply 'Westwood'.

Then I notice Jason Connor, from IT, lounging on a large sofa a little way down from the sign. He must have been drafted in to help cover any technical questions at the meeting. I imagine there'll be a few and I don't expect to see much of Don for the next week or so. I try to pretend I don't see Jason, but he's too quick, waving immediately. He rises and trots over.

'Hey there,' he says with a glint in his eye. 'Should be an interesting meeting, huh?' He actually seems excited.

'Hmm,' I respond.

'You know, I reckon they've seriously underestimated the resource requirements for IT. We're going to need a much larger head-count than you guys have been thinking.'

I just stare at him, my cheery mood already starting to evaporate. Clearly he thinks he's going to charge into this meeting and stir up all sorts of trouble. He probably thinks Don hasn't tried hard enough to retain more of the IT staff. Over his shoulder I can see Brendan still berating the poor person on the other end of the phone.

It's going to be a long day.

But then Bobby appears from a stairwell, saving me from having to chitchat with Jason, just before Jonathon Green and Sean Peterson slip in through the front door to-gether. Bobby walks towards me, nodding to the others in greeting as they make a bee-line for the double doors beside us. John shoots me an odd look as he throws open the door. I can only imagine what they must all think of me after yesterday's experience. He bowls through the door with Sean close behind and Jason follows them into the room, without farewell. Bobby greets me casually.

'How are you feeling today? Any better?'

'Heaps better, thanks,' I tell him with a confidence I don't really feel. 'How about you?'

'Couldn't be better,' he fires straight back. I don't believe him. Rescheduling this meeting so quickly for today seems very risky, as the bomber appears to have a very serious grudge against someone in our management team. But who? And why? Regardless of whoever is being targeted John has insisted that we move ahead with the merger. If it gets delayed then all the staff from both organisations will suffer, not knowing where they stand for employment. We need to do everything possible to end the uncertainty quickly, to get back to business, to sort everything out. In truth I think he's under pressure from the Board to get things resolved. I'm sure he doesn't really want to be here today either.

So here we are, coming together again – only twenty-four hours since our last effort to meet at the Marina Café. Personally, I don't think it's the smartest thing to be doing. But I do tend to agree that the merger, and its restructure of personnel, needs to be resolved. Mind you, I had half expected a visible police presence here, but there isn't a uniform in sight.

'So how's that psychic radar working today?' Bobby asks. 'Are we in any danger?'

I'm not sure whether to laugh or cry. It feels good to have someone like Bobby believe me, but it's also such a heavy burden. 'Don't do that, Bobby. You can't rely on me. I have no idea.'

'I've seen you in action, Lily. Don't put yourself down. You've got something very special going on in there,' he gently taps me on the forehead. 'So, if it's okay with you, I'm gonna stick close to you today, because if anything bad starts to go down I'm pretty sure you'll be the first to know.'

'But what if I'm not?' I tap my own forehead, 'What if nothing happens up here? What if there's already a bomb waiting for us,' I stop, feeling scared. 'This is a really bad idea. We shouldn't be getting together again like this, not so soon.'

'But we have to Lily. John's right, we have to move this along. We can't just delay the merger and leave all those people in suspense. We owe it to them to finish this.'

'Come on,' he says, taking my hand. 'Let's go do this thing.'

His hand is warm against mine and I feel myself flush a little, suddenly remembering why I did agree to come today.

There is a large rectangular desk in the middle of the huge meeting room. Many of the seats are already taken and a murmur of low conversation greets us. No one looks up – they probably can't meet my eye. Because of what happened yesterday at the marina they probably don't know whether to thank me or have me burned as a witch.

Bobby releases my hand and gestures that I should lead the way. Very gentlemanly. I do a quick head count. I don't see Brendan – he must still be out on the phone – nor do I see Hector Lawson. Did he get appointed or not? Nikki isn't here today either. I wonder if she refused to come. She was pretty shaken up yesterday. Even with Bobby close by I wonder again why on earth I agreed to be here today.

I'm just about to sit down when there is a movement behind us and someone places a package on the tea and coffee table to the left of the doorway. I quickly dismiss the curious feeling that prickles through me and sit down, glancing around at the men at the table, shuffling through papers and making small-talk. Then Sean Peterson, who has been making himself a coffee, calls out.

'Who's this for, Reuben?'

I spin around in surprise. One of our mailroom guys, Reuben, has just dropped off a package and is leaving the room. I watch him stop and turn slowly. Reuben blinks through his thick glasses and speaks very softly. I can only just hear him.

'It's from Westwood, arrived this morning. The note said it was for morning tea here. So I bought it over.' It's the longest speech I've ever heard him make. Then he shrugs and turns back to leave.

'Hang on, Rube',' calls Sean, as he picks up the package. 'There's no note on it. Do you still have it?'

Reuben hesitates for a moment, half turning back, and then says: 'It's in the car. I'll get it.' He turns away again and heads towards the door to the lobby.

—don't let him do it, he's telling fibs—

I jump in my seat and almost scream. The bomber's mother is with me yet again. The bomber is telling lies, but to who?

I stand up too quickly; my chair topples over behind me. Heads turn sharply my way and Bobby says something but I don't hear it.

—tell him this is wrong, tell him to stop—

Tell who? I want to shout out. I look around the room quickly. Everyone is frozen in place, staring at me in surprise. My eyes find Bobby's and he understands immediately. I look over at Sean who is holding the package and frowning at me strangely. I turn to Reuben who has stopped at the doorway and is looking back at me. He looks baffled. I feel my legs go suddenly wobbly; my heart leaps into my mouth.

—he'll listen to you, I know he will—

As Reuben disappears through the doorway I find myself moving without thinking. I stumble over my upturned chair and snatch the package from Sean, quickly running out into the lobby. The little man is almost at the exit as I shout at him.

'Reuben, wait. I think this is the wrong package.'

He freezes.

I can literally hear my heart hammering wildly in my chest as I cross the lobby uncertainly; holding the package out in front of me like the extra distance between it and me will actually make a difference. The words in my head seem somehow grateful now, but still insistent. Driving me to act.

–he doesn't mean to be bad–

I'm shaking like a leaf when I reach Reuben, but he hasn't moved. He stands motionless, his back to me, just inside the doorway.

'I'm pretty sure that this package is the wrong one, Reuben. Would you mind taking it back please and seeing if you can find us the right one.'

I actually press it into his back to let him know that I'm right behind him.

For an eternity nothing happens.

We just stand there like that, still as statues. Me holding the package out against his back, him frozen in place, hunched over slightly, reaching for the door. I realise that we are about the same height and I try to picture the back and head in the hoodie that sped away in the cruiser yesterday. Is Reuben the bomber or am I making a complete fool of myself?

He starts to turn around. He looks annoyed. His face is blanched with angry splotches and he is grinding his teeth.

Oh shit. What have I done?

–he's all upset now, such a temper–

The words come in sharp and clear, straight into my mind, and I know. I'm instantly certain that this funny little man before me is the bomber and that I am, right at this moment, holding one of his bombs in my hands. The wave of terror that sweeps through me is nearly incapacitating and I almost drop the package.

I try to focus on what to say next. Then I suddenly remember that the bomber uses some kind of remote control to trigger the device. I quickly look down at his hands which are clenched into fists at his sides. Both are white with pressure. But they are both empty.

–he doesn't mean to be bad, he's confused–

I try to speak again, but struggle to find my voice. He's staring into my face with such intensity that I almost take a step backwards. He doesn't look confused to me.

'This is the wrong package, Reuben. I'm pretty sure . . .' I finally manage to mumble.

He continues to stare at me, his eyebrows knitting together. I hold my ground as his face goes a deeper shade of purple. Then I become aware of other people around me. Someone is moving up stealthily behind me and I can hear someone else on a phone nearby, calling emergency services, asking for the police. Reuben hears it too and suddenly snatches the package from my outstretched hands, quickly tucking it under one arm. When he speaks his voice is quiet and strained. I can barely make out the words.

'You're right. It's the wrong one.'

Suddenly the main hotel door in front of me bursts open. Hector Lawson stops in his tracks, confronted by the unusual scene before him. The lobby is unnaturally silent. Reuben is blocking the entrance. Hector looks at me and at Reuben's back and sees the package under his arm.

When I look back at Reuben he is holding a small plastic box in his free hand. It's black, with a large blue button. It looks like an ordinary garage door opener. His expression is hard to read.

'How did you know?' he whispers to me, inclining his head slightly.

Hector is frozen where he stands and, suddenly sensing the tension in the situation, starts to back away. I can feel someone else moving ever so slowly up behind me. Without looking I know it's Bobby and I draw some comfort from that.

Then I think about Grammy, and the comments she made on Sunday afternoon. She told me that I had to face my fear, and that this would help to set things right again, or something like that. What exactly did she say? Is this what she meant? Facing up to the bomber? Or did she mean something else entirely? I try to push the thoughts aside. I need to concentrate.

'You mother told me,' I reply in a whisper also. 'She's upset. She's been worrying about you. She doesn't like the bad things that you've been doing.'

He frowns and sneers at me. 'My mother's dead,' he says, shaking his head.

I should leave it at that, but simply can't. Something is driving me to try and reach out to this confused and dangerous little man. He has a bomb in one hand and its detonator in the other and he is clearly unstable. I should leave it, but I just can't. The words come out of me from nowhere.

'Yes, I know that. But she's still watching over you. She can't rest because she's so worried about you.' I pause for a beat and then add, 'She wants you to know that she doesn't blame you for the accident. That it wasn't your fault. And that she's still proud of you, but not of what you're doing with all these bombs. She wants you to stop.'

He frowns at me, shaking his head again. 'You're crazy.'

'What you're doing,' I say more forcefully, halting him again as he starts to back away, 'it's breaking her heart. She doesn't want you to get into trouble. She knows you feel guilty about the accident, but she just fell.'

Now he seems unsure.

He looks back at me, frowning and wary, but he also seems intrigued. I don't have the faintest idea what accident I'm referring to. But he seems to know. He understands.

But it isn't comforting him. In fact, it seems to be making him even more upset.

'You lie,' he says flatly. 'Everyone lies to me.'

Then he darts away. He's deceptively fast. Nobody moves around me. They have all seen the package, and they've all seen the small plastic box in his hand. Nobody moves a muscle. With feet that feel leaden I slowly step forward into the doorway and watch Reuben jump quickly into a small, light blue sedan and start it up. He glances around quickly, checking that no one is pursuing him, and then he drives away.

Bobby is suddenly at my side. Hector is still standing rigidly, holding the door open, rooted to the spot in fear and surprise. He mutters a soft expletive and sinks to the ground, parking himself firmly on his bottom.

'Which way did he go?' Bobby asks in a serious tone.

I point north, towards Wilton. My mind is still reeling, desperately trying to catch up with everything I've just done and said. It takes a moment to realise that I've just confronted the bomber, that I've just been chatting with the man who has been trying to kill me. My insides turned to ice and I reach out for the door frame to hold myself up.

'The police are still ages away, I'm going to go after him,' Bobby announces. I feel my eyes fly open in surprise. What? I grab his arm with my free hand and hold on tight.

'No! Just let him go. We know who he is. Let the police go and get him.'

'He's got to be headed home. The office is the other way, so where else would he go? If we don't follow him he could grab his things and disappear. Then he'll come after you and the rest of us again. The guy is unstable, we have to go after him.'

'He's got a bomb, Bobby. Don't be stupid,' I plead.

'I'm going. You can either come with me, or stay here.'

With that he pushes past me, pulling free of my grip on his arm, and jogs quickly around the side of the hotel. I stand there for only a second. I can't let him go on his own.

I leap into the passenger seat just as Bobby starts to reverse his car out of its parking space. He grins.

'Good girl,' he says. His eyes are animated. I throw on my seatbelt, shaking my head in disbelief. What are we doing?

As we pull out he tosses me his cell-phone.

'Use that, find out where he lives.'

'What? How?'

'Call Lauren or Claire, he's an employee of HBS. His home address will be on file.'

'Oh.' I'm impressed. He's a quick thinker.

I make the call. The receptionist puts me through to Claire and I quickly explain that I need a home address for Reuben, the mailroom guy. It suddenly occurs to me that I don't even know his last name. He's just Dave's quiet little colleague.

'What's all the drama?' Claire demands. 'Why do you need his address?'

'Because he's the bomber.'

'Yeah right, and I'm the tooth fairy.'

'Just get me the address, Claire, and fast please.'

Bobby is heading vaguely north as we wait for the information. I can hear Claire muttering as her fingers tap heavily on the keyboard. Finally she comes back on the line and reads out an address in the heart of Wilton.

'Lorneville Drive,' I tell Bobby.

'I know it.' He immediately accelerates and is looking for a left turn. 'Call the police. Tell them where we're heading. Maybe they'll have a car in the area.'

I dial the emergency number and am immediately connected to an operator. I ask for the police and after a quick transfer begin telling the woman who I am, who we are pursuing and where we are heading. She fires short and sensible questions at me while Bobby drives like a maniac. She tells me to stay on the line. Next thing I know we're flying past Wilton Comprehensive and turning right into Lorneville Drive. I scan the house numbers.

'Further down, on the right,' I tell Bobby, who seems to have already figured it out. Then we're slowing and we see the light blue sedan parked a little crookedly in the driveway of a row of three old council units. There is a large sign outside the row of units, promoting the fact that the site will soon be developed into luxury split-level townhouses – by none other than Cassidy Construction, Steve Cassidy's brother's company. Construction will be commencing soon.

The unit looks still and quiet. I look at Bobby and raise my eyebrows in query.

'Now what?'

THIRTY-EIGHT

Reuben is more than just furious.

His blood boils with rage as he drives frantically and aimlessly. He isn't thinking clearly, but he knows he can't head back to work.

They know it's him. Shit. That stupid, stupid girl. What the hell did he do that could possibly have given him away? How the hell did she work it out? Shit.

He'd been prepared. He had a simple and believable story ready to go. The bloody bean-counter bought it. That Peterson prick accepted that the package was from Westwood. They all believed him. No one else took any notice whatsoever, except for that bloody girl. That bloody stupid girl. God-damn her.

He clenches the steering wheel in fury. While he drives without thinking he isn't surprised to find himself passing the big old school and turning into Lorneville Drive. He's heading home. Where else can he go? He will go home and clear his head, come up with a new plan.

He's still trying to understand how the girl knew about him as he pulls into the driveway and hurries inside. He takes the package with him, although he isn't sure why. He needs to come up with a plan. He knows he won't have long, but he should have enough time to come up with something clever.

He moves quickly from room to room, his mind reeling, his anger and frustration enveloping him further and further. He still can't make sense of it.

How the hell did that stupid girl know about the bomb, about his beautiful device? And worse, how did she known about his mother? And about the fall?

He has never told anyone at work. He didn't invite anyone to the funeral and he'd even called in sick rather than tell anyone. He didn't want their sympathy. They'd have just made fun of him like they always did. So there was no way that girl could have known about his mother.

He goes into the garage, where he keeps all his tools, and places the package down on the workbench alongside the other device he created last night. He is making them bigger now, enjoying the increasing scale of destruction. He runs a finger gently over the open device, savouring its simplicity and the awesome power it contains. He almost smiles, but then he remembers the girl again and his mood darkens once more. She makes him furious.

How dare she say that his mother forgives him for the accident. How dare she presume to tell him what his mother is thinking? Mother never forgave him. How could she?

He looks around his garage and starts to lurch back into despair. This is the place he feels the most comfortable. His own safe fortress.

Fighting back the misery he tries to focus on the task at hand. He needs a new plan. He needs to be two steps ahead of them, just like before. He has to run, and hide, quickly.

He will need clothes and money. He darts upstairs and drags a gym bag out of his bedroom closet. He starts grabbing shirts and socks and underpants out of his drawers and then burrows into one drawer to find his hidden cash reserves. He curses silently as he flies back and forth around the small room, grabbing things and throwing them into the gym bag. Then he stops.

He moves swiftly to the window.

A police car has just pulled up outside. Shit.

THIRTY-NINE

As we sit there trying to decide whether to approach the unit or not a police car turns into the road ahead of us and pulls to a stop at the kerb. They are across the road, in front of us, and have stopped just short of the driveway that Reuben's sedan is parked in.

We watch two uniformed officers quickly take in the scene, the passenger talking into a radio receiver, obviously relating their arrival and reporting our presence. Bobby starts to open his door and the driver abruptly holds up his hand in a clear 'stop' signal indicating that we should stay in our car. Bobby closes his door and points at the unit with the old sedan out front. I watch him mouth the words 'in there' twice. The policeman points too, acknowledging Bobby's direction. The two officers confer for three or four minutes before the passenger finally climbs out of the car and starts to make his way over to us.

—no baby, don't do it—

The words startle me and I spin around, expecting to see Reuben emerging through the door. But nothing seems to have changed. What is he doing in there?

The policeman reaches our car just as an incredibly loud explosion tears through the unit. Its windows blow out and glass showers the front lawn, the blue sedan, the footpath, the police car and the road. The garage door arches violently and buckles outwards, not quite tearing free from its frame as a wall of flame erupts behind it. The policeman flies over our bonnet and disappears from sight. I feel our car rock, shaking from the force but no windows break. I scream.

Then Bobby is holding me and I have that all-too-familiar buzzing sound in my ears once again. I look out and see smoke billowing from the shattered windows of the unit, seeping around the twisted remains of the garage door, drifting from fresh cracks in the walls. The policeman in the car is cowering across his front seats, talking rapidly into the radio, his car covered in random debris but otherwise unscathed. I spin to look out my passenger window, finding the other policeman on the ground, starting to sit up. He's shaking his head, dazed and deafened, but otherwise okay.

—oh no baby, no, no, no—

Then Bobby is leaping out of the car and running. I don't understand where he is going. I start to open my door but the policeman is in the way. I turn back and clamber quickly over the driver's seat, righting myself just in time to see Bobby cut sharply into an alleyway between a couple of houses across the road. I stumble at first and then find my feet and race after him.

As I reach the entrance to the alleyway I see Bobby sprinting out the other end and turning sharply left. At the end of the alleyway I realise that I have emerged into Fraser Park. We are less than a kilometre from Wilton Marina here. I catch sight of Bobby again, up ahead, jogging along and looking into the backyard gardens of each house he passes. He seems frantic, like he's lost something important to him. I call out and he stops, staring into a back yard just ahead.

'Bobby, wait,' I call out again and finally reach him. I stop just short, catching my breath. I'm pretty fit, but I'm not a sprinter. He turns to me.

'Stay back, Lily. He may still be alive.'

FORTY

He sprints downstairs, dragging the gym bag behind him.

He darts back into the garage and locks his eyes on the two devices there. He feels in his pocket and comes out with the black plastic box. It's a simple garage-door remote control. He'd disabled the door to this very garage a few months back to see how the system worked and he'd been surprised at its simplicity. It would be easy to use for his own purposes.

He moves quickly again – time is against him now. He slips the package he has bought back from the hotel into his gym bag, zipping it up quickly. Then he turns to the open device and makes a couple of simple adjustments. With his fingernail he pops the back off the little black remote. He makes a minor adjustment there too and clips the cover back into place. Leaving the open device in the garage he walks back up into the main entranceway.

He sees the police car again. They're still inside, relaying messages back to the station, probably waiting for back-up. He doesn't have much time. He slips down the hallway to the back door, his gym bag over his shoulder. He never planned for this; he simply never considered it a possibility. But he is resourceful.

He flings the back door open, but remains where he is standing. The steps always stop him here. The back steps and the washing line. He hasn't been able to use them since. These days he sets up his clothes to dry on a rack in the lounge rather than venturing out the back door.

He freezes for only a moment, but it feels like forever. The images rush through his head once again. Every time he comes out here, every time he tries to use these back steps, the scene replays itself over and over and over. He just can't make the images go away. Despair grips him like a vice.

Pulling the door closed behind him he sits down on the top step wearily, the gym bag dropping to his feet. He tries to fight the feeling of hopelessness. Consciously he knows that if he stays where he is he will be caught – and that is inconceivable. He has to get away.

But he can't seem to make himself stand up – the weight on his shoulders is oppressive. His will to fight is draining away as he struggles with darker emotions. I must not fail, he tells himself, imploring his feet to move.

But the misery is deep and strong and all he can manage is to slide down one step. This strengthens his resolve and he grits his teeth, forcing himself to slide down another step.

The police are coming. He needs to distract them. So he reaches into his pocket and withdraws the black plastic garage door opener.

After a moment he takes a deep breath and slides himself down one more step. This is as far as he can go. He knows he is too close but he can't push himself further.

He raises the remote control device and slides his thumb across the blue plastic button.

Then he presses it down firmly.

FORTY-ONE

I suddenly realise what Bobby is doing. He starts to move and I grab his hand quickly, in an effort to hold him back. He tries to shake free of my grip but I hold on tight.

We're standing directly behind Reuben's unit, which is now heartily ablaze. Smoke and flames pour out of broken windows and from a rectangular space where the back door is completely missing. Fortunately the wind comes from the park behind us, blowing the thick smoke out over Lorneville Drive. Every now and then, as the smoke ebbs and billows, I can actually see right through the small house – straight up a short hallway and out through the gap where the front door had previously been – to the road on the other side.

Directly in front of us is a short chicken-wire fence that frames a tiny flat yard featuring nothing but an old rotary clothesline and a small tin shed. A long set of concrete steps runs from the yard up to the gaping hole where the back door used to be. A man lies face down at the foot of the steps. It looks like Reuben, but it's hard to be certain. He isn't moving.

Bobby is trying to climb the low fence to go over to the man, but I hold him back.

'Wait, Bobby,' I implore. 'Please don't go in there.'

He frowns at me. 'We need to check on him.'

'No we don't. Let the police do it. Stay here.'

I'm suddenly terrified. I don't know why. I should be relieved in some way, but I feel sick, and my knees start to give way beneath me. I lean forward, needing to balance myself against him. 'Don't go in there, please.'

—don't leave him there, help my baby—

I cling to Bobby as the words invade my mind. They make me angry. I feel certain that another bad thing is about to happen. I feel overwhelmed and angrily decide that I'm sick of having my thoughts interrupted.

As I lean into him Bobby takes my weight and stares fixedly into my eyes, searching for some explanation for my determination not to let him go into the yard.

—he needs help, please—

I snap, squeezing my eyes shut and shouting irrationally. 'No, we can't help him!'

The words come back at me so quickly my eyes fly open in shock.

—but no one else can, please help him—

Bobby is staring at me, wide-eyed. 'Lily?' he asks cautiously. I'm amazed. The last words in my head were clearly a response to my shouted refusal.

'He's beyond help now. We can't help him,' I say more softly. I'm looking at Bobby, but he seems to realise that my words aren't meant for him. He says nothing.

—please, he's just confused, he doesn't understand—

'She's not listening to me,' I say to Bobby. 'She thinks he's just confused.'

—he is confused, it wasn't his fault—

'She can hear me,' I murmur in amazement, to nobody in particular. Bobby just keeps staring at me, like he wants to understand but isn't sure if he can believe what he thinks he's hearing. 'What wasn't his fault?' I ask clearly.

—it was an accident, I just fell, he blames himself—

I can scarcely believe what is happening. I'm conversing with a dead woman I have never met. Holding a conversation with a spirit. But Bobby interrupts me.

'Lily, look . . .'

I follow his gaze back towards the burning unit. The man is sitting up. It *is* Reuben – he looks dazed and blood is streaming down his face. His glasses are askew, forced up on top of his balding head. We watch in horror as he searches around on the grass beside him till he finds a black gym bag and reaches inside. He pulls out some clothing, possibly a t-shirt, and uses it to wipe his face. Then he pulls his glasses off and carefully wipes them clean. As he slips them back on he presses the t-shirt to his head to try and stem the bleeding.

Then he becomes aware that we are watching him.

He stops moving and just stares at us. I can tell that he recognises us as his expression turns to a grimace. He shakes his head and just sits there, glaring at us.

—please talk to him, help him understand—

Then I hear the sirens, lots of them. Many different kinds. Police, Fire, Ambulance. All coming quickly closer, descending on us like a swarm of angry bees. If Reuben can hear them he doesn't react. I assume his hearing will have been damaged from the blast, as mine had been so often in the last week.

'We have to talk to him,' I finally say. 'His mother needs to talk to him.'

The look on Bobby's face is priceless. My sudden change of heart has completely flummoxed him. I try to smile reassuringly, like I know what I'm doing, but I'm sure it's not convincing. He nods anyway and looks over at Reuben again. He still hasn't moved.

—it wasn't his fault, you can make him understand—

Bobby steps easily over the fence and reaches a hand back to help me across. I don't need it but take the hand anyway, clambering over quickly. We both stop then to gauge Reuben's reaction. He's moved now, shuffling back to the base of the steps, pulling the gym bag along with him. He looks defensive and hugs it to his chest.

—I just fell, it was an accident, nobody's fault—

I take a step forward and then another as Reuben begins checking his pockets and searches around on the grass for something. He suddenly appears to spot what he has been trying to find and pitches forward. I stop in my tracks as he snatches a small black object up off the ground. He seems to grow in confidence and draws back to the steps, pulling the gym bag up over his shoulder and clasping the small black thing to his chest.

Bobby puts his arm out to restrain me, but I gently push it aside and press on. Part of me knows what I'm trying to do is insanely dangerous, but I am driven to reach out to him. I know better, but I just can't help myself. We make it to the washing line, only a couple of metres from Reuben, who is now picking at the black object with his fingernail, when I stop.

—he's a good boy really—

The absurdity of the statement makes me want to argue with Reuben's mother. Clearly she is wrong. Reuben is not a good boy – far from it. But he needs help and I know that I am the one who has to try. Shaking my head in disbelief at my own daring, I step forward again.

'Reuben,' I call to him. I know from experience that he will be at least slightly deafened. 'I need to talk to you.' He doesn't even look up, just continues fiddling with the little black thing. That's when I recognise it from our brief meeting at the hotel.

It's the remote control for his bomb. A sick feeling runs through me. I hesitate, suddenly desperately uncertain. But then the police arrive and the atmosphere changes again.

'Stay where you are. Raise your hands in the air where we can see them.'

The voice is amplified, authoritative, and I instinctively obey, freezing where I stand, my hands travelling upwards. Reuben is looking past me to where the cops have taken positions, his frown deep and set.

I turn to peek back over my shoulder. A uniformed policeman is crouching in bushes a few metres back from the wire fence. Another man, who seems to be wearing darker blue combat clothing and a helmet, is leaning out from behind a large tree trunk. He's aiming a rifle at us. I stop breathing.

—oh my baby, don't let them hurt him—

Bobby gently places a hand on my other shoulder. I turn towards him and see another two dark-clothed men lurking behind trees in the park behind him. They both have rifles too and they're also aiming them straight at us.

I freeze, looking up into Bobby's eyes. He doesn't seem as frightened as I feel, but he isn't moving either. Then his eyes drift across to Reuben and I very, very slowly turn my head to follow his gaze.

Reuben is still sitting at the base of the steps with the unit burning furiously behind him. Its hot this close, but the wind continues to drive the worst of the smoke away from us. Reuben is alert and watchful. He has finished fiddling with the remote and is holding it casually in his right hand. He's clearly angry, but he also seems grim and determined.

—please stop him, he's going to do something silly—

'How can I stop him? He doesn't believe anything I say.' I speak clearly, desperately. 'He doesn't believe I can hear you.' Both Bobby and Reuben's eyes turn to me just as the man with the loudhailer booms out behind us again.

'Nobody needs to get hurt here. Just remain calm and follow my instructions.'

I look over at Reuben who seems to be making up his mind about something. I see his thumb slide gently over the big blue button on the remote control and he hugs the gym bag a little tighter. He must have another bomb. But where?

—tell him I forgive him, it wasn't his fault—

'But I've told him that,' I say frantically. 'He doesn't believe me.'

Then Reuben stands up and walks defiantly towards Bobby and me, quickly closing the space to almost touching distance. He's staring at me, an angry frown on his blood-streaked face. I feel myself shift backwards, just a half-step, and I bump into Bobby who also moves back with me. Our hands are still raised and I feel one hand brush the steel-tube clothes-line. Bobby has to duck slightly to stand next to me beneath it. I feel cornered and scared, but am glad to have Bobby beside me. Then the policeman's commanding voice booms again.

'Stay where you are. Don't move. We are armed and will take action if you move again.'

Reuben ignores the voice as if he hasn't heard it and glares at me, then at Bobby, then back to me again.

'How did . . .' he starts to say, but falters. He uses his free hand to rub the side of his head and poke around in his ear. In the other hand he holds the remote control out in front of him – for all to see. He obviously can't hear properly. He shakes his head carefully and speaks again, more loudly than necessary, given the distance.

'How did you know?' he asks me bluntly.

I can't answer. A sudden wave of fear washes over me and I remain frozen, my hands still raised in surrender. I try to take it all in but simply can't. There are armed policemen at my back, pointing guns at me. The unit before me is well ablaze and smoke pours from it, but fortunately the wind is pushing it away. And there is a desperate and obviously crazy man standing in front of me with yet another bomb. My mind goes blank and I can't formulate a response.

'Reuben, this doesn't have to end badly,' Bobby sudden-ly speaks up beside me. 'We understand what you're going through. We want to help you.'

The police have gone quiet, watching our every move. I still can't speak. Reuben glares at Bobby for a moment and then ignores him, looking back at me ferociously.

'How did you know?' he repeats, even louder this time.

—tell him that I'm here, tell my baby I forgive him—

I try to open my mouth, but nothing works. I just want his mother's inane babble out of my head. I want to be home in bed. I shouldn't have come here, this is crazy.

'She's psychic, Reuben,' Bobby quickly tells him, 'Lily can hear your mother. She is watching over us right now.'

I am stunned, as is Reuben. He gapes at Bobby incredulously. His expression changes again and again while he tries to digest this bizarre revelation. It clearly does not compute. His eyes fix on me firmly.

'How she . . .' he hesitates. 'How she . . . died. How did you know that?' he asks.

—I fell, down the steps, it wasn't his fault—

Around me everything goes quiet. I can hear the crackle and hiss of the fire and Bobby's ragged breathing beside me, but Reuben's mother's words are still clear. And then somehow I know. I know it all. I understand his rage and I know that he wants to kill us, Bobby and me. He blames us for everything that has gone wrong today. He had wanted to destroy Jonathon Green and his entire management team, but we will have to do. Destroying us will be enough.

The realisation washes over me and I almost panic. We have no chance.

He has the bomb in his gym bag – I'm suddenly certain of that too. The remote is firmly in his grasp and he is ready to end it all. The police don't matter, the burning house doesn't matter. He knows it's over, but he wants some answers first.

FORTY-TWO

'Your mother doesn't like what you're doing, Reuben,' I say softly.

'What?' he shouts angrily.

I raise my voice. 'She fell down the steps. It was an accident. She was going out to hang out the washing – your washing – and she slipped and fell. It wasn't your fault.'

He stares at me. This time he's heard me fine.

'She'd asked you to do it, but you refused. You were busy with something else. So she went ahead and did it, but she slipped and she fell . . . and hit her head . . . and died.' I hesitate, trying to gauge his reaction, but his face is now a mask. 'But she doesn't blame you. She doesn't blame any-one.' I pause again, unsure of myself. 'And she misses you.'

He doesn't react immediately. I feel Bobby shift slightly beside me. He lowers his arms and once again places a hand on my shoulder, offering unspoken support. I lower my own arms and hug myself tight, trying to draw strength from within. The police voice calls out again but this time I don't register what he says. Neither Bobby, Reuben, nor I move. We just stare at each other as the tension mounts.

'How can you know this?' Reuben suddenly demands.

–tell him I called him Robin sometimes, my little boy wonder–

I meet Reuben's eyes. 'We're not lying to you, Reuben. I have a psychic ability. I can hear people and sometimes I just know things. Your mother, she . . . speaks to me. She told me about the fall, and she told me that she used to call you Robin sometimes, rather than Reuben. Her little Boy Wonder, she said . . .' I tail off uncertainly, but his eyes grow to the size of saucers and he takes a half-step back, away from me.

'You can't know that,' he shakes his head. 'No one knows that.'

—sometimes he is Thor, the god of thunder, his little secret—

'Your mother just told me that you are also sometimes Thor, the God of Thunder. But it's a secret.' I pause as I watch the mask slip again. I see the confusion and hurt shine through. His expression quivers and contorts as he tries to make sense of my words. Clearly this means something to him, but he's struggling to accept it. 'I don't know what it means, Reuben, but your mother told me that. She really is here. We can talk with her if you want . . .'

He shakes his head furiously, refusing to believe. He seems annoyed that I appear to know so much, and he looks as if he thinks I am just trying to fool him.

'No, it's not true. You lie, you stupid girl. You're lying!'

I'm terrified, but I need to convince him that I understand, that I want to help.

'I'm not lying, Reuben. I know why you did all this. That man from the council, up on the carpark. You made that bomb – you're good with your hands. He was taking your home from you, so soon after your mother . . . after your mother left you. You tried to talk to him about it, but just couldn't, so you chose to punish him.'

He blinks and frowns as I continue on, almost babbling, scared but determined.

'And then you heard about the merger at work, at HBS, and you realised you might lose your job too, as well as your home. It made you angry – your whole world was collapsing. You felt betrayed so you made another bomb . . . to destroy the management team. To stop the merger. They were the decision-makers. They were responsible.'

I feel crushed by a wave of burning shame as the depth of my involvement abruptly hits me. The placement of the bomb between my desk and the meeting room had been very deliberate. He wanted to kill not just the management team, but Janet and me too. I was definitely a target. I feel sick, but force myself to keep talking.

'But it didn't stop them . . . I mean us. We just kept on going. Ploughing ahead, without thinking about the hurt we were creating . . .' Bobby moves slightly closer, squeezing my shoulder. I draw strength from him and carry on.

'So you went to Commonwealth, and took out your competition, to help keep your job safe.' I look to Bobby for confirmation. 'The two men who died, one was the Sales Manager, but the other was their mail guy, wasn't it?'

He keeps his eyes on Reuben, but nods slightly. I turn back to Reuben.

—he didn't mean any of it, he's been so confused—

'The Sales Manager being there was just a bonus, wasn't it, Reuben? Another suit; another bloody manager. He wasn't your target, but you were happy to kill him too.'

The words taste bitter as I say them.

It's very still and quiet around us. Other than some muted popping and crackling from the fire it is deathly silent. I have Reuben's complete attention. He appears transfixed as I press on.

'But then you realised that we may not even need a mailroom person any more – as almost all our communications are moving to email – so you blamed the IT team, namely Don Swain, and you blamed Bobby and I for not understanding how important you are to HBS. For how hard you've worked, all your life . . .'

Something attracts Reuben's attention behind me. Police officers moving around, I suppose. Bobby's grip tenses but I don't look around. I am compelled to keep talking, to get it all out.

'And then you learned about our sailing plans and about the meeting at the Marina Café. You were clever, you knew no one would expect lightning to strike twice in the same place. But it went wrong, because of me. And this morning, at the hotel, it went wrong again . . .' I suddenly can't finish and the words just dry up.

I lean into Bobby, wishing I didn't know any of this. I feel so responsible. There must have been more that I could have done. If I'd tried to talk to him at work, or found a way to handle the redundancies better somehow, then maybe it might not have come to this. Tears start welling in my eyes.

Reuben finally breaks the silence. 'You've been spying on me.'

I don't know how to respond.

—don't give up, please help him, he's not a bad boy—

Their both deluded, mother and son. I'm out of my depth. I don't know what to say.

Reuben steps forward, shaking his head, and swings the hand with the remote control up in front of my face. Waving it at me, he slides his thumb across the button, taunting me.

'If you're so smart, tell me where the device is hidden,' he sneers.

'It's in your bag,' I say quickly. I could reach out and touch it.

He pauses, making a face. Then he waves his arm out towards the park, to where the police are positioned amongst the trees. 'But you're wrong. It's out there. Right beside them. I can kill them all now if I want to.'

I say nothing. He's goading me.

'Or maybe it is right here in my bag,' he crows, stepping closer to me. 'Maybe I'll bring the thunder down right here, right now. Take you and your boyfriend with me.'

Bobby tenses beside me. Smoke from the burning unit turns and begins to drift across us. The policeman with the loudhailer remains quiet. Why isn't he trying to take charge? Doesn't he realise there is a bomb here?

'Or maybe,' Reuben continues, 'I'll just let you hold my bag and see what happens.' He holds the bag out to me. 'Take it,' he orders and I reach out instinctively. I want to just drop it but my fingers won't work. It's terrifying. I know I'm holding a bomb.

'We're leaving now,' he turns suddenly and calls out loudly. 'If you try and stop us I'll blow everyone to hell.' He raises his arm above his head, holding the remote up for all to see. He signals simply with his free hand that I should follow him as he starts to move slowly towards the park.

The loud, authoritative voice finally returns.

'Just stay where you are and let's talk it through.'

—stop baby, don't hurt anyone else—

I cling to the bag, wanting desperately to just throw it down and run away as fast as I can. 'I'm not coming, Reuben,' I say defiantly. 'Please, just give yourself up. It's over. Your mother doesn't want anyone else getting hurt. Especially you.'

He spins to face me. 'But everybody's already been hurt. Don't you see that?'

'Yes, I know. Too many people have been hurt already. So let's just end this now, right here.'

'But there aren't enough of you. Someone has to stop you all.'

Stop you all? Who else is he referring to?

Bobby moves up behind me. 'I can make it stop, Reuben. If you'll put down the remote I can promise you I'll keep your job safe.'

'Liar,' Reuben snaps. 'You couldn't, even if you wanted.'

'I can work things out with John Green, and with the people at Head Office. We can stop the merger and let everyone just keep their jobs. You'll be a hero.'

Reuben pauses and actually seems to consider this. But he quickly shakes his head, and shouts angrily.

'You can't. You lie. It's far too late – we've all had the letters. And why should I trust you anyway? You're just another filthy, money-grubbing liar.' Reuben points at us, the fire from the unit reflected in his tormented eyes. 'You did this,' he screams. 'You don't care who you hurt.' He glowers at us. 'Now I don't care either,' he snarls.

He turns on his heel abruptly to face the police, raising his hand again to display the remote control. I can see the blue button clearly as he presents it for inspection.

'Don't try and stop me,' he shouts. He takes a small step forward towards the park, waiting for a reaction from the police. They don't disappoint.

'Stand your ground. No one leaves this area until all weapons are disabled.'

Then Bobby does something completely unexpected. He takes a quick step around me, reaches up to the clothesline above us, and spins it with a mighty heave. The steel beam that I have been standing under whips away, slamming forcibly into Reuben's upstretched arm. The small black plastic remote pops out of his hand and spins through the air.

I have a sharp premonition of being blown apart by a tremendous explosion as the little black box hits the ground and triggers the bomb in the gym bag I hold.

I scream in terror.

Reuben cries out in surprise and instinctively clutches his now smarting wrist to his chest.

The little black plastic box hits the ground. But it doesn't break, nor does it set off the bomb that I hold. Instead it simply bounces and rolls, stopping face up near the fence that separates Reuben's unit from the park.

The big blue button seems to stare at us maliciously.

Bobby stumbles and falls to his knees as he tries to get past me. Reuben realises what is happening and darts forward, bending down and hurrying to get to the remote first.

Then there is a thunderous crack and Reuben abruptly spins back towards us, twisting in the air and landing on his back. He screams in surprise and pain.

–nooo. no, no, no. not my baby–

Reuben writhes momentarily, a stain of crimson spreading across his chest. He looks down at himself, convulses once and groans softly, and then he too is still.

Three armed policemen rush over, guns raised. One moves quickly to stand over Reuben, training the gun on him while a second one kneels down and checks for a pulse. The third one stands over the top of the fallen remote control and aims his weapon at Bobby who stays where he is, slowly sitting back and raising his hands skyward.

After a few moments, the second man stands and makes some kind of hand signal, prompting the man guarding Reuben to lower his gun.

Apparently Reuben is no longer a threat.

FORTY-THREE

People are everywhere. It's chaotic yet again.

Bobby and I are escorted to a picnic table in the park nearby where we sit, side by side, facing the burned-out unit. One of the armed policemen stands guard over us while order is slowly established. The man with the loudhailer fires off orders, securing the scene and keeping the neighbours at bay. More senior officers arrive and quickly establish themselves. We watch as the fire is put out, the crowd of curious neighbours pushed even further back, and a police forensic team begins to poke around the area. We sit in silence, both lost in thought.

I can't really take it all in. The bomber, Reuben, has been killed and I don't know how to feel about that. Should I rejoice now that I, and all my co-workers, are safe? It doesn't feel right somehow. I feel responsible.

Natalie Dowd arrives and moves around the scene: talking with people, gathering information. Eventually she comes over to us, to try and fit all the pieces together. She doesn't seem annoyed that we haven't been separated. She sits down across the table and asks us simply to tell all.

So we do.

Bobby goes first, explaining everything as he experienced it in a calm and logical sequence. Natalie doesn't interrupt and once he finishes she turns to me. I try to do the same, but I know my version of events will again raise more questions than it will answer. I find it hard to believe myself as I sit there describing how I took the bomb off Sean

Peterson and basically gave it back to Reuben, sending him on his way. It sounds stupid, not matter how I phrase it.

'So you had another premonition?' Natalie asks.

'Well . . . yes. Pretty much.'

'I see.' She pauses for a few moments, clearly weighing it all up, and then asks me to carry on. I do so cautiously. I try to stick to the facts and the sequence of events and try to avoid delving too deeply into the 'psychic' parts of the story.

When I reach the end Bobby takes my hand.

He says, 'We didn't do this to him. You shouldn't feel guilty.'

'But I do, don't you see?' I implore. 'He was part of our team. I should have taken the time to talk with him and help him understand . . .' I choke on my words. 'We were responsible for him.'

I fight back the tears. Natalie is watching us. She clearly doesn't know what to think. I can tell she's trying to decide if I seriously have some psychic gift or if we are actually guilty accomplices – trying to deflect blame away from ourselves.

At that point a uniformed officer and another man in dirty white overalls drift over to our table. They whisper to Natalie with some urgency. The forensic search must have found something important. Natalie stands and starts to go with them, but then stops, turning back to us.

'Wait here please. I have more questions for you both and I'm going to need you to come down to the station again shortly. We'll get your statements down in writing. Then we'll take things from there. All right?'

'Are we under arrest?' Bobby asks.

She fixes him with a firm gaze, considering the question carefully.

'Not at this stage,' she says, then turns and walks away with the two men. We sit there for a minute, lapsing back into silence. I realise that something is bothering me, but can't put my finger on it.

'You know, I didn't feel him go,' I finally say quietly. Bobby doesn't respond. 'When Reuben died I didn't feel him pass on. He didn't speak to me.'

'Have you felt that before?' Bobby asks carefully.

'Yes, I have.' I try to remember how it had been, out on the edge of the pier when Sue had passed over. 'I felt Sue going, the other day. She said goodbye to Don. I heard her and I felt her going, but not today, not with Reuben. Why would that be, do you think?'

It's a question he can't possibly hope to answer. I don't expect him to, but he tries.

'Maybe he just didn't say anything.'

'Maybe.'

'Or maybe he just didn't come close enough to you? Perhaps there's a distance rule. You needed to be physically closer to him.'

'I was closer to Reuben than I was to Sue. And his mother doesn't seem to be here any more either. Do you think they left, or moved on, together?'

He shrugs, 'I don't know.'

'Neither do I. It's really weird.'

'Yep. There's a lot of that going around.'

I smile a little despite myself. Bobby still has his arm around me and it's nice, a little more than comforting. I snuggle in a little closer. He hugs me back and I feel him looking around the park. Suddenly he stiffens and turns back towards the burned unit.

I look up, wondering why he has become uncomfortable. Something is wrong and I instinctively know it isn't Reuben's spirit or the police that are worrying him. It's something else. Something more personal.

I crane my neck to look over his shoulder, behind us, and it's only then that I realise where we are sitting. It's the same picnic table Bobby had been sitting at the other night when I was out running. That's how he knew about the alley between the houses earlier. He grew up around here.

Then I spot the older man. He's tall and grey, heavier set than Bobby but even from nearly a hundred metres away the resemblance is clear. He is standing on the verandah of a rather large and almost grand old house across the road. The house is familiar; it's the one that Bobby had been staring at that night.

Bobby's father is watching the thinning smoke rising through the trees from the burned-out unit.

'Maybe you should drop round and say hello later,' I suggest in a measured tone.

'I don't think so.' He replies, his face set. Then he softens a little, looking a little sly. 'Besides,' he says, 'I already have plans for later.'

'Really? What plans?'

He looks down at the table coyly. 'There's this girl I was hoping to take out later, for a meal maybe, after the police are finished with her.'

'Oh,' I say. 'Is she nice?'

He nods, and gives a small smile. 'Very nice.'

'Oh,' I say again. 'Is she pretty?'

The smile broadens. 'Uh-huh, very pretty.'

'Hmm, so no one I know then.'

He grins. 'Oh, you know her, Lily. She's very smart, very intuitive, but a bit slow on the uptake sometimes. Tends to need dead people to point things out for her.'

'Oh,' I say yet again. 'I know her. She's not so pretty.'

'She's a bit self-delusional too.'

I smile then, but look into his eyes meaningfully, 'Aren't we all?'

'You think I'm deluded?' he sounds surprised.

'You pretend that you don't miss them, but you do.'

He frowns at me. 'Enough with the parents, okay? Or you might not get that meal.'

I have to physically bite my lip; the compulsion to keep pushing him is so strong. It just seems such a shame. But he's so damn stubborn, and he's clearly still not ready to try and heal those old wounds yet. He may not be ready for years. I give in and fall silent again, happy enough to be in his arms.

But I crane my neck again, looking back over his shoulder. I watch Bobby's father drift back inside his big, stately home. I can sense his regret; he's intensely sad. I think briefly about going over and telling him that Bobby is right here but resist the urge. Bobby isn't ready. It wouldn't be right.

'So what are we talking about here?' I ask. 'Lunch? Dinner? A mid-afternoon snack?'

'I guess that depends on how long we spend at the police station today.'

'I don't want to go back to work . . .'

'Neither do I, but I'll have to call in at some stage.'

We don't get to finish making any plans as Natalie Dowd suddenly returns. She's ready to take us both down to the station, once again. We still have much to discuss.

<h1 style="text-align:center">FORTY-FOUR</h1>

I normally don't like airports as even a terminal as small as Hawthorne's is generally bustling with emotion and tension. Earlier, in the departure area, it was harder. But at least now, here in the arrivals section, I'm feeling a little better. As I watch another flight come in there is hugging and laughing and crying, but of the joyous kind. It's actually kind of nice.

It's Friday today. I can barely believe that only two weeks have passed since I survived the first explosion that now marks such a significant change to my life. And only eleven days since I first met Bobby – and less than an hour since I lost him.

My cell-phone rings, just as the screen on the wall announces the arrival of Dad and Cheryl's flight.

'Did you remember to restock his liquor cabinet?' Megan asks playfully as I answer.

'Some of it, but I'm hoping he'll forgive me when I tell him my tale of woe.'

'Well, it's quite a tale. Got to be worth at least one bottle of gin?'

'Yes,' I agree, 'at least.'

'Did you decide what you're going to do at work?'

'Yes, actually, I did. I'm going to take the money and run.'

I try to sound casual as I say it, but in reality it's been one heck of a tough decision. But it's decided now. I'm not going to re-apply for my job at Westwood. I just can't do it. I just don't think it's what I'm meant to do with my life.

'Woohoo,' she replies. 'That's a big call. You sure?'

'I've already confirmed it in writing, so yes, I'm sure.'

'Okay. So now what?'

'I haven't decided yet. One thing at a time.'

'Mmm. And this Bobby guy. Is he going to stay and sweep you off your feet?'

I pause and allow my mind to wander. Megan's already heard all about my last few days' debauchery. I smile to myself as I recall how it all played out.

After he was released from the police station on Tuesday, Bobby returned to the Mt Wallace Hotel to find the meeting still in progress. He then had to explain everything that had happened to the team. Once that was cleared up he'd become embroiled in the ongoing restructure debates. It was very late in the afternoon before he called to apologise and explain that he simply couldn't leave and that there was no way we could get together for a meal – our date – that night. I was a little hurt but didn't complain. I was just glad that I didn't have to participate in the great debate myself.

But I did take the initiative and boldly asked Bobby if he would commit to dinner at my place after work the next night. He agreed without hesitation.

Dinner went well. Very well, in fact. I feel a warm glow as I remember it. We ended up in bed together and it was as good, if not better, than I had dreamt it might be. Afterwards we talked on and off almost until dawn. It was very special – and it didn't end there. After work yesterday we went out to dinner and ended up at his room at the Mt Wallace Hotel. I haven't had much sleep this week, but I'm certainly not complaining.

Earlier today Bobby tried to convince me to come to Auckland with him. His words were cautious but his sincerity was clear.

I understand that there is too much history for him to stay here, and his job is based in Auckland – and he understands that I now have a whole new family awaiting me at Bluff Creek, but he made the offer anyway, and genuinely.

Officially I'm still undecided, but the reality of saying goodbye only minutes ago has me leaning heavily towards paying him a visit . . . and probably very soon.

I let out a deep sigh and finally respond to Megan's question. 'No, he flew out about an hour ago.'

'Oh, I'm sorry. He sounded nice.'

'Hmm . . . yeah. He is.' But I don't feel up to talking about Bobby right now. The ache inside me is still too raw. Before she can respond I change the subject, knowing that Megan will want to hear this. 'Hey, guess what? Natalie Dowd stopped by work today to visit me.'

'What did she want?'

'Well, she sort of wanted to update me. She told me that they had dug into Reuben's background and discovered that I was right about some things.'

'Really? What things?'

'Umm, well, apparently his mother did die six months ago, pretty much exactly as I described – falling down their back steps. And the timing of the first eviction notice from the council, it fits in perfectly with the first bombing attack. The guy who was killed was the same guy that signed Reuben's eviction letter.'

'Oh wow, you nailed it! And did she also tell you that Steve used to live in another council unit on Lorneville Drive? He used to live about a dozen houses up from where that last bomb went off.'

This does surprise me. 'No. How do you know that?'

Her voice is a little smug. 'I've been snooping. Did you really think I wouldn't?'

'You should be careful. You don't want to get fired.'

I hear a soft snort down the line. 'Nah, never happen. Anyway, he moved out a week or so ago and went to a flat over one of the shops down at the marina. Do you think he knew this Reuben guy? Do you think they were working together?'

I don't need to consider this, immediately feeling certain there is no connection. I doubt Steve would have ever even given the poor little man the time of day.

'No,' I respond, 'they weren't.'

'Hmm . . . did she say anything else?'

'No, not really. And she didn't really offer any thanks, but I could tell she was grateful. Otherwise, you know, why would she bother to come and tell me at all?'

'That's nice. Good on her.'

There is a pause. This time Megan changes the subject. 'So what time does the flight get in?'

'Pretty much now, actually. I'd better get going.'

'Boy, I'd like to be a fly on the wall at your place tonight.'

'Yeah, it's going to be interesting.'

'Maybe you could invite me over the day you introduce Greg and Cheryl to Grammy?'

'You know, you get less and less funny each day.'

'But you love me anyway . . .'

'I have to go, Meg. Their flight's landed.'

'Righto. Well, send my love, won't you? Are we running Sunday?'

'Absolutely. Unless Dad grounds me once he hears what's been going on.'

'Ha. That'll be the day,' she says, and hangs up.

People have started to appear through the arrival gates. I sit upright and try to focus on the here and now. My parents will walk through any minute. Together, probably hand in hand. Still in love after all this time. I briefly envy them and then suddenly I know what to do.

I know – in both my head and in my heart – that I will be making a trip to Auckland in the near future. If there is a chance that Bobby and I can be together then I will do my best to make it happen.

I nod happily to myself. My mind is set.

I have so much to tell Dad and Cheryl. So much has happened while they've been away – things that I feel certain will forever shape my life.

The phrase feels familiar. Shape my life. I remember Grammy saying something like that to me recently. Something about a challenge having being chosen for me, and that it would not destroy me, but help to shape me. Were her words actually a clairvoyant prediction or simply wise counsel?

Regardless of which, I know – without a shadow of a doubt – that she was right.

* * *